KING OF DIAMONDS

Nancy!
Enjoy the ride!

Nan Spingler

KING OF DIAMONDS

AN ALL ABOUT THE DIAMOND ROMANCE

NAOMI SPRINGTHORP

King of Diamonds
An All About the Diamond Romance
Copyright © 2018 Naomi Springthorp
Published by Naomi Springthorp
All rights reserved
ISBN 978-1-949243-03-1
Cover Photographer: Randy Sewell of RLS Model Images Photography
Cover Model: Chris Mayo
Graphic Designer: Irene Johnson johnsoni@mac.com
Editor: Katrina Fair

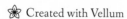 Created with Vellum

This book is dedicated to everyone that loves the game of baseball and appreciates the players in those pants!

THANK YOU

Thank you to the romance writing community for being so supportive. Every single one of you is special in your own unique way. Your knowledge, friendship, and camaraderie is priceless.

Thank you, Bex Dane, for sharing your extensive knowledge and helping this newb through the process.

Thank you, Cassandra Robbins, for being a real live person when we need it.

Thank you, Katrina Fair, for putting up with all the crap I've sent you and not complaining about my text messages at all hours of the night.

Thank you, Irene Johnson, for pulling all-nighters and being my art guru.

CHAPTER ONE

In the last couple months, my life has gone from being totally in control and an independent, self-sufficient entrepreneur to having my fantasy baseball boyfriend become real. Yes, a professional baseball player loves and wants me. And, it's not just any player, it's the catcher I've been fantasizing about for years, my boyfriend in my head. It's utter insanity! I'm seven years older than him and he has women waiting for him in his room on road trips. I've seen it firsthand on more than one occasion. He can be with anybody he wants and he's not interested in those women he finds waiting for him. No, he only wants me. Until it got all fucked up. Indirectly and accidentally, but fucked up nonetheless. We broke us and I'm not sure if we can ever be the same. When you break something fragile it shatters and there's no putting it back together. When you break your favorite coffee mug you can glue it back together, but it'll never be the same. It might still hold your coffee, but you can see and feel the cracks. It's broken and you're simply refusing to let it go.

I'm standing on the stage at the Batter Up. I just finished singing my final song in the karaoke competition and I'm overcome with emotion. The wild card round and I chose "Thinking Out Loud". What was I thinking? That's our song and he's been in my head everyday since I left him in LA. It was less than two months ago, but it feels like forever. I wasn't thinking. I was simply doing what he wanted. No matter what, I want to make him happy. Our song was one of the three options Mike at the Mic gave me and before I could consider the options, Rick was in the back of the room yelling out "Thinking Out Loud". I had already decided I wanted him back, well, that may have been him helping me there, too. I can't believe the things he does for me even though I left him, refused to talk to him, didn't reply to his texts, and avoided him and everyone he knows for most of two months. I even avoided watching the games, except for my stupid moment when I had to see his face and wished I didn't as I watched him get kicked out of a game. He was persistent with daily texts and voicemails, along with sending me flowers and having a limo service pick me up for the finals tonight. I pushed him away. I get it, now. He didn't give up on me. I need to embrace my girliness that's been driving me crazy and trust in him. It's not weakness, it's risking my heart. But, after being without him—I'll give him my heart completely. Honestly, I'll give him about anything he wants and be happy doing it. Anything to be with him. I didn't expect him to be here tonight. I wasn't sure when or if I'd ever see him again, other than in his catcher's gear behind the plate. Now, I'm in a private hazy world with Rick pulling me down off the stage to him and I hope he never let's me go...

Rick holds me tightly to his chest, breathing me into him as the music plays out. I missed him. His arms around me, his warm breath at my ear, and his words that cut straight through to my heart. "The only thing that matters is that I have you near me," he whispers in my ear.

Mike with the Mic starts in, "Another outstanding performance from Sherry. She really has ruled this contest from the beginning."

Rick whispers in my ear, "I don't want to let you go," as he sets me back down on the stage. I don't want him to let me go.

I'm directed to go backstage and the rookie, Chase Cross, drags Rick back to the table with the team.

I'm backstage and I don't care about the contest. I want to be with Rick. He needs me. Maybe, I need him. We all have our personal issues. I need to remember who he is and what has happened in his life. We don't want to hurt each other. We need to trust each other. I didn't think a text from Joey would be a big deal and he didn't invite Ava to his room. If he needs to go for a run, so he can clear his head, well at least he told me and didn't disappear into the night. He did come back and want answers, he didn't leave and it was over. No, that's what I did. Just like me. Drill it down to the base of the problem and not be able to get over it or around it or focus on anything but it. Damn it! Why is this taking so long?

Mike with the Mic pops backstage looking for me, "Sherry? I've called you out three times. What're you doing back here?" He stares at me oddly and crooks his head to a questioning angle. "Never mind, you did great. Can you come out on stage now, please?"

Mike leaves and I follow him out, stepping up onto the stage. "Thank you everybody for coming out tonight. The crew here at Batter Up and I appreciate your patronage during this contest. We know some of it has been hard to listen to, while other contestants like these two standing here made up for it in spades. The bartenders have surveyed the crowd and put the votes together." A waitress walks up and hands Mike a napkin. He turns to us and says, "One of you got 55 of the 60 votes. Amazing results. Congratulations, Sherry! You've been the one to beat since week one."

I'm speechless. I manage to mutter out, "Thank you." Not concerned about the competition at all. It's not important right now.

"It's okay sweetie, go do what you need to do," Mike encourages me to do what's in my heart.

I search for Rick, and he's back at the table with the other Seals. I go to him, but Cross stops me before I get there, "I'm not letting you get any closer to him unless this is a good thing. Are you going to fix this?" Chase questions.

"I'm going to him and not running away, so we can fix us. He's not alone in this," I tell Chase.

"You better be sure about that because his ideas for fixing it are crazy," Cross warns.

"I like crazy," I smile at him, and like the troll under the bridge he lets me pass.

I approach Rick slowly, gazing into his eyes and hoping to find our connection. "Hi. Do you want to get out of here?"

He stands up, "I'll go wherever you are," his eyes on me heavily.

My eyes start to tear up and I'm getting all girly again. I need to keep some of my wits about me to get through this and not lose it. I reach out for his hand and he takes mine. I lead him out of the Batter Up and retrace our steps to the bleachers at the Embarcadero. A peaceful place with a great memory and a beautiful night sky. A place where we can be alone. We walk silently. It gives me time to consider what I want and what I want to say to him.

We climb up the stairs of the bleachers and sit down together. He starts to talk, but I stop him. "I need to start. You didn't trust me when I've given you more of me than I've ever given anyone else. I trust you more than anyone else and it hurt because of it. Everything I've done that I'd never do screamed at me internally. You didn't trust me, and finding her in your room—It was too much. I needed to get away. It hit home with me because I don't trust people, but it was never a question with you. You never saw that part of me. I trusted you from the moment I saw you step on the baseball field for the first time. You have history, it was evident pretty quick that relationships haven't gone your way. I learned how bad women have treated you. I saw the hurt on your face then and I heard it in your voice when you called me drunk. When I told you there's only you, I meant it. I need you to trust me. I'll never hurt you intentionally." I wait for a response to my ramble, with more to say.

Rick takes a deep breath, "I have to know if you believe me." He stops and searches my eyes. "I need you to know you're the only one for me. Ava is nothing and I've never given any other woman my room key, only you. I'll never cheat on you."

"I have to. You're not one of those players." I gaze up at him and smile, while my eyes fill with tears. "I don't know if I can handle the life of a professional baseball player, it's why I ran. You didn't trust me and it weakened my heart. I couldn't see what was happening right in front of me. I couldn't trust my heart and believe in you." I look down and taste my salty tears as they fall across my lips. "I've never needed anyone." I gaze up at Rick, letting him see my tears, "I love you and I need you."

He immediately put his arms around me, holding me tight, his face in my hair, "I love you, my queen. Always you. Only you." He pulls me into his lap and we sit on the bleachers together quietly, needing to be together. I didn't know how much I needed him until I felt my heart start beating, deprived of the ability for weeks. He places his hands on my cheeks and presses his lips to mine softly.

"I'm sorry. I'll do my best to never hurt you. You haven't done a thing to make me not trust you. You've given yourself to me freely. That's all me and I know it. I've thought about it a lot and I trust you with everything, breaking all my rules. I've never been this possessive. I've never cared this much or felt this way. The first sign of another man made me boil." His face turns red simply saying the words. "Nothing is the same without you. I only want to be with you. I need my queen back."

"I freak out when I start acting and feeling all girly, and you make me girly. My whole life I've thought it was a weakness to be girly, but now I'm learning maybe it isn't. It's my happy tears and the fluttering in the pit of my stomach and needing someone else —needing you. Many things I'd never considered were all of the sudden things I might want. I come with baggage and you'll have to deal with it," I'm shaking at my honesty.

Rick pulls me tight to his chest, "I love you and your girly moments. None of the rest matters."

The girly part of me takes over and I don't let my brain talk me out of it. I need him to know I'm his. I need to know it can be the same. I need to feel that he still loves me and show him how much I love him. I need to remove this protective shield I've built around myself tonight and bare my heart to him. I lean in and whisper in his ear, "I still belong to you. I'll always be yours. I'm sorry I freaked out."

He tightens his embrace, "I overreacted. It's not all you. I love you. Please say you'll never leave me again."

"I promise I'll never leave you again," my heart tries to leap out of my chest as I gaze into his eyes.

He kisses me and his body relaxes, "I was afraid I'd never hold you again. I need you."

Why would I ever leave this man? How did I let this happen?

"Please take me home and hold me all night, every night, my king."

"Anything for you, my queen. You're all I want and all I need," he smiles against my lips and kisses me senseless. His heart warms and beats against mine.

I message the limo to pick us up and gaze up into Rick's blue eyes, hoping the sadness will disappear. My new goal: before I sleep, my man will be happy again.

He holds my hand, not letting go as we walk out of the park and the limo pulls up. The driver opens the door and Rick instructs him to take us home. The driver puts the privacy glass up and Rick sits with his arms around me, just looking at me.

"I want you to know I belong to you. I'm yours. Please make me yours again. Make love to me." I need him. I search his eyes and see his brain is getting in the way of his heart and heat. What do I do? I don't want him to think I'm pushing him for sex. He needs to know it's more.

Rick gives the driver a destination change. This man always has a plan. A few minutes later we pull up to an apartment building and the driver opens the door. Rick pulls me out of the limo along with him. We walk in and get to the elevator, my body is on fire with elevator memories and I can't help but wonder how he'll handle this. He presses the button for the third floor and the growing tension in his hand is evident. "We're on the elevator," I point out simply and that's all it takes. His hands are all over me and he's holding me against the wall with his body. "Pull the elevator stop." I feel him get hard against me.

"No," he says as he takes a deep breath to gain control and the elevator door opens. "I promise I'll make love with you all night. Please work with me here. There are a couple things that need to happen before I'm out of control, and Sherry—you make me forget what control is." He leads me to an apartment and unlocks the door. "I told you I would take you to my place." Rick claims me with his mouth while we stand in the hallway and I put my arms around his neck. His need and desire shoot through me. He picks me up and continues to kiss me as he walks through the door and kicks the door shut behind him. He leans his forehead to mine. "This is my place and I've wanted to carry my woman through the door for years. I've never brought a woman here. None of this furniture is mine. I rent it furnished and with maid service. It's not home. It's the place I keep my stuff. I haven't been living my life. Living started when I first touched your lips at the Locale. You're everything to me."

"Come home with me and never leave," I offer my home and my heart. The brightness starts to come back to his eyes. "I want to go on road trips with you. I want to be at every game, behind home plate cheering for you, supporting you."

He smiles at me and I have hope for us, "Is there anything else you want, my queen?"

"You, my king. Please take me home."

Rick pulls me close, running his hands up and down my sides and searching my eyes. I feel like he's looking for something, but I don't know what.

He locks up and we head back to the limo. His lips on me from the time the elevator door closes until we get home. I want him inside me. I want him to come home. I need us to be the same. His kiss is more heated on the elevator up to my place and I run my hand along his hard length. I pull the elevator stop and drop to my knees, unbuttoning his pants and freeing his hard love. He grabs my arm and pulls my mouth to his, kissing me with need and holding me against the elevator wall with his body while he pulls my belt off hastily and slides his hand into my pants. He gets harder at the touch of my wet heat. I'm entranced by his kiss and don't even notice he puts himself away. The elevator starts moving and he picks me up to take me with him, not taking his lips from mine as he carries me home. Rick unlocks the door and kisses me, repeating what he did at his apartment and carrying me through the door. "This feels right, our home," he says as he walks into our bedroom and lays me down on our bed.

I sit up to take my boots off and he watches me. I continue to undress, removing my socks, taking off my jewelry, pulling off my pants, and slipping my top off, leaving me in my matching black satin string bikinis and bra. I move to the bathroom, to wash off my face and brush out my hair, so I can be me and bare for him.

I go back to the bedroom and Rick is lying in our bed, naked. I step out of my panties and unhook my bra, letting it fall to the floor. I climb in bed, needing him and wanting him urgently. I want to climb on top of him and mount his hard length, but he stops me. I'm so frustrated and needy. I want him inside me. "What the fuck!" Pent up tears start to run down my face. "Why won't you let me have you inside me? I need you. I need to have you. I need to feel you love me like it was before I fucked everything up!" There it is. Everything in my head out where he can hear and see my girl crazy. "I told you I have girl baggage! Damn it!" I move away needing to hide my emotions in the shower, but he grabs me and pulls me close.

"I don't know what's going on, but I'm not letting you leave this bed. Now, baby, let me love you," he says as he holds me. His hands hot on my skin as they caress my breasts and he licks from my neck down to my sex. His beard tickles my heat as he licks my sensitive nub. He moves down burying his face in my hot wet sex, licking my wetness with his tongue and slowly caressing my clit.

"Oh my god!" I cry out. Rick stops and pulls away. Leaving me wanting more.

He glares at me with an evil grin and says, "Who am I?"

"My king. Rick, my king!" I answer quickly, needing his attention.

"Tell me more. Tell me what you want," Rick tortures me.

"I want you inside me, my king. Only you." He goes back to licking my needy center, over and over, sucking and nibbling all around it until he dives back into my wet folds. Taking his tongue as deep as he can and driving me crazy. "Please can I have you inside me?" I beg and he slides a finger in me. "Please, my king. I need you. I want to feel you. I need your love inside me. Only you my king. Love me. Please love me. I want to feel you push into me. I need to feel you come inside me. Please, my king—make me your queen."

He sucks and licks knowing exactly what to do to set me off, but won't do it. He climbs my body and claims my mouth with his. His hard length rubbing between my legs, he reaches down and rubs my clit hard while he strokes my tongue with his. I'm out of control. "Rick, I love you." He slides his hard cock into me slowly and I'm done. I see the fireworks I've been missing as he strokes into me deep and deliberate while he kisses me.

His kiss slows, he lightly sucks on my lip as he moves his kiss to my neck and whispers in my ear with his low sexy voice that drives me crazy, "I love you, baby. Only you, my queen. Tell me it's only me. Tell me you want me. Tell me everything in your pretty head."

"I'm only yours. No one else will ever have me, only you. I want you always. I never want to be without you. I want to be with you forever. I love you. I want to..." I catch myself before I say something crazy, something I wasn't aware I wanted.

Rick pounds into me harder and faster. He's almost there. "You can tell me anything, baby. I'll never leave." He's getting harder and stretching me slowly with his thick length.

"I love you, baby." I claim his mouth with mine. Trying to tell him things I can't say in words with my actions. With my tongue on his and my hands on his body. I dig my fingers into his strong upper arms and cry out his name uncontrollably. My orgasm pulling at him and drawing him as he pushes in hard and holds himself at my deepest point feeling me squeeze him over the edge.

Rick wraps his loving arms around me and holds me tight to his chest. "I missed you, baby. I'm never letting go."

All I can do is smile. I didn't break us.

CHAPTER TWO

The smell of coffee came earlier than I wanted it to on Thursday morning. My alarm had already gone off and I turned it off, thanking it for waking me to the gorgeous love of my life wrapped around me. I need a remote to turn the coffee smell off. The aroma wins and I start to get up for coffee, but I'm grabbed and pulled back into bed.

"I don't think so," and he puts his lips on mine tenderly, rolling me under him and taking me with his hard length. "Good morning, my queen," he says with a huge smile on his face. "I missed being with you, but I missed your sweet talk when you're asleep the most. I need to wake up with you in my arms every day."

I can't believe I'm saying this and moving this quickly, but I'm all in. "We can make that happen. Are you moving in with me today? Sounds like a good thing to do on your off day," I suggest. I really need to figure out what I say in my sleep. Suddenly he renders me speechless with his motions and all I can do is feel. His hot breath on my ear, describing what he's doing to me slowly as he does it sends me over the edge quicker than it should and I'm calling out his name.

"Yes, my queen. Now, you're going to come for me again, with me when I'm ready. Feel me push into you and rub you with my love, then take it away, over and over, feel the friction, our heat. Feel me push all the way into you, harder, faster. Touch my cock and feel me entering you, sliding in and out. Feel my length get harder for you because you feel so damn good around me. Yes, that's all you Sherry. Only you do this to me." Rick pushes on my magic buttons. "Okay love, for me now…" and we both go off like shooting stars. He has so much control over me, I don't understand—but I love it.

Rick pulls me on top of him and holds me to his chest. Quietly he tells me, "I want to move in with you. Do you want me and my stuff here? Do you want this to be my home? I don't want to push you. It's a big change and we have challenges."

"I want this to be our home. I want you here with me," I say with a huge smile on my face.

"That's what I want, too," so happy and relaxed.

"It's date night and if you're moving in today, I'll make dinner here for your first night home. Is that okay? Date night is usually your thing."

"That's perfect. I'll shower and get Chase to come get me, so I can make him help carry. I have errands to take care of, too. That should leave you enough time to get your work done." He gets his phone and gives Chase the address. "Chase says I'm crazy. He's right, I'm crazy in love with you. I have my keys."

I pull on shorts and a tank top, then check the kitchen for supplies as I make up my dinner menu and start in on work while Rick gets ready to go. I handle a few business emails and check my messages. I have a couple of texts:

Text from Sam – I haven't heard from my brother. Please tell me he's with you.

Text from Mom – How are you doing? How did your singing thing go last night?

Text to Sam - He's here. Neither one of us are leaving. I'll tell him to call you.

I walk into the bathroom to talk to Rick while he's in the shower and get distracted by the view. Damn! I need to write things down before I walk into a room where he's naked.

"Babe, Sam sent me a text and I told her you'll call her. Also, um, my Mom needs to meet you," I say as an afterthought.

"Can you go to lunch Saturday? Maybe you can invite your Mom down and then you two can have some time together between lunch and the game. I can get you an extra ticket for Mom if she wants to go to the game." Why doesn't he freak out about meeting parents?

"We aren't playing LA, she's not going to want to go to the game," I hang my head in shame yet again.

"Tell her I want her to go to the game and we can get dessert after or get her a room for the night," he suggests and I know what I need to do, I know what makes my Mom tick.

I shouldn't put it off any longer, I call Mom.

"Hello?" she answers.

"Hi, Mom. Would you like to drive down to have lunch Saturday and maybe stay for the baseball game? I know we aren't playing LA."

"I'd love to meet you for lunch, but I'm not interested in a Seals Game," she says.

"I'd like you to go. Rick wants you to go to the game, too."

"No, I don't think so," difficult mother.

14

Rick takes the phone from me, "Hi ma'am, I want to take you and your daughter out to lunch and I'd love it if you'd go to my game. It would mean a lot to me and I'm sure Sherry would enjoy spending the afternoon shopping with you or going to the spa or something. Maybe both if you'd like to stay the night Saturday. I'm happy to get you a room." He continues, "I love your daughter, she's the best thing that ever happened to me and I'm not letting her go." He listens, "I can't wait to meet you. Sherry will get everything set up and get you the details. Thank you, ma'am," and he hangs up leaving me in awe.

"Please book a room for your Mom for Saturday night, some place nice that she'll like. She wants to go shopping after we have lunch and loved the idea of spa day on Sunday with her daughter. She agreed to go to the game, so I'm going to get you two tickets behind home plate. Lunch downtown or somewhere else and you can drop me off at the stadium?"

"You're amazing. Lunch somewhere else." I say knowing where Mom will want to go shopping.

"Perfect. Then you can take my car and park in my spot when you get to the stadium," Rick says nonchalantly.

"What? I can't park in the players lot," minor freak-out.

"It's fine. It'll impress your Mom and you might as well get used to it because I'm moving in, so you get a stadium access pass," he continues like it's everyday business.

I repeat, "What? You're killing me with all this."

"Get used to it, babe. Life of the baseball player. Not part of what you imagined? I wondered about your fantasy. Maybe add that to date night tonight?" he says laughing. He plants one of his no-way-you-can-forget-me kisses on me and says, "I love you, Sherry. I'll be home later."

What did I get myself into? I'm in it and I'm not giving it up. Baseball player craziness is better than being without him. I never want to be without him.

I take a quick drive to the public market to pick up a couple of dry aged steaks from the butcher, some baby potatoes, broccoli and cauliflower from the produce girl, a wedge of parmesan from the cheese guy and a quart of Kahlua ice cream from the creamery. The ice cream is for me, not for dinner.

I get home and unload my groceries. I mix up some brownie batter adding the coffee I didn't drink this morning instead of other liquid and let the batter rest while I preheat the oven.

I have a couple of hours to get some work done, book a room for Mom, book spa time for Sunday and get the brownies baked, then I need to clean up, set the table, and cook dinner. Date night needs to be perfect.

I drop chocolate and peanut butter bits on top of my brownie batter as I place the pan of chocolate deliciousness in the oven to bake and set the timer for 30 minutes.

I book a room for Mom and spa time for both of us at the Brighton. I know she's always wanted to go to the spa there. The spa is on the roof, it features a covered pool and a tasty spa menu. Plus, it's not too far from the stadium and it'll be easy to take her there after the game.

I hear my door open, no knock or anything, "Hey babe, Chase is with me. Unloading my stuff from his truck." He walks over and gives me a quick kiss.

Total girl moment. Rick came in like he lives here, because he does. No knock. No hesitation. It's his home.

Chase adds on, "Hey babe, you baking something for me? Smells good." He walks over and gives me a peck on the cheek.

(Note to self: Need to be prepared for multiple baseball players at all times.)

Rick gives Cross the evil eye. "My woman."

"I know, but I'm being nice if she bakes," Chase says.

"Chase sweetie, I'm baking brownies and they're almost done," adding to Rick's torment.

The guys make a few trips up unloading while I take the brownies out to cool and finish up my last few work items for the day. I look at his clothes and boxes of stuff in my place, correction —our place, and consider how I can clear some space for him in the closet.

They take off to handle a few things and I shower before I start dinner preparations. I put on a short tropical print sundress with ties over each shoulder, made of a silky material and one of my favorites I bought in Hawaii. I work my way into the kitchen to start prep for dinner. I find my apron and pull the ties around to the front. I set the steaks out to get to room temperature and gather my veggies, cheese, herbs and spices. I wash all the veggies, toss the baby potatoes in olive oil, black pepper, garlic salt, marjoram and thyme, and set them aside on a baking sheet. I chop the broccoli and cauliflower into bite-size pieces, bagging up the stems to make a broth later. I grate up some of the parmesan and preheat the oven. It's date night and I want it to be special. I set the table simply with a candle and the frame I bought in Colorado with my favorite selfie of us together. It puts me in a romantic mood and I consider which playlist to go with. I need to make a new one that includes "Thinking Out Loud," "Come Home," "Never Tear Us Apart," "All Right Now." I want to invoke memories of everything good. I place the potatoes in the oven to start baking and watch for when they start to soften, and cut out a few brownies about three inches square. It's warm in the kitchen, so I tie my hair up on the top of my head leaving my neck and shoulders bare. I take the potatoes out of the oven and squish them with another pan on top of them, making the skins crack and exposing the soft white inside. I dust them with parmesan cheese and consider eating all of the brownies and ice cream while I wait for Rick to get home.

Rick gets home a while later and finds me at the closet. I've already moved my clothes around and started hanging up his, and added his books to my bookshelf. He puts his arms around me and smiles contently, "Chase is back, he followed me up mumbling about brownies." He kisses me like he's been gone for weeks and leaves me heated.

I smile up at him, "I've got Chase covered." He follows me to the kitchen and I have two brownies on a napkin waiting for Chase. Rick's very interested in my short dress, apron, available neck, and bare feet. "Chase sweetie, come on into the kitchen. I've got something for you," I call out.

Chase was there instantly, who knew he'd be easy to control with baked goods? Rick was standing behind me, his hands appreciating my hips. "Dude, I don't need to see that. But, I'd like a brownie, make it two brownies."

I hand him the brownies and thank him for helping Rick move in. "I'll remember and bake extra next time."

"No problem. You two need to get a room, but you're already in it. Awkward. I'm out of here. See you tomorrow, dude," and Cross was gone with brownie in mouth.

"You want to get cleaned up and I'll finish dinner?" I ask Rick thinking he just moved all his stuff and it's a hot day.

"I'd rather start with dessert," he says as he runs his hands over my body and claims me with his mouth.

I see the heat in his eyes and untie my apron "No, you should leave that on," he says as he goes for my neck, kissing, nibbling and sucking. He gets hard against me and I rub against him with my hips, driving him hotter with my sway and the feel of my body in his hands. He reaches under my short dress to find me going commando. "Fuck me." He drops to his knees putting his mouth on me, sucking hard at my sex while holding me to him with both hands on my ass. The immediate heat and intensity of his mouth and hands on me have me out of control, at his mercy.

"Oh Rick! More! Please more!" I call out to him and it drives him further. Sucking harder and sliding a finger inside me until I convulse in pleasure calling out his name.

Rick bends me over and thrusts his hard cock into me from behind, holding me up with his arm around my waist. "Baby, you're perfect. So tight around me, you were made for me." He's moving fast and the friction keeps my orgasm rolling. His need for me showing in his wild abandon. He's so hard and completely in the moment. I can't help myself and I begin pushing back against him, meeting his strokes and intensity until he grabs my hips and takes full control. Pounding me on him hard and fast, digging his fingers into my hips and not letting go until he cries out a guttural moan, biting down on my neck as he comes hard and takes me into oblivion with him. We should've ended up on the floor. Rick somehow had me leaning against him, my back to his front—both of us gasping for air. "I love you, my queen. It's only like this with you. I've always been in control, but something about you makes me lose it and drives me fucking wild. I don't just want you, I need to have you, I need to touch you, and I need to have you wrapped around me."

I turn to him unable to put words together and kiss him deeply, claiming him as my own. I feel his body sigh in relief and he puts his arms around me, holding me close.

After my recovery, I send him to shower and work on dinner. I toss the veggies with the potatoes, adding a bit of olive oil and salt. I place the tray back in the oven and turn the broiler on. I place the steaks on the broiler tray and make sure I have my tongs ready. I turn on my new playlist and place the steaks in the broiler for a few minutes, then flip them over for a few minutes more. I pull the broiler tray and cover the steaks with foil. I check the veggies and move them around the tray, leaving them to cook longer.

Rick comes out of the shower dressed in a snug fitting black

T-shirt and board shorts. The damnedest things make me lose it. I feel the drool building up and preparing to drip down my face. It's unbelievable, luckily Rick is hungry. "It smells good in here. Can I help with anything?"

"Nope, everything is about ready. Have a seat." I point to the table.

He inspects the table, glaring at it unacceptably. He moves the chairs so they are on the same side, next to each other. He lights the candle and picks up the framed photo. "This is perfect," he says looking at the photo, "Crowns for the king and queen." Rick adjusts the place settings to satisfy the new seating configuration before I get there to serve dinner. What was I thinking? It will always be this way.

I put the steak on his plate and dish the veggies next to it, adding more parmesan to the veggies once they're plated.

We sit down to eat together, in our home, where we live together. Leaning on each other and making googly-eyed faces at each other like teenagers.

I clear the plates and stick them in the dishwasher. Rick sets "Thinking Out Loud" on repeat. He comes to me in the kitchen and puts his arms around my waist, "Dance with me." He holds me close and we sway in each other's arms. This may be the best thing ever, his strong arms around me, my head leaning on his chest, his smile against my cheek and our hearts beating together. I love this man.

I make a dessert plate with brownies, Kahlua ice cream, chocolate sauce and whipped cream with only one spoon, and we stand in our kitchen feeding each other, licking whipped cream from each other's lips, sucking chocolate sauce off each other's fingers and kissing until I find myself being carried to bed.

CHAPTER THREE

W e lie next to each other in bed and he says, "I'm ready to hear about your fantasy."

"I don't think you really want to hear about my fantasy. You didn't even want to be a baseball player with me and that's where my fantasy begins," I wait for denial.

"I want to hear it from you. I want to know everything about you. I don't want us to have any secrets. Nobody else matters, only us," he says as serious as a heart attack.

It's silly, but I can't get the secret I'm keeping out of my head. Sam said hide it and she probably knows best. But, I need to stick with honesty and I refuse to risk this by keeping a secret from him. I can do this. "Okay. I'll tell you about my fantasy, but first I need to confess a secret. I'm not going to say it's something silly or it doesn't matter, so I didn't think I needed to tell you. It's not bad and it's not good, it just is."

"Tell me and get it out there," he says slightly unsure.

I made too big of a deal about it because it's been hanging out in my mind. I had no idea what affect it was going to have on me.

21

"I have a pack of pregnancy tests hiding in the cabinet and it's Sam's fault. So, don't freak out."

"Is there anything else you want to share about that? Like, why? Or, how my sister fits in this?" he questions maintaining calm, but I can see his level of relaxation has changed.

"Uh, yea. Sam told me to buy a multi-pack and take a test, because I was being extremely emotional and the pill isn't 100% effective. She actually suggested the pill might not be able to handle the sperm of a professional athlete," I share the whole reasoning behind it.

He smiles, "Well, it's true professional athletes like myself might as well be super heroes."

I watch his train of thought change, "Did you do a test?"

"Yes, I did a test on Monday," I take a deep breath because I haven't said it out loud and I know how I feel about it will show. I hate being a fucking girl that shows her emotions even when she doesn't want to. "It was negative." My eyes start to well up and I do my best to somehow suck it back in without Rick noticing.

Rick pulls me to him and holds me against his chest. A few minutes of silence pass and he speaks in the most sincere tone, "Thank you for telling me. Please don't keep anything from me."

"I promise. I won't keep secrets from you. I have always and will always be honest with you." I take a deep breath, "I didn't know I wanted it until I was sad when it was negative and I didn't tell anybody. Well, Sam knows it was negative. I sent her a picture." A single tear rolls down my face. Damn it! This girly stuff! "Sorry, I didn't mean to lay all of that on you."

Rick's hold on me tightens and he takes a deep breath as he kisses my forehead sweetly. "Someday, baby."

"Tell me about your happy fantasy, my queen," trying to steer our conversation into a different direction, and I oblige.

We snuggle under the sheets together and I tell him about my fantasy. "I've had a fantasy baseball boyfriend ever since you made it to the majors. I didn't look at you and consciously choose my fantasy. I'd never had one before. It just happened. I started having dreams about the fantasy. What he'd feel like to touch, from his hair to his hard body. What his beard would feel like when he kissed me. How his lips would taste and his salty neck after we'd worked up a sweat. How it would feel to have his hands on my skin. Would they leave a heated path or goose-bumps? The feel of his tongue against mine, his mouth claiming me, taking my body as his and having his way with me, driving me out of control. Waking up in the morning, imagining it was real and checking in the bed next to me to find I was alone. I never spoke to him, but I was at every home game cheering for him more than the rest of the team and wearing only his jersey. I wanted his autograph, but I refused to single him out and specifically go after him and only him. I was waiting for my opportunity at a fanfest or autograph signing, and it'd been years without happening. I was afraid he wouldn't be anything near what I imagined, or I'd speechlessly lose my marbles when I got close to him. I avoided one of the things I wanted most, him. Men would ask me out and I even went on a handful of dates, but they were all compared to the fantasy and reality was tossed aside. I learned that fantasy is what you believe you want, and there was no reason why I should settle for anything less, other than it didn't really exist.

"One night after a winning game I felt froggy and saw an opportunity to get a couple autographs, so I went for it. I had a drive to complete my collection and was only missing a few of the current players. I cut through the seats to the dugout while the team was celebrating on the field and hung out a few minutes. I always love to watch the on field interviews after a winning game, and this was the perfect location for it. The rookie walked up to me, I got his autograph and he started talking to me, but I had no idea what he said. I was completely oblivious. I'm pretty sure he saw me drool as I focused on my fantasy who was standing only twenty feet away. I swear I could smell his manly, rustic scent in the air. I tried to recover, told him I needed the autograph for my collection and that he'd been doing a great job this season. I stood there getting my wits about me, while I watched the interviews. My fantasy completely ignored me and walked right passed me to the locker room. I was devastated because both of my fears had come true within a few minutes—my fantasy ignored me, making me consider he might not be who I thought he was and I became a blithering idiot. I gave up. My heart sank. I turned from the field and started for home. Then somebody yelled for a blonde in a Seno jersey and I thought to myself 'Huh, I'm a blonde in a Seno jersey... I should turn around, but they can't be yelling at me' and I turned to look anyway. The rookie was standing there looking straight at me. I walked back to the dugout, he handed me a note and was gone. I remember reading the note and thinking 'I can't date a ball player.' I had mixed emotions about meeting a man at a bar at midnight. But, none of it mattered because it was my fantasy and if I didn't go I would regret it more than any dumb thing I might do with a guy I met at the bar. It was my fantasy, rules had to be forgotten. This was one of those nights that could define your life. I'd make the most of the night and enjoy it, because it was only going to be one night. That's what baseball players do, right? Especially, when you're invited to a bar at midnight? It's a one night stand and I don't do that, but for my fantasy I'd see the night through and follow his lead or I'd always wonder 'what if.'"

Rick caresses my skin as I speak, "The interesting thing is that I learned something. I was wrong. Reality is better than the fantasy in every way."

"Proof we are meant to be together, baby," he says and claims my lips showing me his emotions. He keeps his arms wrapped around me and I fall asleep in his arms.

I wake up at about 3:30 and can't sleep. I get up quietly and go in the other room to do some work. I know Friday is going to be a full day and Saturday isn't going to have time left to make up for it. I check my email, social media, and to-dos for the day, update some photos on my social media and price out options for a few new trip requests I've received. I go back to the trip Rick asked me to plan for us and review the details, updating the airfare to first class and adding an oceanside couple massage. I'm fidgety and can't make myself sit still. I hit the pan of brownies, picking at the bits and crumbs around the edges. I'm awake and I don't want to be. I want to be sleeping and wrapped in my gorgeous man's arms. But my brain and body aren't agreeing with me. I finally take the time to get my Instagram started and post a few photos my customers have sent to me. I sit and read my new Hawaii magazine from cover to cover. Still not sleepy. What the fuck? I've never had trouble sleeping. What am I freaking out about? Time for a recap: I wanted my hunky boyfriend to move in and he did. All secrets have been shared. Great date night. Ate more brownies than I should have. All caught up on work. Had amazing sex. Okay. It must be that Mom is meeting Rick tomorrow or, oh shit! Sam told me to do another test. Nerves anyone? I don't want to do another test. It made me sad and I don't want to reinforce sadness. Maybe next week or if I'm late or something. Why am I worried about Rick meeting my Mom? He was great with her on the phone and even got her to do what he wanted, when I couldn't.

"Babe." I hear called from the bedroom.

Shit! I don't want him waking up alone or getting any strange ideas. I get up and walk into the bedroom to find him sitting up and squinting at me. "Hey. I couldn't sleep."

He reaches out and grabs my hand, pulling me to him. "I can

fix that." He puts his lips on mine and pulls me over to lay on top of him while he kisses me and kisses me and kisses me. He caresses the curve of my back and runs his other hand through my hair. Touching me possessively, lovingly. Then he starts to tell me a story, "There was once a king who was lonely and sad, but hid it from everyone around him. His court lacked loyalty and had lied to him. His army was his family and they always backed him up, constantly looking out for him—especially the newest and youngest soldier. His castle was empty and the only maidens who wished to visit his royal mattress were merely in search of a conquest or royal title or treasure. The king focused on his kingdom and ruling his army. Ignoring the loneliness which nagged at him, the parts of him which seemed to be dead and his worry about having a royal heir. He went into battle almost daily with his army, calling the shots from the battlefield and being an active participant. Unafraid. But, hid himself away from his personal world inside the castle and maintained special armor protecting himself from his disloyal court and the greedy maidens. Always in need of a woman who loved him and trusted him. A woman to make his queen, for only him to worship. To be his only one and give him an heir. One day after battle, his newest and youngest soldier came to him saying he had found the woman for his bed. The king chastised his young soldier for being focused on pleasure and sowing his oats, but the soldier insisted the king had been sheltered too long and must attempt to remove the armor. The king agreed to send for the maiden his trusted soldier spoke of and from the moment he touched her hand he felt he was under a spell. He left her in his sitting room to consider his battle plan, and when he returned he could do nothing but kiss her. He wondered what this spell was, what potion this woman had with her. Oddly, she tried to break the spell, seeming afraid of it. When the king saw her walk he had to have her. He had to touch her. He had to know her intimately.

He needed this witch to want him and need him. He needed her to be unlike the other maidens. He would leave for battle and be unable to concentrate on the war. Her kiss mesmerized him and her body had left him addicted. He wanted her in his castle and he wanted her to rule beside him, but the intensity of the spell had caught them both off guard. The king had become enraged, questioning, and she fled in the night. The king was miserable and needed to have her. He needed her to be safe and protected. He wanted to do things he'd never done before and would send his servants to do nice things for her since she didn't want to be in the presence of the king or talk to the king. The amazing woman finally allowed the king in her presence and was accepting, but had demands. They would live together in the castle and if the king was going to war, she would be at the battlefield. This spell-casting woman did not demand treasure, she did not care about title even when I referred to her as my queen. She was not after the royal seed. Yet the king could not help himself. The king had to have her in his bed repeatedly." Rick kissed me tenderly. "I love you my queen, may I worship you now? I promise to grant all of your wishes in time. I just want to pleasure you." He pulled the blanket up over us and took me to a new world, worshiping me until I could no longer stay awake and my brain gave up.

CHAPTER FOUR

I woke up in my favorite place Friday morning before my alarm went off and before the coffee was brewing, there was a man holding me tight and talking. Does he tell me the same things I say in my sleep when he thinks I'm sleeping? I wonder. I'll probably never get to know. It doesn't matter, he's here with me. Though, this morning he's having a quiet conversation with himself while I sleep. "My sweet, beautiful, Sherry. I hope I deserve you. I hope I give myself to you as freely as you give yourself to me. I want to know everything your heart desires. I want to take care of you and give you everything. I've only ever loved you and I don't know what I'd do if you weren't with me. I never want to experience it again. My happiness, my love, my life." I absorb his words and the soft whisper he says them in, enjoying his possessive arms around me. He fills me with the love and confidence I need to be part of his world.

The damn alarm goes off and I smack the snooze button, but it'll only give me nine minutes. I pretend it never went off. Rick squeezes me and kisses my neck, then whispers in my ear, "Good morning, my queen. I love being here with you."

I roll toward him, squishing my naked breasts against his chest and put my arms around his neck. "Good morning, my king. I love you being here with me." I draw a line down his throat with my kisses. I feel his hard length on my leg. I reach for the alarm and turn it off. I grasp him and lightly stroke him with my hand, receiving a very happy response. I slide under the sheet and continue to run my hand up and down his length. I lick his tip, tasting the moisture there. I trail my tongue along his thickness and swirl around the tip as I suck him into my mouth. I take him all the way in my mouth, pulling my lips and tongue along his shaft.

"Babe, come to me so we can come together. I want to love you," he says as he sits up and pulls my lips to his. I grab his hard cock and slide it inside me. He's exquisite, filling me and stretching me. "I love the way you take control of my dick like it's yours. It is yours."

He moves inside me, pressing up into me. His arms holding my body to his and his lips claiming mine possessively. I feel the whisker burn on my face as we move together, slowly stroking and building the heat. His tongue hurried as it moves against mine. He needs this and he's trying to hold back. I run my fingers down his back and bite his neck hard right at the collarbone. "My body's yours, baby. Don't hold back."

He searches me with flames in his eyes, seeking permission. He lays me back on the bed as he begins to pound into me with need. Harder and harder, he slams into me over and over. Hard and fast and fucking amazing. Driving me to my own orgasm without any other contact, simply his hard love filling me again and again. I tighten around him, squeezing him and he continues with a few last hard strokes as he sends himself into oblivion with me. His face is red and he has perspiration on his temples. I reach for his mouth with mine and kiss him thoroughly as we both come down.

I smell the coffee brew and apparently so does he, "Want to walk over to the Yolk for breakfast with me before I go to the stadium?"

"For sure," I say as we both get out of bed and get dressed.

We walk to the Yolk and have a tasty breakfast with easy conversation. I love how he always holds my hand when we walk together and always sits on the same side of the table with me.

Walking back from the Yolk, Rick starts giving me information, "I need to be at the stadium by noon today. That's early for a Friday because I need to get a full work out in and I have some things to take care of at the stadium. I'd like you to be at the stadium in time for batting practice today. I had the membership team hold your seat for you, but I prefer when you sit behind home plate and I can hear you throughout the game. Can I bribe you because I know you have friends in your section you want to hang out with? I can get you all passes for early entry today, so you can all be in the park near the dugout for batting practice. Then you can hangout with them in the member lounge pregame before you come sit behind home plate. Also, any tips about your mom before I make reservations for lunch tomorrow?"

"You don't need to bribe me, my king. I'll be there for you and cheer for you. I promise, I'll be there yelling for you. But, Batting Practice might be cool and I'm sure my section peeps would appreciate it. They might forgive me for ditching them. Mom is pretty basic when it comes to food, she likes any place with salad options. Am I riding home from the game with you tonight?"

"Whatever you want, babe. You can drop me off and drive my car, so you can use my parking spot. There will be an envelope for you at will call."

I message all of my section peeps about meeting for early BP and try to get some work done, while Rick starts to unpack.

Rick walks up to me ready to go to the stadium, "Are you ready?"

"No, go and I'll meet you there before BP," I suggest, realizing I should've been paying attention to the time.

Rick puts his arms around me, "Okay, but be early for BP," as he gives me one of his unbelievable you-can-never-forget-me kisses. I reciprocate diving into his mouth with my tongue and moaning into his mouth with need. I don't want him to forget me and I want him punch drunk, exactly how he leaves me.

About 20 minutes later I get a text message from Rick.

Text from Rick - You drive me crazy. I'm walking into the clubhouse with a hard-on and I had sex pregame. I love you, my queen.

I love that I'm able to do that to him. I'm sure the team will enjoy some fun at Rick's expense over the hard-on.

Text to Rick - I love you, too. See you this afternoon, but can't wait to come home with you.

My phone rings and the caller ID says it's the stadium, "Hello?"

"Hi, this is Carter from the Seals. I'm looking for Sherry."

"This is Sherry. Is everything okay?" wondering what's up.

"Everything is fine. I'm a clubhouse assistant and Seno has given me some things to take care of for him today. I need some details from you, would that be okay?"

"Sure thing. What can I do?" wondering what he's up to now.

"I'm supposed to have a jersey made for your mom and need to know what size. While I'm at it, what size jersey do you wear and do you have a preference on cap styles? I also need your date of birth for your access card and do you know how many people will be joining you for BP today?" he rattles off questions.

"Mom wears a women's extra large. I wear women's large in

jerseys and usually get a men's jersey. I prefer adjustable caps and don't mind snap-backs. My birthday is May 3 and give me a minute to get you a head count," I say trying to figure out who's going. I check through my messages to find out who can meet early for BP. "Ten people will be joining me," I tell him. He thanks me and asks me to have will call contact him when I get to the stadium. Rick really put him to work.

Since I already have the phone in my hand, I decide to dial up Mom and give her the plan for the weekend. "Hello?" Mom answers the phone.

"Hi, Mom! Thought I'd give you a call with the info for this weekend. How are you today?"

"Everything seems to be fine today. Is Rick the guy who was carrying you over his shoulder in that internet picture?" she asks.

"Yes, Mom. Rick is the only baseball player and the only man in my life. You have a room at the Brighton for Saturday night and we have a reservation at the spa Sunday morning."

"I guess I do need to meet this guy. He said he loves you and he's not letting you go," Mom recounts.

"I know, Mom. I was there listening when you went along with him after telling me no." I point out the part of the conversation that irritated me.

"Okay, so what's the plan?" Mom asks.

"When you drive down tomorrow go straight to the Brighton. They'll let you check-in and park your vehicle there. Your reservation has an early check in for Saturday and a late check-out on Sunday. Everything is already paid for including valet parking. We will pick you up to go to lunch." I give her instructions and hope she listens.

"Where are we going to lunch?"

"No idea. Rick is handling that part himself. When he says he wants to take you out, he means it. He picks the place and everything. He does the same thing on date nights," I say and giggle. I like how he plans it all out and I'm along for the ride.

"That worries me. He's controlling," Mom frets.

"He's not controlling, but he has certain things that are just him. It's kind of nice to get in the car and let him have everything planned. You have to meet him," I say gushing.

"I thought you were giving it time or something? What's the current standing?" she wants details.

"You need to meet him, Mom. I love him. I'll give you the details in person tomorrow. Rick said he's getting a reservation for 11:30 lunch, so we'll pick you up about 11:10." I can hear her deciding she should back out, so I get off the phone quickly.

"I don't know..." and I cut her off.

"I've got to pick up another call that's coming in. See you in the morning," and I hang up.

I get ready for the game, and head to the trolley station feeling like a million bucks. Happy to be treating my baseball peeps to early BP and amazed at the man who's making the unnecessary bribe happen. I love how he wants me there early and behind the plate for the game, for him. I should be upset he's choosing my seat, but it's all about supporting him, and it's like being at the game with him. He wants me there. I never thought this would happen. He wants me there. He wants me cheering for him. He needs me.

The trolley gives me too much time to myself. Yes it's public transportation, smells like pee and/or barf at any given moment, could have transients wandering through, and it's still the best way to get to the stadium. It evokes baseball for me. It's part of my game process. It's all part of the event. Getting to the park. Getting stadium food. Getting to my seat in time to watch my guys warm up. Today I'm trying to enjoy the ride and take in the beautiful San Diego coast route on the green line. It's changed so much over the years. The Wyland artwork on the building near

Little Italy is still there, but you can't see it with the new building built next to it blocking the way. The juxtaposition of the Tuscan accented apartments followed by the contemporary art and then the Spanish details of the Santa Fe Depot, it's San Diego defined. The trolley stops have been refurbished and even the lines have changed to be more accommodating. New public park areas have popped up a few places along the green line. No matter how I try to distract myself, my head is filled with my team and the way it's being stripped naked of the players we all cheer for. It's an annual thing, the trade deadline. And, it's bittersweet. Sad to watch deals that get our favorites traded, but I always look forward to the rookies coming up. Most years that's in September when its time for the expanded roster and the teams bring up guys to give them a taste of the big leagues. This year, it's happening in July. Because, well... trades gutted us. It's the right thing in the long run. There's no telling how the next three seasons go. Games could be a disaster. It's horrible! Everything's in my head as I walk up to the stadium and the organist is playing "Yesterday" by the Beatles. Couldn't be more right on. Trade Seno and it could gut me, too.

I walk up to the will call window and ask them to let Carter know I'm here. After a few minutes, a short bald man walks up to me with his hands full.

"Hi, Sherry? I'm Carter," he introduces himself.

"Hi! You need help," I observe.

"Only when one of the guys assigns me on a mission and today it was Seno," he laughs. "Okay, so here's your access card. It doesn't give you free rein of the stadium, but it does give you access when employees have access and it does allow you access to the players parking lot when you're driving the registered vehicle, Rick's Challenger."

The photo on the access card is cropped from one of the selfie pictures Rick took in Colorado. He kept them with him. It makes my heart warm. I'm such a freaking girl. I'm never going to under-stand how he has this effect on me. I've never gotten gooey over any man.

Carter continues, "This is your Mom's jersey for tomorrow." He holds up the extra large women's jersey already personalized with SENO and the big 6. The regular team uniform the team will be wearing tomorrow. "This is your full set of jerseys. Seno wanted you to have the jersey to match the team for every game, so here is the regular team jersey, the alternate jersey, the Sunday jersey, the away jersey and the matching caps." He trades me the jersey and cap I have on for the alternate jersey and matching cap. Everything of course with the big 6 and SENO emboldened across it.

"Are you kidding me?" I'm ecstatically happy. My fandom is showing.

Carter smiles at me, "You really are a fan. You two are a perfect match. I do see a wardrobe problem. I'll get that fixed and leave everything in Seno's car. You're early for BP, do you have names? I can leave passes for your guests at will call."

I give Carter the names and send them all a quick text. He gives a note to somebody at the will call booth and directs me to follow him into the stadium. He takes me into the belly of the stadium to a room with all kinds of uniforms and things the team wear. He pulls out the matching hoodies for each jersey, handing me the one for tonight's game. Oh my god! I'm spoiled! I'm having a hard time maintaining myself.

"Let me take you to Seno and he'll escort you to BP."

Is this really happening right now? Trying to maintain myself and not let my total fan freak-out show. Carter is leading me through the stadium, up to the field and into the dugout. He yells into the clubhouse, "Seno!"

A few seconds later Rick comes walking up the stairs into the dugout and he's heading straight for me with a purpose. The only people in sight are the grounds crew setting up for BP. Then it happened, a repeat of our first kiss in the corner of the booth at the Locale. No words, his lips on mine. Claiming me all the way to my toes with his intent and lighting me up like an erupting volcano. Damn! As much as I don't like how he makes me girly, I hope this never stops.

The team starts to come out for BP and Cross starts in, "Dude, you better stop that shit. I know she's hot and spunky, but you'll be hitting BP with a hard-on and I've already seen too much of your dick today," laughing under his breath. Martin follows close behind him making smooching sounds at us.

Rick gives him a dirty look and realizes BP is starting. He walks me to my acceptable viewing area behind the dugout and introduces himself to all my peeps before he gets to work. Carter hooked my peeps up with caps that have Seno and the number 6 on them. Everybody loved it! Cross came up and gave autographs with Seno after BP. It was great!

After BP, my peeps and I all go to the lounge for $5 beer and free popcorn. Six "thank you" beers is too many, but I take them and drink them all. My baseball peeps are the best.

I find my seat behind home plate in time for the guys to come out and warm up. I'm in row two directly behind home plate tonight. I'm loopy from the beer. Rick waves at me and smiles when he comes out early to warm up our starting pitcher. Lots of hoopla going on pregame tonight and I'm not into it in my current state. I may need another beer. Luckily this section has seat service and I'm riding home with my boyfriend. Then it hits me, this is my first game back after leaving LA. The last couple of days have been amazing and so much has happened so quickly. What the fuck am I doing? Am I dating, no, living with a baseball player who I left only weeks ago? And, he's meeting my Mom tomorrow! What am I thinking? This has disaster written all over it. This whirlwind of craziness is getting the best of me and I need to take control. No more following my girliness allowed! My brain is trying to take over and I can't let that happen. This isn't a brain situation. It's a heart situation and I'm learning that's ruled by my girliness. It may be the most illogical thing I've ever done in my life, but it makes me happy and I'm risking my heart, not my brain. Maybe I shouldn't have any more beer.

A large choir walks onto the field and sings the National Anthem. The next thing I know Rick is standing at the net in front of me, smiling at me, and making motions at me like I'm drunk. I might be. I wave, smile, and do the sign language "I love you" back at him. Yelling, "Make it a win, babe!" He laughs and shakes his head as he turns around to get down to business.

The lineup is familiar other than they've squeezed Mason in. We're playing the hated San Francisco Sissy's this weekend. We need to get some wins and a sweep would be a great thing. Our ace is pitching tonight, so the game will probably go quick. The first five innings go by with no score for either team. Two of our players have been hit by a pitch, both Rock and Mason. The team is acting restless and defensive. They want to retaliate and are trying to keep a collective cool. Skip doesn't allow that crap in his dugout. Top of the sixth inning with two outs and our pitcher, Grace the Ace, lets one rip that gets away from him high and inside, skimming the edge of the hitter's helmet brim. The San Francisco dugout empties onto the field after our pitcher. Rick runs to get ahead of it and guard his pitcher. The rest of the guys on the field are there almost instantly as back up and the Seals dugout empties. Cross is at Rick's back with Mason ready to go. It's a rumble, except only hot muscular ball players are allowed to participate. Half of them know they're not supposed to fight while the other half are hooligans who don't care and want to fight—the San Francisco half. Rick has his game face on and takes control of the situation. A couple of the San Francisco guys go at him with fists ready to go, but he calmly says something I can't hear. The umpires take forever to get out there and do anything.

The hitter takes his base, daring Grace to throw at him again. "Throw at me again, meat, and I'm coming for you."

The umpire gives both teams a warning, and the next guy up strikes out. Bottom of the sixth was uneventful, we got a couple of hits but nobody scored. Bottom of the eighth, still no score with one out and Mason hits a home run bringing in Cross. Martin strikes out and Rock pops out. Top of the ninth, San Francisco responds with a homer and two hits. The runners attempt to steal and Rick picks the runner off trying to steal second base, ending the game with a 2-1 win for the Seals.

Hannah is on the field ready to do her thing. She grabs Mason and Seno for her post-game interviews. Seno tells her it's all the new rookie Mason and backs off, not wanting to get into an interview about the potential fight and what he did to avoid it.

Rick walks up to the net behind home plate and I hop over the seats into the first row to meet him. He puts his hands on the net and I reach mine up to his, holding hands through the net. "I'll be ready in about twenty minutes." I smile and nod as he takes off for the locker room. I wait for the crowd to clear and go to the elevator, using my card to get to the garage. I find Rick's car and climb into the front seat. The bench seat is comfortable and I'm buzzed. Rick finds me sleeping in his front seat and he's annoyed. "I couldn't find you and you're asleep in my car. I looked out here and didn't see you." I say something though I have no clue what came out of my mouth. "Never mind, let's go home buzzed girl." He climbs into the car and I use him as my pillow for the ride home.

I wake up and I'm being carried over Rick's shoulder into the elevator. "You can put me down in the elevator," he might want some elevator action.

"No. I'm not putting you down until we're home," he says in

a tone I'm not familiar with.

"Are you okay?" I ask unsure.

"I am now. I couldn't find you and it reminded me that you know how to hide from me." His brain is playing games with his heart.

"I'm right here and I'm not going anywhere. Remember? You moved into my place and made it our place. You don't need to worry. If you want to worry about something, it'd be how to get rid of me."

"Don't even joke. I don't want you to ever leave," he says seriously and sets me down so he can put his arms around me and kiss me senseless. We get home and he unlocks the door, locks it behind us and takes me to bed.

Rick holds me close, whispering in my ear, "I love you, Sherry. You're my only. Never leave me." He kisses me softly, then again tenderly, but not stopping. His lips on mine sweetly, sucking and nibbling at me like I'm his favorite dessert. He keeps kissing me while I kick off my sneakers and he pushes my jeans off. He can't help himself. I know what he's feeling now. He needs to feel me and know I'm here, we're here together. I reach to help him with his pants, but they're already gone. He continues kissing me with need and takes me as his slowly. Pushing into me all the way, his body relaxes when he's finally home. He lays his head on my pillow next to mine, his weight delicious on top of me.

I put my arms around him, "I'm yours, Rick. I'm not going anywhere, unless I'm going there with you. There's no one else for me. I love you, my king," in the sweetest voice I've ever heard come out of me. Still don't have a clue where it came from.

He turns to me, with the biggest grin ever and his lips are back on mine while he makes love to me for hours, never taking his lips off of me and sending me to unknown places more than once.

CHAPTER FIVE

I wake up early, nervous about the two most important people in my life meeting and go for the always soothing frosted chocolate mini donuts. I inhale almost half a bag of the heavenly bites and climb back in bed quietly hoping I wasn't missed.

Rick reaches for me, "Where'd you go?" as he pulls me to him and puts his lips on mine. He licks my lips and sucks my tongue into his mouth with a low groan. "Were you eating chocolate?"

"Mini frosted chocolate donuts," I confess. "Do you want one?" I offer as I pick up the bag I had dropped at the side of the bed for easy access. He takes three from the bag and I pop another one in my mouth before they all disappear.

"Why are you up so early?" he says with his mouth full.

"Not sure. Maybe I'm nervous about you meeting Mom," I say knowing that's exactly the problem.

"No reason to worry. Your Mom will love me. I promise. Mom's always like me." He says with confidence.

"You don't know my Mom."

"All your Mom wants is for you to be happy and if that means there's a man involved, he better treat you right. I already told her I love you and I'm not letting you go." He stops. He looks at me seriously, gazing into my eyes. "I mean it. I love you and I'm never letting you go," he says realizing I may need to hear it. He kisses me and makes me feel like the only woman in the world.

I smell the coffee calling me, get two cups and take them back to bed with me, along with my laptop. Rick looks at me appreciatively and frowns, "Laptop in bed?"

"I want to do a quick email and social media check. Same as almost every other day, but I want to stay in bed with you, too," I smile and gesture to my still mostly naked body. "I have to keep up on business and I did share my donuts with you." Rick groans at me. "You'd prefer I did it somewhere else? I can take it in the other room."

"No," as he puts his hand around my ass and snuggles up against me. "You don't need to worry about that stuff. I'll cover everything for you. I want to take care of you."

I ignore him because I don't work that way. I need to be able to take care of myself. I'm independent and don't want to answer to anyone about what I do with my money.

I check my messages, email and social media. I have a few texts, some emails and a new social media post. One of my customers posted pictures of the trip they're on right now on my page and tagged all their friends—I love it! I read my texts:

Text from Sam – Tell me everything is okay. Rick didn't call me.

Text from Adam - I'm in San Diego for work this weekend. I'm hoping you've gotten over your boyfriend and would like to spend some time with me.

Text from Mom – I packed my bag and I'm getting ready to leave. Not sure about this, but I want to see you. I'll be at the hotel waiting when you get there.

Oh, crap! A text from Adam. I thought, okay, maybe hoped he'd given up on me. I can't hide it. No secrets. "You didn't call Sam!" I tell Rick and hand him his phone.

Text to Mom - See you soon, Mom! You'll see everything is perfect. Love you!

Text to Adam - Sorry, I'm back with my boyfriend. He's the only one for me.

I debate with myself, remembering what my Mom taught me about keeping things to myself that just hurt people. When another text pops through.

Text from Adam - I'd never hurt you like he did. Give me a chance, my Angel.

Text to Adam - Goodbye.

I immediately block Adam, so the messages don't continue and he doesn't decide to call. It would be bad and escalate quickly.

The spam meter on my email is going crazy this morning, so I take a minute to go through and delete the junk mail.

I turn to Rick, take his phone and dial Sam because he hasn't managed to do it yet. She answers, "It's about time baby brother!"

"Hi, Sam," I say with a giggle. "I told him to call and I handed him his phone and he still didn't do it. So, you've got me instead. I can hand him the phone if you want."

Rick closes his eyes and shakes his head, "Why did I intro-
duce you two?"

"I can hear him in the background and that verifies he's alive.
I did watch the game last night and I could see he's back in
playing form. That's good enough. But, I'd like to know what's
going on there," Sam says still worried.

I'm not the one who should tell her he moved in with me. I
mouth a question at him silently, "Are you going to tell her you
moved in with me?"

"You tell her," he says out load where Sam could hear him.

"I've been directed to tell you that your bro moved in with
me and we're together and I love him. And, if I'm the one who's
going to talk to you then I'm waiting until he isn't here
watching and listening to me do it." Rick takes his phone
from me.

"Hey Sam," Rick says apparently not approving of the direction I was taking the call. "I'm meeting her Mom today and it's a
busy day. I'm good, actually I'm better than good. I'll call you
soon," and he hangs up wanting to use the time we have left this
morning in a specific way. But, I stop him because I need to tell
him about Adam.

Here I am needing to tell him something I thought wasn't
going to matter. Maybe I should've told him about Adam before
he moved in or when we were telling secrets. I don't know. But, I
need to tell him before he finds out on his own. I didn't think it
mattered. I'm not ever going to see the guy again. Honestly, I
thought he was gone. He hasn't texted me in days and he has a
busy schedule. Hot as he is, why would he waste time with a girl
who's hung up on another man?

"Um, I need to talk to you about something."

Rick stops and stares at me, unsure of my tone. "Okay. What
kind of something?" He already doesn't like the conversation.

"It's not bad, just filling you in on details you missed while we were apart." Realizing this is almost the worst possible timing, but it can't wait.

"Sherry, I don't think I like where this is going."

"I'm sure you won't, but listen to me for a minute. I met a guy when I was drunk in a bar in LA. I didn't have sex with him or anything. We had dinner at a cafe. We danced together at the bar and he kissed me, but I left. I didn't give him my number and he doesn't even know my name. I was extremely upset at the time, honestly hating men."

"Yea. Keep going." Rick is not happy and trying to stay calm.

"He got my number from Joey when he saw him at the bar the next night and started texting me, calling me daily while I was on my road trip. He kept telling me he wanted to spend time with me and I kept telling him I wasn't interested, that I was still getting over my boyfriend. I know you don't want to hear that, and I found I couldn't get over you. He was in San Francisco when I was driving through there and met me for dinner. He told me it wasn't a date, but it was like a date. We didn't kiss or anything. It was only dinner and I kept going on my trip." I stop trying to read his reaction.

"Is there more?"

"He drove up the coast and met me at my hotel one morning. He took me to breakfast and explored a beach area with me one day. He asked for more. He asked me to spend the weekend with him at his place in San Francisco. He kissed me. I turned him down and he dropped me off at my hotel. That's it other than a couple calls and texts while I was driving home. I told him some-body else has my heart."

"But? Why are you telling me this now?"

"He texted me this morning and he's in San Diego for work and asked me out. I told him I'm with my boyfriend and I blocked him. I can show you the texts. I'm not interested in him at all. I thought I needed to get over you. I thought you were with Ava.

He was a distraction." I pull up the texts on my phone and show Rick before he can say he wants to see it or not. I don't want him having any questions. "He never meant anything to me. I've only ever loved you, my king. I don't want to hide it from you. I figure it's better to tell you about a text from a guy than to let you find it."

He takes a deep breath. "Thank you for telling me. We were both hurting and I know you were confused. Shit, Ava was naked in our room. I don't like it. I hate the thought of another man touching you, kissing you, wanting you," his anger showing.

"None of it matters. We're here together now and we'll always be together. I didn't want him. I only want you. Believe me, trust me. I thought we were over."

Rick pulls me close, his voice low and shaky, "I know, my queen. I was afraid we were over, too. I didn't know what to do without you. I couldn't find you. I needed to know you were safe. I was worried about you being on the road trip alone and I didn't know where you were. I wanted to leave the team to go search for you. A part of me was missing. I couldn't sleep. All I could do was think about you. I hate how this guy was persistent and he's still trying. Where is he? Give me his number."

"I've already handled it. I have no idea where he is and I've already blocked him. I'm sure that's the end of it. I'm sorry. He's nothing."

Rick grins, trying hard to get over it quick, "Now, where were we..."

Text from Sam - You horndogs!

But, I can't respond because Rick has his arms around me and is claiming me with his lips. I'm not complaining. It's amazing and much better than him dwelling on Adam. Win-win. I wrap my legs around him as he carries me with him to the shower. He turns on the shower and turns his back to the cold water, keeping me warm. Slowly kissing me. I taste the chocolate and coffee on his lips. I run my fingers through his hair and feel his hard body against mine. His muscles holding me up like I'm nothing. I want him badly. His abs against me and the occasional bump of his penis near my sex increase my desire. His hands roam my body and his touch draws me into his world. I hear words around me and don't recognize that they're coming from my own mouth. "I need you. I've always loved you. I'll always be yours. Please take me now. I need your love. I need you to need me." I kiss every part of him I can reach and dig my fingers into his muscled shoulders. It's happening and I don't know where it's coming from. My need has taken control of my actions. My words affecting him.

"I'm crazy for you. I take good care of things that are mine," he says as he slides me down his body and leans me on the shower wall. He spreads my legs with his and drops to his catcher's squat. He puts his hands on my hips and runs them down my thighs as he moves closer, kissing my legs, and up my thighs. He feels my wet heat and touches my folds with his fingers, sliding one in. He latches onto my clit with his mouth, sucking and licking me until I move my hips. He has to have me. He stands up and lifts me to his body, sliding me onto his hard length exquisitely while he holds me tight to his wet body. "You're mine," he says as he repeatedly slides in and out of me. His body quivering as he pushes hard up into me and I scream out his name. The feel of him inside me, touching me, is beyond sensational. I close my eyes and see fireworks. All I can hear is our heartbeats. It hits me all at once like a rocket. I shudder and shake uncontrollably, calling out his name over and over. He follows almost immediately and presses tightly against me. We stay there pressed together against the wall, not wanting to separate and making this time together last as long as it can.

Eventually the day must get started. We have plans today.

We use the shower for what its intended and get dressed for lunch. I pull on my jeans and my "Talk Baseball To Me" top, prepared to put my jersey on over it for the game. Rick dresses in jeans and he looks so good, I want to eat him up! Can I keep him like this and always have him walking around in jeans and no shirt please? He pulls on a gray long sleeved button up shirt with bright blue flecks in the material from the closet and rolls the sleeves up. The flecks make his eyes shine. The only thing sexier is when he's in full catcher's gear and his eyes pierce through his mask.

"You're beautiful, babe. Are you ready to go?" He asks smiling.

"Almost," I finish brushing out my hair and grab my game bag, so I'm ready. He locks the door behind me as we make our way to the elevator.

Rick and I hop into his car to go pick up Mom and I remember I'll be driving his car around this afternoon. I pay attention in case there's something quirky. He pulls me over next to him and rests his hand on my knee when he isn't shifting. I'm starting to understand the attraction of the bench seats. We drive to the hotel and pull up in front to find Mom sitting on the bench outside. She won't recognize the car, so I get out of the car to meet her.

"Hi, Mom!" as I give her a big hug. I turn to lead her back to the car, but Rick followed me and he's standing right behind me. I turn to him and he sees my nerves. He slides his arm around me and gives me a peck on the cheek. "Mom, this is Rick Seno."

Rick reaches for her hand, "It's a pleasure to meet you, ma'am. Your daughter is wonderful."

"Its good to meet you, too," Mom is unsure about Rick. "You didn't have to go to this trouble for me, sweetie. This place is too nice," as she looks at me.

47

"Rick said to pick some place you'd like and he covered everything," I look at him and smile proudly.

"Ladies, please allow me to take you out to lunch," he gestures to his car. I climb in the front seat and scoot to the middle, leaving room for Mom. Rick holds the door until we are both set before he walks around and climbs into the driver's seat. He pulls out of the Brighton and drives down Harbor, passing the Maritime Museum and turning toward the airport on the way to Shelter Island. We park at a Polynesian building and he walks around to open the car door for Mom and I. He chose another tropical themed restaurant with a view. He grasps my hand and entwines our fingers as we walk to the restaurant. "I think you ladies will like this place. They have a great salad menu and a mini buffet. It's all Hawaiian inspired." He smiles at me as he says Hawaiian. We walk into the restaurant and they seat us immediately at the table with the best view of the bay. Rick sitting next to me as always.

"This is a nice view. I've never been here," Mom trying to make small talk and not successfully, but I appreciate the attempt.

We order and I comment, "I love the Hawaiian thing they have going on here and the buffet looks so tropical. I want to try everything." Rick gives me a squeeze.

"I appreciate you driving down, ma'am. It means a lot to me that you're willing to go to my game tonight. I know you're not a Seals fan and I'd like to eventually convert you to the Seals from LA," Rick hopes to get Mom talking.

"I always take advantage of time with Sherry and if she's spending time with you, then I need to meet you," Mom lays it out there. She's been negative about men for as long as I can remember. I've always assumed it's because my dad ditched us, but she's never said anything about it.

"Mom, I love Rick and he's moving in with me. He's not like

the other guys and he's not what you think when you think base-ball player. He's a fabulous catcher on the field and only my man off the field."

Mom stops and looks at me, then at Rick. "You both look happy. I'm happy if my daughter is happy. I don't want Sherry hurt. What do you mean when you say you're not letting her go?" Mom says glaring at Rick.

Rick gets a big grin and says, "I mean that I want to be with her always, I hope someday she'll allow me the privilege of making her mine. I'll do whatever it takes to make her happy and keep her that way. I never want to be away from her again." He looks to Mom for her reaction to his honesty.

"This all seems so fast to me and I know Sherry needed time. I'm not sure what to think," Mom shows her concern.

"I was wrong and shouldn't have left him in LA. I freaked out..." and Rick cuts me off.

"We both handled the situation poorly and the time we were apart taught both of us how much we want to be together," Rick refuses for it to be my fault.

"True," I chime in.

"Rick, please call me Shar. My daughter can be difficult. I'll be happy to go to your game tonight and we'll see from there."

"Thank you, Shar," Rick keeps a positive conversation going.

We eat and overall I'm maintaining myself, no freak-outs. Though I was in my own world there for a bit when Rick was telling Mom what he meant by not letting me go. I'm not complaining in any way, shape or form, but what a time to be smacked in the face with a huge reality check. Does he really want us to be permanent? Partners? ...Married? He's moving in with me and we're sharing a closet and an address, not just a bed. Is this my life? How did this happen? I don't chase baseball play-ers! Then again, he didn't want to be a baseball player with me and I made it okay for him to be a baseball player. Talk about fucking confusing! People think women are crazy and mixed up, they should try a big league baseball player sometime. Warrior on the field of battle. Calling the shots on the field. Doesn't want to be that person unless he's on the field. Needs me. (Okay, rant within a rant... He needs me? It makes me so happy that he needs me, but really? He needs me? I'm seven years older than him. I'm not always easy to deal with. I'm independent. He wants to pay my way for everything, he doesn't think its necessary for me to work, and I can't imagine allowing anyone to pay my way and not being in control of my own everything, well except sex maybe. Yes, definitely sex. He is the king, that's not just a cute pet name. And, he needs me! More than that, he loves me.) With me, he wants to be that person. For me, he wants to be that person. My personal warrior. My professional baseball player. My king. Focus Sherry!

"I need to get to work, ladies." He pays and we take his car to the stadium. He pulls into the player's garage and parks the car. Rick gets out of the car and pulls me out the driver side with him, handing me his car keys and pressing his lips to mine, lightly sucking on my lower lip in the process. He whispers in my ear, "I love you, baby. I wanted my hands on you all through lunch and it's killing me. I know that's silly, I was sitting right next to you." He claims me with his mouth, sending electrical shocks through my body. "Go, your Mom's in the car. Her jersey is in the back-seat. Have fun with your Mom and I'll see you pregame, my queen." He plants one of his there-is-no-way-you-can-ever-forget-me kisses on me and waves as he disappears into the stadium. I get into the driver's seat and start up the car.

"Are you sure you should drive after that?" Mom says laughing. "Seriously, you look like you're in a daze, flushed."

I laugh, "He always leaves me punch drunk. He's so sweet though, Mom. The words that man whispers in my ear, I can't even explain. I don't know how to handle his request to take care of me. I've always taken care of myself."

We take off out of the garage and head out shopping for a couple of hours. I'm enjoying his Challenger, the stick and the rumble of the engine. Very much like him.

Mom and I have pleasant conversation all afternoon. She actually offers helpful advice and tells me I'm an adult and need to do what's right for me.

"So, to recap, he lets you drive his custom car, he wants to cover all of your expenses, he wants to live with you at your place, he's not interested in other women at all, he's a big league baseball player, kisses like sin and probably does other things just as well or better, and he's solid muscle. Not to mention he wants to keep you and I believe him when he says he loves you. It's written all over his face."

"Does that mean you'll wear a Seno jersey tonight? He had jerseys made for both of us to match the uniform the team is wearing tonight."

"Absolutely, but I'm still an LA fan," Mom smiles.

"Fair enough, for now!" We pull up to the stadium and I flash my access card, so I can park in the player's garage. We park and I get our jerseys and my game bag out of the car. We enter the stadium and walk to the section behind home plate where our seats are.

Text from Rick - Order whatever you want, your seat is permanently set up to charge my account. Love you, babe!

Text to Rick - You don't need to do that. I can handle my own. Mom agreed to wear your jersey. Make it a win! Love you, too... My king!

Text from Rick - I don't need to, I want to. I know you can take care of yourself, but you shouldn't have to. I want to take care of you, my queen.

Text from Rick - Buy your Mom some popcorn and a beer or something.

My mind goes dirty and I reply.

Text to Rick - What else do you want? Exactly how do you want it?

But, no reply and he walks out onto the field.

"There's Rick, Mom." I say pointing to the hottest man ever in full catcher's gear. "How do you like the seats?"

"He moves with a different attitude on the field, doesn't he?" witnessing his intensity. "These seats are nice, but too expensive. Is this where you usually sit?"

"My normal seat is over there, field level down the first base line. Rick gets me a seat behind home plate because he likes to hear me cheering for him and he can make faces at me from this distance. He's serious out there. He wants to make it a win every game, less than that is unacceptable."

"I can see that. He makes his mind up and does it. Determined. Good qualities," Mom shares her insight.

CHAPTER SIX

The team is out stretching and warming up. A marching band marches across the field and plays the National Anthem, and it's time to play ball! Rick walks out and gets in position behind home plate, throwing the ball to the pitcher a few times and around the infield as San Francisco's first hitter swings a bat in the on deck circle.

The Seals score first in the bottom of the third inning with Mason hitting a home run. Bottom of the fourth the score is still 1-0 Seals with two outs and runners on first and second. Seno is up to bat and the runners are Cross and Martin. Martin has a huge lead off of first base and nobody is holding Cross at second base. The first pitch to Seno and the runners go on the pitcher's release, a called ball that's probably a strike. Both runners safe at second and third. I yell out, "That's it boys! Steal'm! Wooooo!" and Rick glances at me. "Let's go Seno! Yeah baby! Knock it out! Wooooo! Bring those boys in!" Pitch two is called a strike. This umpire is making bad calls at the plate. Pitch three Seno swings because who knows what the umpire will call it, he connects and breaks his bat. There's a loud crack. Rick runs and the ball chops through the infield over the head of the first baseman all the way to the corner where it rattles around long enough for Rick to get to third, and Cross and Martin to score! 3-0 Seals. Rick is celebrating at third clapping his hands in a manly way. The next hitter comes up and pops out, leaving Seno at third.

The game is going smooth and is still a shut out at the end of the sixth inning. I make a quick run to the bathroom before the seventh inning stretch, and get back to my seat in time to stand up and sing "Take Me Out To The Ballgame" with Mom, swaying together and singing out. I love that Mom is a baseball fan, even if she does root for the wrong team.

The rest of the game was fairly uneventful. Our pitcher in good form, followed Rick's calls and pitched a complete game. Rick and Martin both got base hits, but nobody pushed them around to score. Final score was 3-0 Seals.

Hannah grabbed the pitcher for the on field interview and they talked about pitching a complete game. The pitcher tonight was brought up a couple weeks ago and this was his first start. We will be seeing more of Rhett Clay, he isn't going anywhere.

Rick turns to me, "I'll be at the car in twenty." He winks at me and takes off into the dugout.

"He's a hoot." My Mom turns to me, "Very attentive and doesn't seem to notice other women at all."

"Yeah, in Colorado he called me down to the dugout after the win and pulled me into the dugout to kiss me. He can be crazy!" I tell Mom as I remember his mother's words from later that evening.

"It's fun. I understand what you mean about needing to meet him. You've both gotten lucky finding each other." Slightly shocked at my Mom's words, I smile and she hugs me with approval.

The crowd clears and I lead Mom to the elevator, using my access card to get to the player's garage. We slide into the front seat of Rick's Challenger and watch as a few of the other players walk out to their cars. Rick wears more gear as catcher and always takes a few minutes longer. We chat about going to breakfast before the spa and how early it'll need to be. Rick walks up to the car and sits down in the driver seat. He leans in and kisses me on the cheek, then looks to Mom "I hope you enjoyed the game, Shar."

My Mom actually smiles at Rick, "Very much. The seats were great. Thank you. You call a good game, Rick. Of course, I always like to see San Francisco lose."

I'm a bit shook, sitting between them and listening to the conversation go on around me. This is my Mom, right? While I sit in shock, they decide we should call it a night and start early the next morning. Rick pulls up to the Brighton and hops out of the car to open the door for Mom. "I appreciate you. I wouldn't have Sherry without you. Thank you." Rick hugs my Mom and she hugs him back. This isn't my Mom. When was she replaced with a look-alike?

"I can see you are good to her and you both love each other." Again, I can't say this enough... Who kidnapped my Mom and replaced her with this sweet woman that looks like her? Why isn't she freaking out about us moving in together? Shacking up? Him being controlling or something? Going off about carrying me through a hotel lobby over his shoulder? She leans down to look in the car, "I'll meet you in the morning, Sherry," and she walks off into the hotel.

Rick gets back into the car and immediately puts his arm around me, pulling me close and kissing me like a fool. His hand moving up my thigh. He rolls the windows up and whispers in my ear, "This was a good day, but it's driving me crazy not having you around me right now. Let's go home, my queen."

Rick strokes my thigh the whole drive home and I sit against him with my head on his shoulder. It's amazing how much this man loves me and needs me. I have no doubt.

We park at our complex and Rick kisses me sweetly on the lips like when he's going to offer me a hand out of the car, but the kiss pushes him further. He's on top of me and we're making out on the front bench seat of his car. His thigh rubs against my happy places as he let's out a hot heavy sigh at my ear, stopping to kiss and nibble there. He's back to my mouth, sucking on my lower lip, biting and tugging at it gently. He slides his tongue into my mouth to dance with mine and I suck on it until he moans, as our bodies continue to rub on each other. "We could take this to the bedroom, my king," I suggest aware the chances we make it from the elevator are minimal.

He focuses, "Yeah, you're right." It takes him a few moments to clear his head enough to move on.

We get in the elevator and I simply say, "We're on the elevator. Anything you want to do here, on the elevator, my king?" Using my sweet, sexy, seductive voice. Rick lets out a groan that sounds more like a lion's roar, I pull the elevator stop and I'm instantly pinned to the elevator wall by his hard muscled body. "Oh yeah, my king. Show me what you want." He unbuttons his jeans and releases his hard wanting desire. He pulls my pants completely off of me and holds me up so my lips can touch his. I wrap my legs around him drawing another roar as he slides me slowly down his hard body onto his rock solid cock. I cry out as he slides in and fills me lusciously. I climb him with my arms around his neck, unable to help myself I bite at his neck and collarbone as I move on him, stroking him with my hot wet sex.

"Oh fuck, you're perfect, my queen." We move together, meeting each other's effort.

I hold on to him tight and lick his neck, kissing and sucking. I hear sexy little noises and realize the needy whimper is coming from me. I want more of him. I want all of him. I whisper in his ear, "Don't you want to bend me over? Take me hard? Fuck me senseless? My king should get what he wants."

A growl comes from within Rick and he strokes up into me hard, biting at any part of me he can reach. He lifts me up over him and licks at my hot folds, biting and sucking at my sensitive nub until I shake with pleasure. He slides me down his body and flips my back to him, holding me tightly against him. His pulse racing, his heart beating, and his cock wanting attention. Rick whispers in my ear, "Let's play a game, my queen. Every time I say something, you say "Yes, please, my king." How does that sound?"

"Yes, please, my king," I respond instantly and he gets harder.

"Good girl. Would you like me to bend you over and fuck you hard, my queen?"

This could get interesting, "Yes, please, my king." Rick bends me over quickly, holding his dick in his right hand and placing his left hand at the curve of my ass. He slides in hard and fast. Pounding into me repeatedly.

"Harder, my queen?"

"Yes, please, my king." I hear his low groan at my response.

"Do you want more, my queen?"

"Yes, please, my king." He's fucking amazing and I can hardly speak.

Rick leans over me and gathers my hair in his hand gently to pull my head back to him. He breathes heavy and hot at my ear, nibbling at my lobe. The solid muscles of his body against me, rubbing against my ass as he strokes into me. He kisses my neck and his whole attitude changes. "Nobody has ever felt like you, my queen. Do you only want me, my queen?"

"Yes, please, my king," I should answer differently, but I don't know where he's going with this and this game came with instructions.

"Never be with anyone else, my queen."

"Yes, please, my king."

"May I love you forever, my queen?"

"Yes, please, my king."

"Never leave me, my queen."

"Yes, please, my king."

"I will make you mine someday, my queen."

"Yes, please, my king." I hear a noise and I'm reminded we're still in the elevator. "My king, we're on the elevator," wondering if he's lost track.

"Do you want me to grab you by your seductive hips, and finish inside you?"

"Yes, please, my king." He does exactly that. He grips my hips and digs his fingers in like he doesn't plan to let go.

Rick leans against the carpeted elevator wall and pulls me back against him. Smacking my ass against him hard with every stroke. "Is this want you want, my queen?"

"Yes, please, my king. Harder." I break the rules.

Rick slams me harder, "That's breaking the rules. Do you deserve to be spanked?"

"Yes, please, my king." He stiffens and raises his hand, but he lightly pats my ass and squeezes my cheeks. He'd never hurt me. "I love you, my king. It'll always only be you. Hold me, love me, kiss me, fuck me. Only your hands will touch me. Only your cock will have me. I know how much you love me and the pleasure you give me is unlike any other." My words go straight to his heart. He caresses my body lovingly, then grabs hold of my hips and slams into me over and over and over, sending us both over the edge.

He reaches around my waist and pulls me back to him, his lips at my ear, "I will love you forever, my queen. Now, pull your pants on so we can go home and I can love you properly."

"Yes, please, my king."

CHAPTER SEVEN

I wake up the next morning with Rick wrapped around me, the same way I fell asleep. I'm loved, cherished and protected. The alarm hasn't buzzed yet and I don't smell any coffee brewing. It's an early morning for both of us since I'm meeting Mom for breakfast before our spa time and Rick has early practice before the 1:40 game today. I lay in silence and enjoy his arms around me, but my head is anything but quiet.

The last few days, the last week... let's face it, in the last two months my life, my whole world has been turned upside down. I guess that's not quite right. My world has been shaken loose and invaded, but somehow that's a good thing. I need to admit the truth to myself and accept it because anything else, well it just isn't going to work. Getting what you wish for isn't always a smooth transition. Fantasies aren't supposed to be real and in reality the fantasy isn't real, even this time since Rick Seno is even better than I imagined he'd be. Fuck me, because he's better than I imagined possible. He's like finding out what a ten on the scale of one to ten really is, when what you thought was a ten turned out to be only a five. I've heard of whirlwind romances and love at first sight, but I didn't believe they were real and I never in a million years thought it could possibly happen to me. I'm an independent woman with a stable head on her shoulders. I'm self-sufficient and I don't need anyone to take care of me. Okay, well, at least I was until a few weeks ago. That's the final straw that broke us when I left Rick in LA—my own insecurities. But, I've learned I can be with my Rick and still be me. Granted, the definition of me has slightly changed. I still support myself with my own business and I can keep my head straight most of the time, but this girliness that takes me over really throws me for a loop and I hate to say it, but I kind of like it. Technically, I'm still self-sufficient and don't need anyone to take care of me—but, this is where it gets sticky because I love it when Rick takes care of me (especially the sticky times). And, I want things I've never wanted before. Things I've never considered as possibilities before. What stable headed, independent, self-sufficient woman all of the sudden wants to get married after only two months? This is utter insanity! For craps sake, I was upset about the negative pregnancy test result! Why on earth would any woman in her right mind be upset about a negative pregnancy test when they've known the guy for less than two months? I should've been more upset about having to pee on the stick in the first place! But now, huh, now I don't want to see another negative because it totally bummed me out. On the plus side, I do get to go to more baseball games and I do get to travel to away games, which I still need to figure out expenses on—It doesn't matter, Rick will take care of it. Damn it! I need to be able to cover my own.

Rick pulls me tighter to him and kisses behind my ear, "Please stop worrying. We want the same things. We need some time to get there, my queen. I promise, baby. I promise." His words are calming, quiet, and sincere. "You always say such sweet things to me in the morning. It makes me happy to know you want the same things I do, and you want them with me. It couldn't be more perfect. I love you, my queen." He snuggles his face into my hair and kisses the back of my neck, while I wonder which parts I said out loud. I've got to get a handle on that. I need to figure out what I say in my sleep and when I change from inner monologue to actually speaking out loud.

The alarm goes off and we both get ready for the day quickly. Rick drops me off at the Brighton on his way to the stadium. I meet Mom in the lobby and we walk out the back of the hotel to the marina, where we find a nice place to sit and have breakfast. We make our way up to the roof and the Spa at the Brighton. It's a very relaxing morning lying around the pool and absorbing the sunshine, while the spa attendants provide snacks, refreshing drinks, manicures, pedicures, massages, facials, and body wraps. She has nothing bad to say about Rick, so I don't prod her and I let it go accepting that she somewhat approves. I leave my Mom and head for the stadium a few minutes after 1pm. I get to my seat in time for Rick to see I'm there for him. He walks back to the net, "You make me feel like a king." He winks at me and turns away to work with his pitcher. His words fill my heart and my worries have vanished.

I yell out, "Make it a win, babe!" and relax in my seat, prepared for a warm afternoon in the sun. I get my hat out of my game bag and put it on, tying my hair up in a knot through the back. I take off my jersey and slather on sunscreen. The sun is warm on my skin, and after the morning at the spa I could take a nap right here. I kick my feet up on the wall in front of me, since I'm in the first row today and I'm ready to enjoy the game.

Tommy's pitching today and he connects with Rick, so it should be a good game. But we're still playing the Sissy's, so anything can happen. The Sissy's fans are probably the worst in the league. They take over half the stadium when they're in town and they're simply obnoxious. Typically, this is a game I'd look forward to tormenting the visiting fans at, well, if I was in my normal seat and not up front for Rick. I'd bring a big bag of peanuts in the shell and shells would be flying at the Sissy's fans, like it was a game! Meli and Samantha would be throwing shells, too. Sandy's wife would be keeping score on all of our hits. We would fake an innocent look if anyone turned around. I can't do that when I'm front and center for Rick, I don't want to cause a problem and I'm not hidden in the sea of people in the seats. If we win today, we sweep the series and the Sissy's aren't happy about it. They've got Billy the Bulldog pitching today, I call him Bitchy Billy because he seems whiny and always has a comment about the umpire's calls. The San Francisco dugout is definitely heated and the game hasn't even started. Rick walks to his position behind the plate with the intensity of a warrior that I love and "You're going to see nothing today, Seno. You're going down!" comes from the Sissy's dugout. Rick ignores them, but his head shakes as he gets to work.

"You got this, my king! Let's go Seals!" I call out, unable to help myself and wanting to defend my man.

But, maybe I shouldn't have because the first Sissy at bat focuses on me as he walks up to the plate, "Hey baby... Angel?" He nods his head at me and blows me a kiss.

Oh, fuck! Adam's a Sissy. How was I not aware Adam is a player? For the Sissy's of all teams! What alternate universe am I in? Two professional baseball players want me? This is nuts. I'm hoping Rick didn't notice, but I know better. Hopefully he ignores it. He doesn't look like the sweet Adam that drove to spend the day with me—a total dick in his uniform. Tommy struck him out on three pitches, all inside and definitely sending a message to back off. He walks the next hitter and we get out of the first inning unscathed. The Sissy's are on the field, and apparently Adam is their new first baseman. This isn't good. This can't go well. Fuck it, this is bad, bad, bad. Shit, shit, shit. Bottom of the second, 0-0, and Rick is at bat for the first time. Don't get a base hit. Please don't get a base hit. What am I wishing for? "Home run, baby!" Rock is on first, Martin is on third and feeling froggy —he wants to steal home and the signs flash around the field. First pitch is low and inside, hitting Rick on the foot and he takes his base, pushing Rock to second. I immediately jump out of my seat to watch him and make sure he's not limping. He appears to be fine. A ball to the foot is nothing compared to all the pitches he takes to the body. I'm glad I told Rick about Adam. He doesn't like it, but at least he's aware and didn't find out when he walked to first. They're chatting it up at first base. I can't hear them, but Rick's body language isn't good. Bravo is at bat, he hits into a double play and the second inning ends, still 0-0.

Top of the third, Rick comes out of the dugout still putting his equipment on and looks at me mouthing "Adam? He's a baseball player." More questioning than making a statement, he's pissed.

I nod and mouth back "I didn't know."

Adam is first at bat and this time he walks straight up to me at the net while the team is throwing the ball around the field, "Hey, Angel. You don't look like the typical baseball skank. I liked that. I thought you were better than that. But, a skank you must be if you're sitting here. I bet Seno is poking you whenever he wants. It's okay, I still want you, baby. Come out with me after the game and I'll show you a better time. I'm sure you remember what its like to spend time with me." He turns toward my Rick, to make sure he hears every word he says, but I already know he's hearing all of it just from his stance. "I remember the feel of your sweet body when I held it against me and your soft lips when I kissed them, how sweet you tasted on my tongue. I didn't push you, you felt like you were worth it. Now I know you're just another base-ball skank." His voice gets quiet, "But I still want to fuck you and fuck you hard." He touches my foot that's still resting on the wall in front of me and I wish I could kick him in the nuts.

"Fuck off, asshole!" I say too loudly. Rick turns and grins at me, trusting that I can take care of myself and trying to let me. Especially since there's a net between us. I end up smiling at the realization Rick trusts me and knows I got this.

Adam the asshole walks up to the plate. Rick's loud and laughing for my benefit, "That's my woman. Isn't she beautiful? Don't even think about looking at her again." Laughing turned dead pan. I detect the unspoken "I'll fuck you up if you say anything to her or just look at her again," in his tone. Actually, it was probably "I'll put you on the DL permanently" in Rick's head. It turns me on when he defends me. I wish it wasn't like this. I wish this wasn't happening on the field.

"You got this guy, Tommy. He doesn't have a bat or balls! He's an out!" I yell out and see Rick look at the ground laughing.

"Yep. Love my woman behind home plate. She's my own personal cheering section." There's some additional conversation at the plate, but its quiet and the volume change is on purpose.

Three pitches, all inside again and the asshole is out. Rick turns to me and gives me a sexy grin with a thumbs up. Tomorrows an off day and it's a good thing because it's going to be a late night, in a very good way.

Bottom of the fourth inning, Rick's first up to bat and the score is tied 1-1. Bitchy Billy has been wandering around the pitcher's mound like he's waiting for directions, but he hasn't pitched a bad game. It doesn't make any sense. First pitch to Rick is way inside, off the plate, and Rick has to step back to avoid getting hit. He shakes it off, swings his bat a few times and steps back into the batter's box. The guys in both dugouts are watching closely, since it appeared Billy threw at Rick—possibly for the second time this game. Billy communicates silently with Adam at first base. From there on everything happens so fast, it's hard to keep up. The next pitch blows across the edge of Ricks helmet, 2 balls. The tension in the stadium is thick and I'm pissed—they're throwing at my man. "Back off meat!" I yell at the pitcher. Third pitch is obviously intentional and hits Rick. The sound is horrible and my Rick drops to the ground instantly. I'm not sure where he got hit. In the arm? Shoulder? Maybe the elbow? I'm out of my seat trying to get through the net to him, but my fear disappears when he pops right up and walks with a purpose toward the pitcher's mound. The catcher for the Sissy's right behind him and the asshole from first running to the pitcher's mound ahead of him.

Oh, fuck. Should I call out to him or cover my eyes?

Skip calls out from the dugout, "Don't do it!" and his teammates join him on the field as both dugouts empty.

Rick doesn't wait for the rest of the team, he yells at Billy, "What the fuck? Do you want to take me on right here?" Billy simply glances at the asshole and Rick hits Adam square in the jaw with his tight fist, knocking his ass to the ground. "Next time you come get me yourself instead of sending a teammate to call me out. And, don't you ever talk to my girl. Don't even look at her again, you fucking asshole!" Rick turns to his team, "Get back where you belong, I've got this." Then he stares at the Sissy's as they all head back to the dugout. "Good, you guys stay out of this unless you want a piece of me." Skip walks out to Rick and escorts him into the clubhouse, while Saben takes his place on first base. He's out of the game and may be injured, but not too bad. I send Rick a text:

Text to Rick - Changing to my old seat for the rest of the game. Text me and let me know you're okay. I'll meet you at your car as soon as you are ready.

Text to Rick - Sorry, I should've kept my mouth shut.

Text to Rick - I didn't know he was a ball player.

Text to Rick - I'm sorry. I never meant to put you in that situation.

Text to Rick - He's a real asshole! I want to kick him in the nuts, but he probably doesn't have any!

Before Rick had a chance to get my texts, Carter is out searching for me. He catches me as I'm standing up to leave my seat, "Rick asked me to come get you. Will you come with me?"

"Of course, is there something wrong? He looked okay." I say concerned as we walk up the steps to the concourse.

Carter isn't answering me and it's starting to make me worry. He leads me to the elevator and down toward the clubhouse offices. As we get off the elevator, he says, "Rick will be fine, he's more worried about you being there by yourself with the San Francisco assholes. He asked me to have you come down and hang out in my office. I have the game on closed caption and I can get you whatever you want. They're treating him right now."

"Can I see him? I need to know he's okay." I didn't have to try to use the concerned girlfriend voice, it was real.

"He's only a couple of rooms away, but I can't take you past my office during game time. Clubhouse rules." Seriously? Rules suck.

I lean out of Carter's office and most of the doors are open. "Rick, are you okay?" I call out down the hall. Going for it. He wants to know I'm here, too.

I get a response almost immediately, "I'll be fine."

I'm happy to watch the game from Carter's office. It's air-conditioned and it was getting warm outside. Sunday afternoon games can get hot, especially during summer. "Hey, Carter. I'm sorry about this. It's probably my fault."

Carter stops and glares at me funny. "It's not your fault they threw at Seno. That's a bad attitude and poor sportsmanship.

They used you as a way to get to him and that's interesting because Seno has a reputation of not being able to shake him."

"This was definitely a unique situation." I don't need to give Carter the details about my history with Adam. "He called me a skank and touched my foot through the net."

Suddenly from the other room, "Next time something like this happens and another man touches you, you break his fingers or stomp his hand if you can't kick him in the groin. No one touches you." So, apparently, Rick can hear very well, he's closer than I think, or these walls are paper thin.

"I don't think it'll be an issue and I doubt Adam ever does this again. I'm betting you dislocated his jaw." I do love how he's my protector, but not that he had to do this on the field. He'll probably get fined and could be suspended. Then again, it might be fun to have him to myself for a few days. I may need a cute little nurse outfit.

Text to Sam - Don't worry, he'll be fine. No details yet.

Text from Sam - He looked like he's okay. Not so sure about the other guy. What was that about?

Text to Sam - He called me baby and blew me a kiss.

Do I tell Sam I kind of dated Adam? I'll let it go with what everybody already knows.

Text from Sam - Oh

Text to Sam - He called me a baseball skank.

Text from Sam - He didn't!

Text to Sam - He offered to show me a better time than Seno.

Text from Sam - Ouch!

Text to Sam - He touched my foot through the net.

Text from Sam - Lucky he isn't dead.

Text to Sam - I may have defended myself verbally and loudly.

Text from Sam - LOL

Text to Sam - More info when I have it. He's 2 rooms away from me and they won't let me any deeper into the club-house. He did yell at me down the hall and said he'll be fine.

Text from Sam - So, are you 2 doing okay now?

Text to Sam - Yes

I review the team schedule on Carter's desk and realize we have away games coming up soon—Seattle, Chicago and LA again. But, I'm in limbo for pretty much everything until I find out what's wrong with him and if he's going to be suspended. I'm not looking forward to LA. I need to research Seattle and Chicago for travel purposes, and find out what hotels we're staying at.

I try to distract myself, but I want my Rick. I need him to be okay. I haven't heard anything from him in at least twenty minutes. The silence is deafening and I don't care about the game. Huh, I don't think I've ever said I don't care about the game. Fine, I did miss a bunch of games when I left him in LA and I missed the game when I was flying to Colorado to see him. It makes sense, he's more important to me than the game itself, but nobody else ever has been. Somehow over the last two months, Rick has become the most important thing in my life. It's an odd feeling when you've never had it before. I lean out of Carter's office and the door is closed now. "Carter, will you please go see what's going on?"

"Sure, let me try to get an update." Carter leaves the room and wanders the halls. Knocking on a few doors, but there's no talking.

I move to the hallway and stand by the door to the office, just looking around to see what's going on overall and notice player's popping into the clubhouse for things. I text Chase and go for luck.

Text to Chase - Hey! I'm in Carter's office and they won't let me see Seno. Can you let me know if you find out anything, please? I know you probably don't have your phone, but I'm going for it. They said he's two rooms over. He was talking to me from there but now the door is closed and he hasn't said anything in awhile.

Carter comes back with nothing. I like the guy, but he's useless. I should've gone for it when he left me alone. Chase hasn't responded to me and it's been about fifteen minutes. I try him again.

Text to Chase - Do you remember my brownies? I also bake cookies and cake. I need to know my Rick is okay. What kind is your favorite?

I get an immediate response.

Text from Chase - I'll check on him as soon as I can. Have to
wait until next inning, only one out left. Chocolate Chip
Cookie Bars.

I knew it. Easily controlled by baked goods.

I concentrate on the game and attempt to wait patiently.
Why is this taking so long, if he's fine? Why am I sitting around
worrying about a guy? Since when do I wait around like this?
This is crap! I'll check on him myself! "Hey Carter, can I get
some ice cream in one of those mini helmets or some popcorn or
something?" Sending Carter on a mission and getting him out of
the way. Carter nods and goes to fetch. As soon as he's gone I
stand up and walk in the hallway a bit, pretending to be
stretching my legs and checking to see if there's anybody around.

I run smack into Chase, "Sherry, what are you... never mind,
follow my lead and be ready to peek in the door." Chase gets
Rick's phone from his locker and walks through the clubhouse
quickly checking in the different rooms, he gives a quick knock
and opens the door to the treatment room Rick is in. He leaves
the door open wide so I can sneak a peek in and gives Rick his
phone, "Thought you might want to see what it looked like. It's
all over the internet." Somehow communicating with Rick that
it's a ruse to let me see he's okay. Rick looks at me and grins.
Chase leaves the door open when he leaves the room, but it gets
shut again. Chase gives me a quick thumbs up and trots back off
to the dugout. At least I saw him and know he's alive.

Text from Rick - Don't worry. I'll be fine.

Text to Rick - Where's your injury?

Text from Rick - They're checking my elbow, my hand, and
my foot. Nothing is broken.

Text to Rick - I'm sure your foot is bruised and elbows hurt like a son of a bitch.

Text to Rick - What's wrong with your hand?

Text from Rick - Cuts on my knuckles from hitting that asshole. Not sure if it's from his teeth or just impact. May need a tetanus shot, he probably has rabies or something.

Text to Rick - I'm sorry. Are you in pain?

Text from Rick - Nothing worse than any other day catching. I should've controlled myself better. I don't have much control when it comes to you. I don't know how long this is going to take. You can take my car and go home, or whatever you want.

Text to Rick - You can't get rid of me that easy. I'm staying here with you, my king.

Text to Rick - <3

A few minutes later the door opens and Rick comes walking out, his elbow supported by a sling and his hand has bandages over two of the knuckles. No limping or anything. He tosses me his keys left-handed, "You have to drive home. My hand is numb." I felt myself go white and he must've seen it. "It's okay. It'll wear off, it's from the local anesthetic they used and I'm not supposed to drive with the sling."

"Whatever you want, baby." I focus on the sling and how closely he's holding his arm to his body.

"Don't worry. It's precautionary. My elbow is bruised and swollen, they want to make sure it's not a sprained ligament. I have to wear this thing for support so I don't make it worse." He rolls his eyes. "It's a bruise. I'm fine."

"Let me check with Skip to see what the damage is and we can get out of here." Rick turns to walk away, but Carter stops him.

"Skip says he doesn't want to see your face for five days. Still waiting on the official suspension and he'll let you know. Billy should be suspended for intentionally throwing at you, too. You need to get your elbow re-evaluated in a few days, call me first. So, get out of here." Carter provides the necessary details.

Rick grabs my hand with his right hand, his numb hand, and makes a funny face at me. "I'm holding your hand, but I can't feel it." I move in close to him so he can put his arm around me instead and he smiles.

We walk out to his car, leaving the stadium before the game is over. I've never done that before. I never would've thought dating a professional baseball player would make me watch less baseball, leave games early, not pay attention to the score—I must be ill. Huh, lovesick? Chemically imbalanced? Lethal combination of pheromones and desire, sounds right.

I'm torn in many directions. He's okay overall, but I'm concerned about his elbow and knuckles. I'm guilt stricken, because this altercation was my fault. He was defending me. Honestly, he probably wanted to punch the guy because—well, the fact he had my number was probably enough for Rick to want to take him out and it went way beyond that. It might be nice to have him to myself for a few days. I wonder how he's going to react to not playing for five days. Will he be grumpy? Will he embrace the time off? Will he blame me? Will we be watching baseball together or does he even watch games? Will there be an Adam conversation?

We get in the Challenger, I lean over and give Rick a quick kiss, "Sorry about all this."

"That guy's a jerk and I should've kept my cool, not let him get to me. You, I want to protect you and keep you safe. You didn't do anything on purpose. You didn't know he's a player. You make me crazy sometimes. I needed to defend you."

"Then we can be crazy together, my king." A little lost with the idea of having five days. We never get more than a day without a baseball game.

I'm suddenly in my head, lost in thought about my Rick. What would've been different if we weren't bound by everything baseball, his training schedule, his game schedule and away travel? Maybe I can take advantage of this time and do things that haven't been possible?

"Do you want to go home to relax and watch the rest of the game or can we make a stop?" It's Sunday and I want to cook. I need to get groceries now that he's moved in and especially since he'll be home for at least the next five days.

"What are you thinking?"

"I want to make you a special dinner tonight and stock up the kitchen. I can get everything for dinner at the public market. I can take you home first."

"You don't need to do anything special for me." Rick turns to me, today has been hard on him.

"I don't need to, I want to," I smile as I throw his own words back at him. "I'll take you home first." He doesn't say anything and it worries me. He's in more pain than he's letting on, or in his head about Adam. "Are you okay?"

He's looking out the passenger window away from me when he answers, "I'm fine, babe." But, I can hear the truth in his voice.

"Never mind. Let's go home, so I can take care of you, my king." I reach for him, resting my hand on his thigh. He doesn't argue.

I pull into our complex and take it slow over the speed bumps. I know what it's like to be in pain and then hit the speed bumps full on, getting shook all around. I park and go to open his door, since his right hand and left elbow are both injured. He opens the door before I can get there and curses under his breath. I'm sure he's a bit sore all over after taking the dive at the plate. There's blood seeping through the bandage on his right hand as he gets out of his car. "How can I help, my king?"

"I'm fine." Louder. Obstinate.

"Let's get you upstairs and make you comfortable." I want to take care of him and he's irritated. I don't blame him. Right hand and left elbow at the same time is a bad combo.

He stares at me in disgust, "I said, I'm fine."

I don't want to make it worse, "My king, you are fine from your gorgeous blue eyes down to your strong, masculine legs. I especially love your Grade A Prime fine ass." I say laughingly and smile at him, trying to disarm his mood.

Rick rolls his eyes at me and I don't even get a smile. We get in the elevator and I consider attempting to put him in a better mood, but I'm not sure where the boundaries are with this mood he's in. I decide to wait and see what he does. Vodka might be helpful, for both of us.

We walk into our apartment and Rick goes into the bathroom, shutting the door behind him. I let him be and go search the kitchen for the magic meal I'm going to cook up for him tonight. I wanted to make steaks and baked potatoes, but there are no steaks or potatoes in the house. The pantry has Arborio rice, pastas, broths, instant gelatin mix, stewed tomatoes, pasta sauce, baking mix, cookies, donuts, and everything needed to bake sweets. I've got basics in the refrigerator, but really only the makings for a good breakfast. The freezer has a couple packs of frozen vegetables, sausage, ice cream, cheesecake cups, yogurt cups, popsicles, vodka, a couple individual frozen meals, and three things I bagged up and froze so long ago that I don't know what they are and can't figure it out through their frost bitten state. Pasta with sausage it is, or we could have breakfast for dinner. Biscuits with country gravy, eggs and sausage. Fresh biscuits will be the magic, breakfast it is.

I walk through the apartment to check on Rick, but he's still shut in the bathroom and it's been at least twenty minutes. Okay, time to check on him. I knock on the bathroom door, "My king, are you okay? I don't want to bother you. I know you've had a bad day and I'm sure you hurt." Nothing. "I just want to take care of you. I love how protective of me you are." Still nothing. There's no water running, so he can hear me. I walk away to change my clothes, but now I'm worried and it makes it hard to be sweet and understanding. I try to maintain myself, but my girliness takes over. "Rick Seno! Say something or I'm coming in there!" I wait, each second becoming more concerned. I turn the door knob and it's not locked. I open the door to find Rick looking at his blood soaked bandages as they lye on the bathroom counter because he took them off. Okay, so I need to stay calm and Rick's an adult. He can take care of himself and he wants to be left alone. He's still bleeding, so I take control. "I know you don't want help, but you can't bandage yourself up with one hand, and that hand is attached to an elbow in a sling. You're still bleeding. I want to help you. I want to take care of you. I'm taking control of this situation. No more of this crap!" I find myself yelling. "We're a team! We don't run and we don't hide from each other! We fix problems together!" Rick stares at me like I've lost my marbles and maybe I have. "Don't look at me like I'm crazy! You basically sat there and told my Mom you want to marry me yesterday, but today I can't be there for you? You know the whole in sickness and in health, in good times and in bad? It's a partnership and it goes both ways!" I go from worried and shaking mad to completely controlled in a heartbeat. I take his hand and pull the bandage the rest of the way off. I grab a clean kitchen towel and a bag of frozen peas. "Bed or couch?" He wobbles his head, but doesn't answer. "Hasn't anybody ever taken care of you? I have a hard time believing your mother didn't baby you. Sometimes you have to let somebody else take care of you. That means me and nobody else, got it?" I lead him to the couch with his hand wrapped in the towel and get him sat down. I press the cold peas to his hand and sit next to him holding it there to apply pressure, hoping to stop the bleeding and take away some of the pain. He isn't talking to me and I don't know why. He's in his head and probably mad at me. "Is the cold helping it feel better?"

"Yes." He speaks!

"Talking is good. Now, how about telling me why you don't want to talk to me?"

"I'm pissed that I let them get to me while I was on the field. That's all."

Let me read between those lines—I'm a weakness. If I wasn't there, he wouldn't be suspended. "We've had an emotional few days. I'm sure you'll keep everything in check from now on. We all have our moments." I stop and take a deep breath. "Or, I can quit going to the games."

Rick gapes at me in shock. "You always go to the games. You love baseball. The Seals are your team."

"All true, but baseball is a game and you're more important to me. I can always watch it on TV." He stares at me funny again. "Don't you get it? You're not a baseball player to me. You're my king, my love, my boyfriend, my lover, my partner, my friend, and my soul mate. Baseball or not, we still have us. I'll cheer for you no matter what you do." I watch him waiting for something, finally the gleam is back in his eyes.

"I want you at every game with me. I won't let it happen again." Rick smiles at me, the first time I've seen him light up since we got home. "Soul mate, huh? Do you believe in that? And love at first sight and shit like that?"

"I didn't until I met you." My answer pops out without

thinking. He leans in and kisses me sweetly, but he's frustrated because he can't use his hands to touch me. I check his hand and he's no longer bleeding. I set his hand in his lap with the frozen peas on it while I gather supplies. I kneel in front of him and take his hand to wrap it back up. I place a gauze pad over the wound and wrap it up tightly. I put the peas back in the freezer and grab another frozen bag for Rick to put around his elbow. "Better?"

"Yes, my queen." He says smiling.

"Good. What would you like for dinner? Pasta, breakfast or pizza?"

"Pizza." He'll always pick pizza. It makes my life easier tonight and I can focus on helping him relax.

I mix up a couple of extra large Screwdrivers and give one to Rick. "This should help you relax and numb you a little." He smiles and takes a drink. I kneel on the floor in front of him to take off his shoes, carefully to not hurt the foot that got hit by a pitch. I pull off his socks. I unbutton his pants and pull them off. Rick just watches me. I take a drink of my Screwdriver and reach my hand around his cock to stroke him. I'm watching him carefully because I don't want to hurt him and he has almost finished his Screwdriver that had five shots of vodka in it. I slam half of mine and set it to the side. I kiss his tip and suck it into my mouth, licking him all over as I stroke him with my lips. I feel his body stretch, wanting more and he's starting to relax. I stroke him with my hand while I continue to suck and lick him. He runs his fingers through my hair with his right hand and feels my head as I move on him. His pleasure drives me to suck harder, move faster until there's no turning back. I hum and take him completely in my mouth while I caress his body with my hands, pushing him over the edge.

He comes hard and lays his head back in ecstasy as he cries out, "Oh Sherry, I love you." I stroke him until he makes me stop.

"Please come here to me, baby." He's only partially with me, more on the drunk side.

"I don't want to hurt you, my king."

"On me, please. Please, Sherry." I reach for my drink, but it's gone. No wonder he's wasted! I make another drink and pound it. "Baby please, I want you to get off wrapped around me."

I don't argue with him, since I want the same thing. I carefully straddle him, trying not to shake his elbow or cause him more pain. I slip his tip into me and slide down his hard length until he's completely buried inside me. I hold onto the couch behind him for support and he manages to get my breast into his mouth. Suddenly sucking hard and stretching it, refusing to let go as I move on him. Biting, kissing, and licking every part of me he can reach. He starts moving as I'm almost to the edge and all I can do is scream out his name as we both go together. I can't stop myself as I move on him wildly and needy. We both cry out and I don't want to stop, he's so amazing. Rick finally touches my shoulder and guides my mouth to his, soothing me with his soft lips and tender caress. Both of us taste like orange juice and vodka. We stay together as I sit straddling him for hours while we make out.

We never ordered pizza. The vodka is gone. I don't remember going to bed. This is what it's like to be with Rick when he doesn't have to worry about baseball. Carefree and reckless. I wake up in bed with Rick holding my hand and it's only 3am. I'm guessing it's the only way he can sleep, otherwise he'd be wrapped around me. He's talking in his sleep, so I listen.

"I love you so much, Sherry. Don't be mad. I want to be with you forever. I want you with me always. Soon we'll make all of our dreams come true. We can do anything together. Don't ever give up on me. I want to protect you and take care of you. Only you, my queen. There is only you." He still sounds buzzed.

I move closer to him and lean my head on his right shoulder, so I can whisper in his ear, "I love you, too, Rick. You're my soul mate. Never shut me out. I'll always be here for you. I have a hard time believing we're real. I dreamt about you for years and you're better than any of my dreams. We'll make our dreams come true. We can do anything together, my king." I watch the smile appear on his face and fall back to sleep.

CHAPTER EIGHT

I wake up smelling coffee before my alarm goes off, so I turn it off and let Rick sleep. I get up and get prepped to make breakfast. I mix up some biscuit dough and brown the crumbled sausage in a pan. I cut out biscuits and put them in the oven. I add flour and milk to my sausage slowly, and stir it in until I get it to the right consistency and the raw flour flavor has cooked out. I crack some eggs into a bowl, add salt and pepper and whisk them up. I heat another pan and melt a little bit of butter in it before I dump the eggs in to cook. I swirl the pan around and scramble the eggs with my spatula. I get a couple plates and coffee mugs, so I'm ready. The biscuits are smelling delicious. I check on them and they're golden brown, so I take them out of the oven. Rick walks into the kitchen with pain showing on his face.

"I thought I smelled you cooking breakfast. It looks great. I'm hungry." He says as he tries to smile.

"I figured you'd be hungry. We never ate last night. I don't remember going to bed. The vodka is gone." I laugh.

"We should probably get more, it helped me sleep last night.

That and the special treatment from my woman." He wiggles his brows at me dirtily.

I dish up breakfast and keep the conversation going, "Do you want to stay in today and relax? I have a couple of errands to do, so I won't be gone long. I can put them off until tomorrow if you'd rather."

"I'd like to get out."

It hits me, "How about we go to the beach and relax on the warm sand for a while, then do the errands?"

"Sounds good, as long as you'll help me shower later."

"Anything for you, my king."

"I like the sound of that. Anything for me. That might get you into trouble."

I'm in a teasing mood, "I look forward to it."

We finish breakfast and get ready for the beach. I put on my black bikini, pulling on denim shorts and a black tank top over it. I brush my hair out and pull it back into a ponytail. I find Rick sitting on the edge of the bed in board shorts, frustrated and trying to take his sling off. I kiss him sweetly and gaze into his eyes, "I love you, my king. Let me help you." I take the sling off and search through his clothes. I find a Property of the Seals T-shirt with the sleeves cut off, leaving it with large armholes and help Rick put it on starting with the left arm to keep it easy on his elbow.

"I'm not going to break." He says sternly and glares at me with his piercing eyes.

"I know you're made of iron, but I don't want to make it worse. I want you to heal quickly, so you can get back on the field." He softens a bit and doesn't argue with me. I help him get the shirt pulled all the way on and put the sling back on with only a slight wince. I grab a couple beach towels and my beach blanket as we head out the door.

It's Monday, the beach is empty this early in the day. I lead

Rick to my favorite part of the beach, over toward lifeguard stand five, and find a patch of soft warm sand. I spread out my beach blanket and sit watching the waves crash. I love the breeze off of the ocean, the sun on my skin, and the warm sand beneath me. The world around me melts away, except for my king sitting next to me as he touches my hand, caressing each knuckle and finger. I turn to him and he's in the same place that I am. The beach is magic. I take off my tank top and shimmy out of my shorts. I fold up my towel and use it as a pillow. I lie back and close my eyes, absorbing everything around me.

"Babe, is this what you always do? I appreciate the view, but it's not safe for you to lay out here in your bikini alone." Rick is already back in protective mode.

"Don't worry, my king. I pay attention to my surroundings and layout close to the lifeguard stand when I'm alone. Thank you for looking out for me. Relax." I choose my words carefully. I can feel his eyes on me and I reach for his hand, wanting to hold it.

"You shouldn't come out here by yourself."

Deep breath. "I'm a big girl and I can take care of myself. I've always taken care of myself. I'm not going to stop living my life. It's always been just me. I've always lived alone and paid my own way. I don't need a keeper. I'm not a child." Can you say DOTM? His grip on my hand tightens. Fuck! Filter on the beach near lifeguard stand five, please?

Before I can speak again, "It's not just you anymore. I want to take care of you. You told me last night that we're a team and took care of me." He looks down, as if he's inspecting the sand. His tone gets quiet and gravelly. "I need you safe. I can't be without you again. Please, Sherry."

I consider the short time we've known each other. All the choices we've made. We both have a learning curve. I never realized how set in my ways I am. "I have to have a life, but I promise to be safe and not do anything stupid. I love how protective you are of me, but we both have different adjustments to make if this is going to work." I heard the "if" as soon as I said it.

"You don't believe we'll make it? I should've known. You gave up on me and started dating. I thought you wanted this as much as I do. I guess it's better to find out now before..."

I cut him off. "Rick, stop. I love you. I want everything with you and I've never wanted anything with anyone else. I'm not always going to say the right thing. I'm still learning how to be in a relationship. I know how to take care of you. I need to learn how to let you take care of me. Sometimes I wonder if we're only a good team when we're naked."

Rick laughs, "We're a perfect team. I like to make you happy. You like to cook for me. You love baseball and I play baseball. You even want to go to all of my games, none of the baseball wives do that or even cheer like you do. You love my sister even though she's crazy. We've made life-changing decisions together. And, of course, the sex is amazing." He has a dirty grin at the end of his rant. I'm good as long as he isn't going down the bad road.

I sit up and kiss him. "We'll get there, my king." I jump up, "Stay here, I'll be right back." I run for the ocean and wade out until I can't touch the bottom. I float, diving into the waves one by one as they pass through, the ocean sharing its energy and playing with me. I wait for my wave and ride it to shore. I walk out of the water feeling like a new woman. Refreshed, I twist my hair and look up to see my man waiting for me with a towel.

Rick holds my towel up for me and I wrap up, "You're so beautiful, even soaking wet." He kisses me on the nose, "And salty."

I lead him back to the blanket, so I can layout and dry off. He sits next to me, watching me. "Lay down, so I can talk to you." He does as I ask and lies on his side, facing me. "Do you remember the last time we were on the beach?" I realize this could take me down a bad road because that was the night that ended with a horrible morning in LA, but that's not my focus.

"I remember Malibu." Flames instantly fill his eyes.

"I'll never forget it. I love the way you plan date nights. You picked me up at the airport in the convertible Porsche and kissed me like we hadn't seen each other in days. You drove us to that Hawaiian themed restaurant on the water in Malibu because they have a dessert you know I'd love, but we never got to dessert. We left the restaurant and ended up on the beach, unable to keep our hands off each other. I stripped down for a swim, but you wouldn't go with me and I ended up underneath you on the sand, then on top of you. I'll never forget how raw it was, you were shaking for me. You needed me. I needed you." I started speaking in my sweet sexy seductive voice, but by the end I had myself breathing hard at the memory.

"I still need you." His eyes and his tone give me goosebumps. "I've never needed anyone, the way I need you." This man does crazy things to me. He can fry my brain with his words. His voice changes, he sounds unsure, "Sherry, do you still need me?"

"I need you more than ever before, my love. Everyday, I need you more." It's the truth. I always speak the truth, but sometimes I surprise myself with the words I say. Huh, I really need to record myself when I'm sleeping. "I wanted to beat the shit out of that pitcher yesterday for throwing at you, and Adam better hope he never sees me on the street or he's going to sound like he's been sucking helium. He'll wish he didn't have balls." I take a deep breath, "I heard the ball hit you and I watched you fall, but I couldn't get to you. I watched you get up and go at the mound like someone was getting the beat down. I saw you dislocate that asshole's jaw with one punch and get escorted off the field. I heard the voice of a worried girlfriend come out of my mouth when I wasn't allowed to see you. All I wanted to do was take care of you and take the pain away. I, I don't know what it is, but it's never been more present in my life than it is when I'm with you now—love, need, our connection, all of it together." I feel tears running down my face and I didn't know I was crying. I was so focused on Rick yesterday, I didn't allow my emotions to affect me. I simply took control of the situation. He needed me to. He was bleeding.

Rick smiles at me, "You really did take care of me last night. I didn't realize how much until you said it. You stopped my bleeding. You made my hand not hurt. You got me wasted, so I would relax and to dull my pain. You made it look easy."

"It's easy, when you want to take care of someone like I want to take care of you."

Rick reaches for my hand and brings it back to his lips, kissing each finger and each knuckle. "I love you, baby. How about you let me take you to lunch? Then we can go home."

I don't want him to overdo it today and hurt. I nod, "I know just the place." We dust off and I pull on my clothes. I take Rick to the public market, so I can get food to cook for dinner while we wait for our lunch. He'd never been there and we end up with all kinds of stuff that wasn't on my list. I stop and run into the grocery store on the way home to get vodka, orange juice and a couple of other things. I want to make sure Rick isn't too sore to sleep tonight.

I get everything put away. I mix up some jello shots and put them in the refrigerator to set up. Orange and grape flavors, both made with vodka. I shower quickly and take Rick to bed with me for a nap. I'm worn out and he needs a break, too.

CHAPTER NINE

I wake up a couple hours later and Rick is sacked out. My nap didn't help. I kept replaying my man getting hit and going down. Every way it could've played out, I played it in my head. Everything from him not going down, to him not getting up. Every time I couldn't get to him. Every time they wouldn't let me see him. Visions continue to run through my head of things that didn't happen. The 92 mile per hour fastball hitting him in the head and cracking his helmet. The ball smashing into his handsome face. The full bone-breaking sound of the impact of the ball colliding into him and the ground when he falls to it uncontrollably. His blood soaking his uniform and streaming from his temple. Knocked out cold. Lying there lifeless. The images and sounds invade my head and won't leave me. Torturing me with horrible things that didn't happen, but now I'm realizing they could. He wants me safe because he never wants to be without me again. I get it now, but he's not going to quit playing baseball. We're going to keep living. Life has risks unless you quit living it.

I whisper quietly to Rick, "You rest baby, I'll be in the other room if you need me. I love you." I kiss his forehead and close the bedroom door as I leave the room. He needs rest. I need a distraction to get my head in the right place.

I was a bad girl today, completely skipping work. Just because the team has an off day and Rick is suspended for five days, doesn't mean I get to vacation. I quickly get my work caught up and handle all of my messages. But, what I want to do is bake. I take a suggestion from Chase, mix up some chocolate chip cookie bars and get them baking. I scrub the baking potatoes I bought for dinner and toss them in a bowl with olive oil, sea salt, and black pepper. I take the steaks out of the refrigerator to bring them to room temperature. I decide to make a compound butter and split the leftover biscuits to toast with garlic. I set a stick of butter out to soften in a bowl and add thyme, marjoram, basil, and some of the soft gooey cheese we bought on a whim at the public market. I smell the chocolate chip cookie bars and check on them, but they need a few more minutes to be GBD (golden brown and delicious). I split the biscuits and spread them with a light layer of butter, then sprinkle them with garlic salt. I pull the cookies out and set them on the stovetop to cool. I place the potatoes directly on the oven rack and turn the oven up to 400, they'll take some time to cook. The butter has softened, so I mix it together thoroughly with the herbs and cheese. I get a piece of plastic wrap and place the butter in the middle, wrapping it up tightly, twisting the ends, and put it in the refrigerator to solidify. I find myself singing "We Belong" by Pat Benatar as I work in the kitchen. I cut up the cookie bars, packaging a few for Cross and find myself scouring the cabinets for something else to make.

I need to keep busy and out of my head because I can't shake the visions of my Rick. The worst of them keep coming back to me and I'm being silly because he's here, in bed sleeping. It's in slow motion over and over. He goes down in the batter's box and he's not moving. I'm watching him for any movement, just to see he's breathing. I can't get to him. I can't be there to hold his head and comfort him. I can't talk to him, so he hears I'm there with him. I need him to know I'm there for him and I need confirmation he'll be okay.

When did I turn into the worrying, needy girlfriend who can't control her emotions? What the fuck is wrong with me? I can't go on the field. The players get the best possible medical attention. Damn it! It truly is a battle on the field and they don't love him the way I do. I hate the Sissy's and that asshole and their stupid ass whiny pitcher. They did this to me. They made me an emotional wreck! I stop and listen to my internal rant and I'm placing blame. The truth is, I opened my heart and Rick filled it. I wouldn't have it any other way.

I open the bedroom door quietly to check on him, but end up climbing in bed with him like a moth to a flame. I wrap my arms around him and kiss him repeatedly. "How are you feeling, my king?"

He smiles at me, like he could be woken up by my kiss whenever I want. "I'm stiff and sore. What smells good? I'm hungry."

"I've been in the kitchen. I've got a plan to help with the stiff and sore. I'll go finish dinner and you come to the kitchen when you're ready?" I move to get out of bed, but he grabs me pulling me back to him and kissing me passionately. "I love you, my king. Let's work on the sore and then the stiff." I laugh, but more than anything I don't want him in pain. He runs his hand over my body and lights me up, trying to get me to change my plan. It's working, but I manage to slide out of bed and scamper back to the kitchen.

"Come back," Rick yells from the bedroom.

"Can't hear you, cooking." But, I could hear him just fine and it wasn't the sound of a man needing help, it was the sound of my man wanting me. I love his desire for me.

I check the potatoes and they're almost done, so I finish the rest of dinner. I season the steaks on both sides with salt and pepper and slide them into the broiler. I place the tray of split garlic biscuits in the oven and find myself singing again, apparently Pat Benatar has possessed me with "We Belong" for the time being.

I hear him get up and he slowly makes his way to the kitchen, still wearing the clothes from the beach. I find something about it sexy. The laid back style with his hair a mess. He stands behind me, kisses my neck, and reaches his right arm around me to pull me back to him. I feel what he wants against my ass and it's an impressive need.

I pull the biscuits out of the oven and flip the steaks over. I hear Rick's stomach growl and the smell of the food is distracting him until after we eat. I retrieve the compound butter from the refrigerator and cut open the baked potatoes, pushing the ends in to make them open better. He eyeballs the chocolate chip cookie bars I have packaged for Cross and starts to open the package, "Stop it, those are for Chase. We have the rest of the pan." I point to the pan and he immediately breaks off a small piece, shoving it into his mouth.

I place the steaks on the plates and set a slice of the compound butter on each steak. I add the baked potato and a toasted garlic biscuit to the plate. I take the plates to the table where the two chairs now sit next to each other permanently. Then I grab the sour cream, butter and compound butter for the table. I sit next to Rick, ready to eat dinner and his brain is working as he inspects me.

"You've been busy this afternoon. Everything looks perfect and smells good." It's not the end of what he wants to say. He kisses me sweetly on the lips, sucking lightly on my lower lip as he pulls away. He gazes deep into my eyes and connects with my heart, I want to melt into him.

I smile, "Sometimes I need to be in the kitchen." I look at him and realize he's going to be challenged to cut his steak, so I take his plate and slice it up for him. He shakes his head with a frustrated grin and eats his dinner. I sit and watch him. I put my arm around him and lean on his shoulder, simply needing him here next to me.

"Are you okay? You aren't eating."

"I will be. I just need to know you're here with me."

"I'll always be here with you, my queen. You keep cooking like this and there may be more of me." He laughs. I get lucky and he doesn't ask any more questions.

We finish dinner and I clear the table. "Orange or grape?" I ask ready to start the relaxing process I have in mind.

"I like both." Ha! I take two of each flavor jello shots to the table.

"Ever done jello shots?" I peer at Rick mischievously. I pick up an orange jello shot, run my tongue all the way around it inside the small cup and suck it down. His eyes heat and I'm guessing it's the tongue action or maybe the sucking action that's doing it for him.

Rick copies me, sliding his tongue into the cup and running it all the way around the shot, then sucking it down. Holy fuck Batman! I get wet just watching him. We both pick up a grape one and watch each other closely as we do the shots. Fuck me! Fuck me! Fuck me! I didn't say it out loud, but it was like I did. My panties and shorts are off in mere seconds, his lips are on mine needy, licking and sucking. I push his shorts down, releasing and stroking his willing cock. I turn around, pressing my ass to his hard cock and his guttural groan shakes me. I bend over and he slides his dick against my ass while he explores my hot wetness with his fingers. His length gets even harder and I whimper with need. His right hand moves to my hip, gliding over me as I move, wanting him. He grasps his cock and slides the tip into me. I want all of him and I want him now. I push back against him and take all of him at once. He moans with appreciation. His hand on the small of my back is warm and guiding. I slide on and off of him, rubbing on him, wrapped around him, the slow friction driving me to the edge.

"Oh, my queen. How are you so perfect? You make me... I just want... I love you wrapped around me," Unable to finish his thoughts he reaches around my waist and bends over me, kissing my back and neck. He's limited without his left arm, but creatively making it work. His hand at my sex, he circles my sensitive center slowly, building my need and I'm a grenade on countdown to explosion. I move against him faster and harder. I can't control myself, I want more and I want it now.

I scream out his name, "More, baby! Please! Rick! Oh, my king!" As I explode and he goes with me. Exploding at the same time, we both cry out at the intensity. He wraps his arm around me tightly and pulls out. I want him inside me, but he pulls me back up to him and kisses my neck.

He turns me to him and devours my mouth with his as he drags me to the bedroom. He takes us both down on the bed and immediately pushes into me. "I need more of you. You're my world." He moves quickly getting faster as he pounds into me, driving me crazy with every movement.

I shudder almost instantly, "You're amazing! I'm yours!"

"Always, baby. You'll always be mine. When you squeeze me like this, it just feels... fuck. I need you with me." Rick slams into me a few times, throwing himself over the edge and shaking in pleasure. He rolls to the side and pulls me back against him. His whole body heaving with every breath as he regains control. His hot breath at my ear, "It's always us. We'll always be together. You'll always be the queen to my king. I promise I'll make you mine. I want nothing more than to make all of your wishes come true."

They're only words, but I believe every single one of them and feel them to my soul. I fall asleep content using his chest as my pillow with his arm holding me to him.

CHAPTER TEN

"Sherry. It's okay. I'm right here. Sherry, wake up. Sherry!"
Rick startles me, trying to wake me up. He searches my
eyes. "Are you awake now? Do you see me?" He takes my
hand and holds it to his heart, so I feel it beating.

"I see you. I like how you're holding my hand to your heart.
Are you okay?" I speak calmly, wondering what's going on.

"You were screaming and calling out my name. You kept
saying you were right here and asking why I wasn't moving. You
kept saying you love me and telling me not to leave. It sounded
like you wanted to get to me, but couldn't. You were hysterical
and I don't want you to be. I love you, Sherry. Were you dreaming?" His voice going from concerned to calming.

I wasn't dreaming. I was having the repeated nightmare that's
been keeping me awake. I don't want to tell him about it. "I'll
be okay."

"Tell me, Sherry. I need to know what's going on. Remember,
we don't have secrets."

I take a deep breath, "It's silly. I'm freaking out and need to get over it. I'll be fine." The chance this is an acceptable response is about zero.

"Whatever it is, it'll be okay. Just tell me."

"I started having nightmares when I was napping with you this afternoon. That's why I got up and found something to keep me busy. I couldn't get them out of my head. Different versions of you getting hit by the ball and falling to the ground. Mostly the worst one and I don't want to talk about it." I come to an abrupt stop because there's no way I tell him how I'm seeing him get hit, fall, and lay there lifeless.

He holds me tight, "I know things can be scary sometimes. It's hard when the team rules make you wait for hours to see that I'm fine. But, the thing that matters most is that I'm here with you right now and I love you." He's right. I kiss him, distracting myself and proving to myself he's right here with me alive and breathing. I reach for his cock and find him to be ever-ready. I climb on top of him, mounting him, and lie down on his chest. Rick lifts the arm in the sling and rests it on my back, holding me to him. I move slightly as I appreciate him inside me, but mostly I lie with my head on his heart. I want to listen to it beat and feel how strong he is.

"I love you, Rick. Can I stay right here, just like this?" I sound needy, like I want to be taken care of. And I do.

He kisses the top of my head. "Whatever I can do to help, my love. I always want to hold you." I fall asleep on him, soothed and protected.

Early Tuesday morning I'm woken by a ringing phone and I don't recognize the ring. I'm still on Rick and he stirs beneath me. He holds me to him and doesn't seem to care that his phone's ringing. "Let me get the phone for you." I say groggily.

"The phone will be there when I'm ready. Right now, I want to be with you." I completely melt at his sweet words and sleepy tone.

"Wow. Say more things like that." I giggle happily.

"We should sleep with you on me every night. It helped both of us relax. You're still on me..." He pushed into me with his morning wood. "The phone can definitely wait." He moves slowly, in and out while he continues to talk to me. "What do you think?"

"Oh," I try to find my voice, but all I can do is appreciate my warm, sexy man, "Phone can wait. Oh, Rick."

"Oh, Rick... huh? Oh, Rick what?" He's in his sexy, horny, teasing mood—I love it!

"Oh, god," sleepy groggy sex is the best. I'm not completely awake and he makes me where I can't think. "You, oh Rick, you just... you make me forget where I am." He pushes into me harder, appreciating my words and the sexy sounds escaping my lips. I move with him and dig my fingers into his hair. "You make everything disappear. It's only you and me."

"Do I really do that for you?" This hot sexy man questioning his abilities.

"Oh, yes! Yes." All I can do is feel him moving, filling me, stretching me. I cry out his name uncontrollably.

"I'm the only one who does this for you, always. Nobody else can have you, my Sherry."

"It's only ever been you. Nobody has ever taken me the places you do." His slow pace continuing, driving me crazy and holding me back from the edge.

Rick growls like he's not only my king, but the king of the jungle and I see the proud look on his face. I kiss his neck, drawing out another low groan. "Not yet, baby." Rick slides out from under me and out of bed.

I'm left confused and abandoned. But not for long, he grabs my ankle and pulls me to the edge of the bed with my legs hanging off. Immediately burying his face in my sex, licking my wet folds and fucking me with his tongue. I'm on sensory overload. He sucks at my sex and I scream out his name. He slides two fingers into me and tongues my clit, lapping, sucking, teasing me until he bites down on me hard and sucks like his life depends on it, sending me into a flying spiral. I hear the sounds coming from me and I'm not in control. It drives him further. Everything goes dark and now he's plunging into me. He's huge, filling me repeatedly, "Oh, fuck me. So, fucking perfect."

"Not yet, please more..." I hear myself selfishly beg him to hold back.

He smiles, my request is an honor he'll happily accept. He takes my breast in his mouth, sucking and nibbling at my nipple, and I'm lost again. Rick strokes into me faster and faster, pushing me over the edge, drawing out my orgasm while he meets me there. He slams into me hard a few times and collapses on me with his lips at my ear, "I love you, Sherry." He kisses my neck and wraps his right arm around me, holding me to him.

I sometimes wonder how I deserve this, him. There are many women out there who would do anything to have someone take care of them, cover all of their expenses, give them great sex, and I mean even if they didn't love them. Yet here I am with my perfect man, my better than any fantasy I ever had baseball boyfriend who worships me as much as I worship him, but I don't want to be kept or have someone else pay my way. Okay, fine, I want the out of this world sex. Only a foolish woman wouldn't. I know he loves me when he kisses me, touches me, slides inside me or, honestly, just holds my hand. I feel it in his eyes when he looks at me. My seat for every game. Traveling to away games. His planned date nights. My stadium access card and Seals wardrobe. His sweet, meaningful, words and gestures. How he always sits next to me at the table. Even his quirks, like elevators, that I admit I love. It has required some adjustment, but no hardship. The horror of having a professional baseball player in my bed every night, what will I ever do? I just don't know.

Rick's phone rings again as we're dozing back off to sleep. He sighs and reaches for his phone to find the stadium calling. He'd rather be home with me and doesn't want to deal with work. "Hello?"

"Hey Seno, Skip wants you to come in this morning and get your elbow checked. Are you having any pain?" Carter calling to take care of team business and I can hear him through the phone.

"Not really, slight soreness and mostly stiff I think from the sling. I'll be there this morning." All business.

"Billy got a five day suspension for throwing at you. The first baseman is on the DL for an undetermined amount of time. Remind me never to make you mad. Also, Seals called up the catcher that's been hot on the farm team to cover while you're out. Saben can't handle four games on his own." I see the shit look cross his face.

I smell coffee brewing and it's almost time for my alarm to go off. I get up and leave the bedroom to go thank my coffeemaker while Rick finishes his conversation. His eyes on me as I pull his dirty T-shirt on and leave the room bottomless.

I take advantage of the time to check what I need to do for work today, check the baseball schedule, turn the shower on to warm, and make a mental list of things I need to discuss with him. I've been thinking about it and since he's moved in and wants to pay, it'll be better to talk about it and have it decided than to wait until he thinks he's just going to pay. I give Rick a cup of coffee on my way to the shower and toss his T-shirt on the bed on my way out of the room.

I turn on some music to listen to while I'm in the shower. Who am I kidding? I put on my *Singing in the Shower* playlist, turn up the volume and close the bathroom door. "Love is a Battlefield" by Pat Benatar takes over my bathroom and I take advantage of the acoustics in my shower as I sing along with her. I love this playlist, it empowers me with strong female vocalists. I dance around the shower singing as I wash my hair and turn to the corner for the best vocal effect on "Million Reasons" by Lady Gaga. I enjoy the water falling over me as 'Til Tuesday's "Voices Carry" comes on and I sing into the water with my eyes closed, feeling the music. I kick it up a notch when "Never" by Heart comes on and I'm ready to get out of the shower when Pat Benatar is back with "We Belong," but it sucks me in and I close my eyes as I sing. I open my eyes and leave the water on for my Rick. I turn to step out of the shower and find him leaning in the doorway watching me with a smile on his face. "I left the water on for you," I grin at him from my eyes and cheeks. "How's your elbow? Can I help you wash your hair or anything?"

"You already do so much for me. I was in a shitty mood after that phone call, but I heard you in the shower and watching you made everything better. I love the way you connect with me and music, you give both of us everything you have."

My cheeks warm and I know I'm blushing. "Let me wash your hair." I open the shower door for him and invite him in. Helping him take his sling off without it getting soaked. I reach my arms around his neck and stretch to kiss him, pushing him into the spray of water with my lips. I love his naked body against mine and the reaction I get from his body tells me he feels the same way. My happy place gets excited and his cock gets hard against me. I shampoo his hair, rubbing his scalp all over and rinse it out. I rub conditioner into his hair and leave it while I soap up his body, rubbing my hands all over him and trapping his cock between my thighs. I rinse his hair, running my fingers through it and pushing my breasts against his chest. I rinse the soap off of both of us and when I drop to my knees to wash his legs, he groans at my release of his cock. I soap up his legs and rinse them off, running my hands up and down both of his legs. I have some fun and soap up his hard cock, stroking it repeatedly and more than necessary before I rinse it off. As soon as I get all the soap off, I kiss his tip and slide my lips over his hard length. I grasp him at his hips with each of my hands, digging my fingers into his deliciously hard ass. It's times like these I truly appreciate his catcher's body, his strong legs and muscular ass. What is a girl supposed to do other than love, pleasure, and worship a man like this? The thought makes me do something I shouldn't. Something that would really piss off my Rick. I close my eyes and blow him like the professional athlete he is, like he's a baseball player and not my man. I take him deep with every stroke and suck hard with every pull, moving on him quickly and with a purpose. Rick leans back against the wall and spreads his feet for balance. He touches my face, caressing my cheek. My eyes are closed, but he must be watching me.

"That's not you, baby. I only want you. I'm still a man, but I don't know. Something is different. I don't expect you to do this for me, my queen." I stop, sit back and gaze up at him. He has a look of confusion. Eyes open and on him, I kiss him from base to tip and swirl my tongue around him, lightly sucking. "That's my baby loving me. It's only ever you wanting to, my queen." I stroke him with my lips and hum to vibrate him. I put my hand around him and stroke while I suck. He gets harder and all I want is him inside me. I stand up and kiss him passionately, demanding. I suck on his tongue and lower lip as I pull away. I turn around and lean against him as I bend over and slide back on to his hard cock. "Oh, fuck. You feel so good wrapped around me." We push and pull together slowly, feeling each other and enjoying the moment. "There's nothing better than you, my queen. I swear you're perfect. We were made for each other. I want you every day. You're my forever, Sherry." I can't even form words, only he does this to me. Suddenly he pulls out of me and takes control, turning me around, he wraps his right arm around my waist and lifts me to him, sliding me down onto his cock and guiding me to wrap my legs around him and hold on. He fucking surprises me with what he can do, and with one arm no less. He claims my mouth with his and I know why. He needs me, he wants to communicate more with me without words. He loves me and he needs me to know, he wants to know I feel the same. It sounds silly because I'm right here with him, but he needs to know I'm here with him, for him, and it's real. Sex is almost a moment of weakness and insecurity we need to surpass, to prove our love. Sometimes I swear he wants it to be more than sex, almost like he has a specific purpose in mind. Other times, like where he's taking us now, he simply wants to love me and everything is in his kiss. He wants a deeper connection and I'm not talking about his dick. His kiss drives the mood and our need. He licks my lips, tasting me with need while he pushes into me. I move on him, stroking him the best I can while I hang onto him. The intensity is getting the best of me quickly. Rick breathing heavy whispers in my ear, "I love you, baby. Can you feel it?" His tone tells me he's not talking about his cock.

"Yes, my love. All over, especially in my heart. I know you love me. I couldn't have a better king." This man just kills me sometimes and I don't know what to say. "Can you feel that I love you?" I wonder if he asked because he doesn't feel it. Tears roll down my face.

Rick presses his lips to mine, over and over. Open-mouthed he slides his tongue into my mouth to dance with mine. His right hand firmly on my back and holding me to his chest, his cock rubbing against my clit with every stroke. He's using his kiss to drive me to orgasm, sucking on my tongue. He moves to my neck, kissing at the perfect spot and when he knows I'm on the edge he sucks hard sending me down the rabbit hole. He leans back against the wall and slides down to the floor. I have no idea what happened. I go dark and I'm surrounded by the firework show with stars and pink bursts. I hear music and I'm relaxed with no worries. Rick kisses me, "Sherry, are you with me?"

I open my eyes and gaze straight into his. He's holding me in his lap. "Why are we on the floor?"

"You let go all of the sudden and I didn't want you to fall, so I leaned back to keep you from falling and slid down to the floor. It was the best I could do with one arm. Are you okay?"

"I'm better than okay. Sometimes you rock my world and I don't know where I go. You should see the fireworks. This time there was music."

"You were singing, my queen." I sing a line from the music I heard and Rick says, "That's what you were singing." I need to get control of this talking and now singing when I'm not conscious. Apparently, "We Belong" is still possessing me.

We get up off the ground, rinse off and get out of the shower. Rick towel dries his hair and pulls on shorts, while I find panties, denim shorts and a Seals tank top. He sits on the edge of our bed and pulls me over to sit next to him. "I know you love me everyday when I wake up feeling like a king. It's all you, your sweet words, how you make me feel. You make me warm all over and I can't control my smile when I'm with you. I meant it before when I told you I wasn't living. Your love gives me life." He kisses me sweetly and slowly, then pulls back while keeping eye contact. "Someday I'll ask because I want to be with you forever, but I'm already committed to you. You're more than my girlfriend."

"It'll always be us, my king." I hug him warmly with my cheek to his.

"So, do you want to watch the game tonight?" I ask wondering how this will play out. I want to watch the game and we haven't watched a game together.

"Yes. I need to go to the stadium this morning to get my elbow checked. Drive me? I don't want to show up without the sling on."

"Anything for you, my king." He pulls a T-shirt on by

himself, but he did put it on his left arm first. I help him get the sling back on and can't wait until I get both arms around me again. I pack my work bag, so I can get some work done while I wait for him at the stadium. He won't be staying there, since he's suspended. I brush out my hair, find my sandals and grab Chase's chocolate chip cookie bars, so I can leave them for him. I cut one out of the pan to eat it with my last drink of coffee, and its obvious Rick has been picking at them. I yell through our home, "I'm ready whenever you are." Rick walks out and hands me his keys.

I drive Rick's Challenger into the player's garage and park. I follow him in and check with Carter to find out where my boundaries are today. He checks the clubhouse and let's me leave my special package for Chase in his locker. Since I'm allowed to wander the seating bowl and concourse, I decide to sit in my season ticket seat and enjoy the view while I get some work done.

Text to Rick - I'm sitting in my old section. Let me know when you're done.

Text to Cross - I left you a present in your locker :)

Text from Rick - Okay. I'll find you.

Text from Cross - I hope it's sweet and baked! Thanks!

Something about my seat always seems right, it welcomes me. I miss my view of the field. I sit field level, but I'm up about halfway and it gives me a view of almost the whole field. The field is a beautiful thing, green, fresh, and perfectly manicured. I can hear the bats connecting with the pitches, the hum of the crowd, the peanut vendor wandering through. In reality, the field is empty other than a few guys playing catch and running around the field like a track. It simply makes me happy. This is the perfect place to work. I open my laptop and work on updating my social media. I add some new photos, update travel specials, and post a picture of my current view to Instagram asking who's interested in a stadium vacation. I check my email and reply to the customers I'm working with. I review my customer's social media accounts for travel posts and photos, anything I might be able to use or comment on for exposure. I prepare an email about planning for winter trips to Hawaii with the suggestion to book early for better rates and give yourself something to look forward to, and send it out to my customer base. I tweet about a stadium vacation using #baseball #SanDiegoSeals #vacation, thinking my fellow fans who follow me might be interested. I review the vacation plans I started for Rick and I, updating them with the best prices, and getting everything set. It makes me excited just thinking about it. I can't wait to spend two weeks in Hawaii with my Rick.

I change gears and review my budget, as well as the away games coming up and check airfare for Chicago and Seattle. As I review the schedule I'm reminded the trade deadline is almost here and it hits me, they brought up the new hot catcher. Rick doesn't want to get traded and the way they've been trading, nobody's safe. I check for the lineup, but it's too early. We'll definitely be watching the game tonight.

Rick sits down next to me. "I see why you like it here. I never see the field like this. It's gorgeous." Spoken like a true baseball fan. "Plus, it's foul ball territory, the seats are angled toward the field perfectly and you've got a clear view."

"I've been sitting in this seat for years. I've never changed. Great view of all the action, total fan section and close to my favorite concessions." I stop abruptly. I may have just had a DOTM moment and I need to make up for it. "But, I love sitting behind home plate. I've been cheering for you for years from out here and you didn't even know it. Now you have no doubt when I cheer for you, I'm closer to you, and I have an awesome view of your ass!" I laugh hysterically because I'm so funny, well at least I think I'm funny.

Rick shakes his head, "My queen, everybody knows when you cheer for me and I love it. It's better than when the whole stadium goes crazy over a home run or even a grand slam. I don't have to be great for you to cheer for me. You cheer for me before I do anything and get me pumped up, and when I do something great you're louder than everybody else. I can always hear you and it feeds my ego every time." Rick leans over and kisses me sweetly, "I didn't know what I was missing."

I notice he's not wearing the sling, "How's your elbow?"

"I'm okay. I need to pay attention for any pain, otherwise I should be able to play after my suspension." He puts both arms around me and kisses me silly, showing me he's fine.

I still feel guilty about his suspension. But, I do get him to myself for the rest of his suspension.

I put my work away and hand Rick his keys. We walk out to the garage and Rick gets in the driver's seat. I slide in the passenger side and scoot over next to Rick, so I can lean against him and rest my hand on his thigh. It's what he likes me to do and wants me to do, it's not just me.

We stop at the Yolk for brunch on the way home and I take the opportunity to handle business, considering I can't concentrate when we get home and will most likely end up naked. "Can we talk about some roommate things over lunch?"

Rick glares at me like I'm crazy, "Roommate?"

Bad choice of words, "Let me try again. Can we discuss a few things? I want to have a plan when it comes to money and traveling." I'm not sure that was any better.

"I told you, I'll pay for everything. Don't worry about it."

"That's what we need to talk about. I don't work like that." I'm struck with a vision of the future and suddenly I know in the future it'll be different. We're partners and it won't be like he's paying for everything. It might not be that bad to be taken care of. "I mean right now. I know it could be different in the future."

"Okay." We find a table at the Yolk and sit down on the same side of the table as always. He puts his arm around me and we order our usual. "What's on the agenda?"

I turn and glare at him because he's picking on me for planning. "Traveling for away games and household expenses. I understand that you have enough money to pay for everything and want to cover it. I appreciate that you want to do that for me, but it'll make me feel like I have to answer to you about how I use my money and I don't want to."

"Okay, keep going."

"My airfare for the away games could be a challenge for me when there are multiple away series during a month. I can't afford the tickets where you want me to sit and I've come to terms with that. Going to the game is kind of us being on a date. Sounds crazy, but it really is like being on a date with you. I spend the whole time with you, right there watching the game and cheering for you and sharing the whole thing with you."

"In my heart, what's mine is yours. I want you to have anything and everything you want."

I put my hand on his thigh, appreciating him and not wanting to get off track. "When I was waiting for you in Carter's office, he was complaining about travel arrangements for the team. I want to offer him my services and handle travel for him. I can do it all for the same cost and make a profit. It should cover the expense of my airfare and make me some extra spending money. If it works out I can offer my services to other teams and make new contacts for doing stadium tours in the future. I don't want to do anything you're not comfortable with. What do you think?" He starts to talk and I add quickly, "I know you don't think I need to work and think it will stop soon, but it's not going to and it doesn't take me that much time. Working with travel is fun for me. I like having my own thing. It's not like I work for somebody else, on their schedule and can't travel with you. I can do all of it."

Diffused, "I don't expect you to give up your business. I know you enjoy it. If you want to approach Carter, you should. Just tell me if you need money. I'm an expensive boyfriend."

"That's the other part, food is definitely more expensive traveling and feeding you at home. I figure the shared expenses are the mortgage, association fees, utilities, and food. I'm happy to keep paying all of it and I can afford it, since you pay when we go out to eat. But, you want to pay for everything, so how about we split the mortgage, I'll pay association fees and utilities, and you cover food."

"Does that make me paying less than half?"

"I'm not sure how much food will be. You're probably paying more than half, but I figure it's easier since all the utilities and everything are already in my name."

"Mortgage? You aren't renting there?"

"No. It's my place. Does that make a difference?"

"No, I love it there." He leans in close to my ear and speaks quietly, "We'll want more room in the future, Elle will need her own room." My whole body shivers and he holds me close, rubbing my arm. "Just thinking of the future, my queen. You said you wanted to have a plan." He throws me off and I've lost focus. Luckily, our food shows up and I have time to recover while we eat.

Rick turns to me, "What if we pay it off?"

"No."

"I know you like to save money and it would save a bunch of money that's getting spent on interest."

"No."

"Why not?"

"It's my place and I've done it by myself." I really need to check my filter, it might need cleaning or something.

Rick runs his hand over his face and takes a deep breath, "This conversation would be a lot easier if we were naked."

"I chose to have it here on purpose. I want to be coherent and not distracted."

"I live there, too. It's our place. Don't you want me there?"

"Yes! I want you there with me. It's just... I don't know how to explain this to you without you deciding I'm crazy." I stop and breathe, "I managed to buy it on my own and that's a big deal to me."

Rick smiles, "I love that about you, my queen. The problem is you're not on your own anymore. It's not only you. I'm here and I don't care how you want to say it, there's a we or an us or partners or team—there are two of us. Two of us doing everything together and to quote a wonderful woman I know 'we're a team'." Son of a bitch! That's twice today he's used my own words against me.

"I'd like to change my definite 'No' to 'Not Yet'. Better?"

"It's progress. Do you have an idea when?"

Pushy bastard. How do I tell him when we're permanent without him being pressured, feeling like he needs to propose? Or thinking I don't have faith in us? Then the tears start rolling again. Damn it! My mouth takes over and I need to get a filter replacement. "What if you get tired of me? Or, realize I have my own special brand of crazy? What if you meet someone you want more? Maybe you'd rather have someone easy. Someone who lets you pay for everything and take care of them? I mean there are..."

Rick cuts me off. "Sherry..." He stops, drops cash on the table and drags me out of the Yolk. He stops in the middle of the parking lot, "You make me crazy," and pulls me to him, plastering my body to his while he kisses me passionately. He pulls back, holding my face so that I have to look at him and listen to him. "The only one of those things that's even remotely true is that I want to take care of you and pay for things for you. I don't want to do that for anybody else, only you. You're the one who makes me crazy and makes me lose control. You're the one who made me need you when all I'd done was touch your hand. You're the only one who's ever made it okay for me to be a baseball player. You want me and love me for all of the right reasons, and none of the wrong ones. Can't you see that we belong together?"

"Say that last bit again. Please."

"We belong together."

I don't know why, but the words straight from the song that's been possessing me strike me and I smile uncontrollably. Is it a sign I've been waiting for or simply my music connection getting the best of me? I can't help myself, I sing the song right there in the parking lot and Rick holds my hands smiling at me like a fool. He picks me up and twirls me around. He's mine. We belong together.

Rick drives us home and pulls me out the driver's side with him. He tosses me over his shoulder and he's mumbling to himself, though I can't make out the words. He carries me across the parking lot with his hand on my ass. We get into the elevator, "Fuck!" Rick yells out and pulls the elevator stop. He slides me down his body and already has his hard cock out and ready to go. He sets me down and presses his lips to mine, demanding, claiming, needing. Sucking on my lips and tongue. Kissing my neck, breathing in my ear, as he unbuttons my shorts and pushes them off, quickly making me naked from the waist down. He keeps kissing me as he discovers how wet I am for him, "Fuck it!" I love Rick in an elevator. He turns me away from him, bends me over and gets inside me as fast as he can. "Ggggrrrrrr..."

I know what he wants, "How do you want it in the elevator, my king? Hard? Fast?" All I get in response is a manly groan. "Oh, you want to take me like I belong to you. Like you just got me back to your cave, caveman style?" I actually feel him get harder at my words and decide to go further. "Oh, I see. You want to fuck me so hard that I can't stand. You want to fuck me into submission, so I'll do whatever you want?" He starts moving quicker. He likes my words. Maybe he needs a challenge. "Do you think you can actually do that? Conquer me? Go for it. Give me everything, fuck me as hard as you want, maybe harder." He slows down and slams me hard over and over and over. I had no idea he'd been holding back. I bend over farther and shake my ass at him. He's fucking me so hard that I have to brace myself, yet, "If you fuck me good enough, I'll do whatever you want."

"Huh," I actually hear a real thought go through his head and he fucks me harder, and harder. He takes my hands behind my back and holds them. He backs to the elevator wall, taking me with him and digs his fingers into my hips. Pulling me back on his cock hard and slamming into me at the same time. He pulls me up to him and, "I'm going to push you over further, so you can watch my hard cock while I fuck you. Every stroke slamming into you. I want you to see how huge I am slamming into your tight hole. I want you to tell me what you see and listen when I talk to you. Nod that you understand." I nod and bend over, but he pushes me farther so my head is between my ankles and I can see him inside me. He pulls out and pushes in, he's exquisite. "I'm going to pull out and you're going to watch carefully. Say yes."

"Yes."

He slides out a couple inches and then a couple inches more. "How many inches do you see?"

"Maybe five and your tip is still in me."

"Good girl. How long do you think I am right now?"

"Maybe seven."

"Keep watching, baby." He slides another inch out. "Oh, you feel good. Keep watching, I need back in for a minute." He slides all the way back into me with no effort at all. He strokes in and out, as I watch him move and see how solid and thick he is. "Do you see how hard I am? How you're pulled tight around me?"

"Yes, my king." I start to cry out.

"No." He slams into me hard five, six, seven, eight, nine, ten times. "Now I'm doing that again harder." And he did, I don't know where it came from and he didn't stop at ten, "You feel so fucking good right now and I don't think I've ever been this big and hard." Fifteen, sixteen, seventeen... "Time to watch again, baby." He nestles in tight, our bodies mashed together and starts to slide out slowly. I watch as he keeps sliding out. "Tell me what you see, my queen."

"At least eight and you're still inside me."

"Yes I am. I'm going to pull out all the way and I want you to reach for my tip with your mouth and suck on it hard. I want to feel how big I am before I slam back into you." He pulls out further until his tip pops out and I reach for him as directed, latching on to his tip and sucking hard. He's big and bulbous at the end of his long thick shaft. He groans, "Oh, fuck... almost there, baby." He pulls out of my mouth. "Tell me you're watching. I want you to see me slam into you. I fucking need you so bad all the time. Fuck me."

"Watching, my king." He lines his tip up and slams hard, all the way in and he's mashed against me again. Stroking over and over, in and out. I start to sway and he grabs me around the waist.

"I've got you, my queen. But, I'm not done until you're ready to give me whatever I want." I don't respond. He keeps fucking me, harder and harder. "Harder, my queen?"

"Yes, harder please, my king."

"Oh, fuck me, fuck me."

My body is out of my control and I'm completely his. I cry out his name with every stroke. He's the only reason I'm still up, I couldn't hold myself up if I wanted to. Where did this come from? Is this off-season Rick? Bad Boy suspended Rick? "Tell me what you want, my king. Whatever you want, anything. I'm yours."

"That's all I want. You, anyway I can get you, my queen." He holds me to him, stroking in and out, and I shake in pleasure. He follows me immediately, as if my orgasm is the final straw pulling him with me. He goes to put himself away and button up, when he realizes he can't let me go. "Babe? Can you stand and pull your shorts up?"

"No and yes."

"It's okay, I've got you. I'll always have you, my queen."

I pull up my shorts and he scoops me up in his arms before I can fasten them. Kissing me immediately. It's like he gets elevator fog and then the fog clears. He gets us home, locks the door behind us and takes me to bed. He stops suddenly and inspects me, "Did I hurt you? I never want to hurt you."

"No, I'll be fine. You literally fucked me until I can't walk. Where did that come from? Just the elevator?"

"I'm suspended. I don't have to be prepared to play baseball. So, you get all of my energy."

Well fuck me. "So, that's off season sex?"

"I guess, yea."

"You were sure demanding."

"I think that was the elevator and you asked for it. You pushed with your words and that always does it for me. Whatever I want after our talk earlier, sounded good. But, Sherry, I want you the way you are. I don't want you to change, then you wouldn't be you." He looks into space, contemplating something, "Did you like it?" His voice quiet and dirty.

"Yes. Seeing how long and thick you are, watching you slide in and out of me. Fucking insane seeing and feeling it." I watch him and see his eyes glaze. "Baby, do you need more?" Next thing I know I'm naked from the waist down again and his face is buried in my sensitive sex. I never thought I'd be wishing for the off season.

CHAPTER ELEVEN

Rick's alarm goes off in time for the game and he kisses me. "Game is on in thirty minutes. I'm going to order pizza and get the game turned on. Do you want to watch with me?"

"I've been waiting for a chance to watch a game with you. I'll be out there in a minute. I like to watch the pre-game and review the lineup. Oh, no anchovies and if you want veggies on your pizza order your own separately."

"Baseball with my woman and she knows her baseball. I like it. Mushrooms aren't veggies in your book are they?"

"Of course not! Mushrooms are delicious fungus. Tell them to bring red chili flakes. Oh, we have jello shots left for tonight, too!" It's going to be a good night. I pull my panties on with my Seals tank top and grab a blanket to picnic with pizza in front of the TV. I get myself settled in front of the TV and research the lineup on Twitter while I wait for the pre-game show to start. "The lineup is pretty normal, just missing you."

"Who's catching?"

"Stray is catching and hitting fifth, Cross is in center and leading off, followed by Mason and Martin. Are you watching as a fan or to breakdown the catcher or what?"

"What are you talking about?"

"The tone of the game. Business or pleasure? Maybe we should go ahead and get started on the jello shots?"

"Might as well. I need to get back to training on Thursday." I line up the remaining jello shots on a tray and bring them to the living room. I grab a grape one, wait for Rick to be watching me and lick around the inside of the cup to release the shot, then suck it down. I want him to be relaxed and have fun while he's suspended, not stress about the game. Rick's eyes go dark as he watches me suck the jello shot and he pulls me to his lips, kissing me with need. I giggle like a school girl and grab another shot, repeating the process. I hand one to Rick, but he's watching the game. I get it. I want to watch the game like I always do, but I don't want my man focusing on a new catcher who is potentially his replacement. Besides, you should never waste jello shots. The doorbell rings and Rick hops up to get the door, "Stay down in front of the couch, the pizza guy doesn't need to see you in your underwear."

"Isn't that how you're supposed to tip them?" I laugh because, well, I'm buzzed on three shots.

"Sherry." Rick scolds me. He doesn't have a sense of humor when it comes to me.

I push it, "What? You never flashed somebody to get free food or maybe beer when you were too young or something? Maybe it's a girl thing."

Rick shakes his head. "Please tell me you don't tip with your tits."

"Sometimes you're no fun. Of course I don't! Relax and have a jello shot."

Rick shakes his head and gets the pizza from the delivery guy. He sits down on the blanket with me and opens this huge pizza with pepperoni, sausage, sliced meatballs, mushrooms, bacon, and ham. The cheese is oozing off of it and the smell is making me hungry. It's hot, so I do another jello shot. I'm not paying attention to the game, but I'm watching it. Mostly, I'm gaging it by Rick's responses and there hasn't been any. There's no score yet and it's uneventful. We're playing a three game series against Houston, and they aren't a big rival or anything. The games will be pretty tame other than the game action itself, and the stadium won't be overrun with fans from Texas.

Seals are at bat, Chase swings at the first pitch and connects with a double to the left field wall. I yell out, "Wooo! Go Chase!"

Rick turns and glares at me, "You know he can't hear you, right?"

"I can cheer for my team if I want!" He shakes his head. "I talked to you through the TV when I would watch games from home. Sometimes I encourage the pitchers with positive words. I also tell the other team they suck."

"What did you say to me through the TV?"

"That depends on what you were doing and when it was." He glares at me strange again. "Always encouraging and positive."

"Why do I feel like you're holding back? Tell me." Joking, now he's in a better mood.

"Well, I've said a lot of things: You're so fucking hot! Tag'm out, baby! He's going, throw to second! Knock him on his ass!"

"That's it? I expected more."

"I changed it up after the Locale, but I haven't watched many games on TV since then. I'm always at the stadium with you. You know exactly what I say at the stadium, you hear every word!" I laugh out loud. "You know more of what I say than I do. I still don't have a clue what I say in my sleep. You should probably tell me."

"No. That's private." He smirks.

"How can it be private if I'm the one saying it?"

"I think it's just for me. If you wanted you to know, you'd remember." I smack him with a throw pillow and he takes it away from me, grabs my hands and holds them up while he searches the depths of my eyes like he's trying to read my soul. His eyes are serious, dark and heavy. "You tell me what you want. You tell me what you're scared of. Sometimes they're the same thing. Some mornings you tell me about your dreams." He turns away and then back up at me, "I love all of it. I love you. I want to give you what you want more than anything." He takes a deep breath and quietly continues, "I want it, too."

Shit. I do a couple more jello shots and lean back to watch the game. Rick reaches for my hand and entangles his fingers with mine as he pulls me closer to him. I'm wasted and do my best to keep my mouth shut. At least I'm getting to watch the game and hold hands with my man.

CHAPTER TWELVE

I wake up to the smell of coffee brewing. It's morning and I don't remember going to bed last night or the end of the game, but I'm in my bed and I'm naked. Rick is next to me sleeping and I remember the conversation we had about what I say in my sleep, but nothing in between other than jello shots and holding his hand. It gives me an idea. I snuggle against him and keep my eyes closed.

"I don't remember coming to bed last night." I say into the room and wonder if the man I'm sleeping next to will respond.

"I carried you to bed." He says in a sleepy voice.

"What do I want?" Pushing my luck, but asking before I get him talking too much.

"You want to give me things. You love me."

"What am I scared of?" I need details.

"Your feelings and wanting to give me things." It's the same as what he said last night, I tell him what I want and I'm scared of what I want.

"What things do I want to give you?"

"You know."

"I want to give you a lot of things. What things do I tell you I want to give you?"

Rick wraps his arms around me and holds me as tightly against him as he can. Wide-eyed and obviously awake, he'd been going along with my ruse. "Maybe you're right. Maybe you need to know. I'm going to tell you, but I'm going to hold you and not let go. You will want to get out of bed and go for coffee or use something as a distraction to ignore it, run from it. I'm not going to let you. You run when you're scared. You've said things when we're having sex, but I think that's almost the same as in your sleep. You want to fill the soft spot in my heart where I've been hurt. You're what I've needed my whole life, you Sherry." He stops talking, possibly reconsidering this whole conversation or maybe trying to put together the best words. "Do you still want to know? You want me to say it?"

"Yes." I need to know.

"You tell me you want me to get you pregnant, so we can have Elle. You tell me you never wanted that and you only want it with me." He tightens his grip and he's right, my flight instinct is trying to kick in. "You know that's a sensitive subject for me and I think that's why you don't say it when you're awake, you don't want to hurt me." He stops again, assessing my reaction. "Then you tell me you're scared of getting pregnant." He stops and waits, like I should say something.

Without thinking, words come out of my mouth and I hear them for the first time as I say them, "It's true, and I want it more than I'm scared of it. The most important thing is that I'm with you." My whole body relaxes and I don't want to run. I guess I just needed to say it.

Rick's eyes light up, "Sherry, tell me what you want while you're awake and coherent. I want to know it's real. I want to read it in your eyes."

I gaze at him and smile, "I want to be with you forever. I want

117

you to get me pregnant, so we can have Elle together. I'm not running. I love you, Rick, and I only want it with you."

He kisses me, like he's breathing me in and I'm his air. "It's even better when you're awake." He rests his forehead against mine. "I want us to have our time together and we'll get to everything else. It makes me so happy to hear you say the words. I have plans for us, my queen."

"Like what?"

"You'll see." He grins at me like a fool. "Can you book our vacation today? And, your away game airfare?"

"I'll book our vacation, but are you sure I should book the away game airfare?"

"Do you mean because I could get traded?"

"Yes. I don't want you to get traded. You've always been a Seal and should stay one. I'll go with you, if you get traded."

"I know you're a fan and know all about trades, but I didn't think about talking with you about it. I guess, I haven't had anyone like you in my life that mattered." He laughs, "You were funny watching the game last night. Naked girl sitting there and second-guessing the coaching on both teams. You were drunk, but you know your baseball." He stops and gazes at me, "You'd really go with me?"

"Of course, think of it as a long road trip." My mind goes dirty. "Think of the silver lining. Do you know how many elevators there are out there, just waiting for us?" I start to laugh, but Rick's eyes go dark and needy. He kisses me with intent and my belly starts to flutter. His hands flat on my back as he holds me to him. His lips warm and soft on mine, while his beard brushes against my face. He holds me and kisses me for the longest time. "I really do love you. I'll do anything for you, my king."

"The game starts at 12:40 today. Want to go get breakfast?" Rick must be hungry.

"How about I cook breakfast for you?"

"Even better." He gives me a quick kiss and we get out of bed. I beeline for the coffee and check what I have to work with in the kitchen.

"Omelette, biscuits and gravy, or my magic waffles?" I call out to Rick.

"Magic waffles?"

"Waffles it is!" He wants to know what makes them magic, but he said waffles and that's enough for me. I grab the bacon, buttermilk, eggs and butter from the refrigerator, and I retrieve my custom waffle mix. Yes, I have my own waffle mix that I put together myself. It's so much better than the box. I melt some butter in the microwave while I beat up some eggs with buttermilk. I add my special dry mix and stir until it's almost incorporated, then add melted butter until I get it to the right consistency. I set the batter aside and warm up my waffle iron. I toss precooked bacon pieces into a pan and toast them up a bit, making sure they're crispy and bringing out some of the bacon grease. When the waffle iron is ready, I brush it with butter, add some batter and drop in some bacon. I close the waffle iron and flip it over repeating the process, but this time I add chocolate bits and bacon. I flip the waffle maker back over and wait for the light to go off, keeping an eye on the steam to make sure they don't overcook. I pull the first waffle and repeat the process again, brushing the iron and refilling it with batter and bacon. I make six waffles total, half bacon and half bacon with chocolate. Rick walks into the kitchen while I'm in the process of making the waffles and he catches me pulling them to pieces and eating them as I make them—a quarter of a bacon waffle, then a quarter of a bacon waffle with chocolate, and he wants to know what makes them magic! Ha!

Rick takes a piece of waffle and gets a mouthful with bacon.

He groans in pleasure, as if he's submitting to the food coma. I hand him a piece with the chocolate and he stares at me stunned. "I didn't think it could get better than bacon. This is delicious."

"Wait until next time. If you're good, I'll make banana and chocolate."

"You're a fantastic cook, my queen. How did I get so lucky?" He smiles at me with waffle shoved in his mouth.

I smile because his words mean so much to me. "I'm going to bake something to take to Carter when I present him my offer."

"Why don't you bake enough for the whole clubhouse when I go back after my suspension?"

"I'm happy to. What do you want me to bake?"

"Cross wants more of those chocolate chip cookie bars. He's been texting me."

"I can do that. What do you want?"

Rick turns me to face him and holds my eyes with his, "I have everything I could ever want." He kisses me and we go back to eating waffles. Tell me again how it is that I deserve this man?

"Do you have any plans tonight?" He smiles.

"Well, there's this guy I've been spending all my time with. But, I might be able to get away. What do you have in mind?"

Rick shakes his head at me, "Date night. I want to take you out, my queen. Can you be ready at 6pm?"

"Yes. I can't wait." I really can't because I love that he plans date night and I'm along for whatever he has in store.

"Tonight is fun, not fancy. It's a jeans night. I'm going to take a run before the game. Please book our vacation." He hands me his credit card. "And, keep the credit card info for booking your away game flights. I want you there with me and I'm paying for it." He looks me in the eye like he's looking a runner back to third and he means business, I'm not making a run for home. He disappears into the other room and I quickly clean up the kitchen, before getting to work. Rick walks up behind me in his running shorts and T-shirt, wraps his arms around me and turns me so he can apply his patented you-won't-forget-me-kiss. He takes off on his run, leaving me punch drunk yet again.

CHAPTER THIRTEEN

I spend the rest of the morning checking my messages and working on our vacation reservations. I get lost in the vacation plans. I can't help but daydream about spending two perfect weeks on the beach with my Rick. I look at the cottage we'll be staying in and the beautiful view of the clear green blue ocean. I scan through the photo gallery of the resort, dreaming about all of the gorgeous sunsets and perusing the updates that have been made since my last visit. I close my eyes and I hear the ocean, I feel the tropical sun on my skin, I smell the fresh pineapple and coconut oil, and I taste the passion orange juice. I imagine us wandering the North Shore exploring together, but mostly it's us lying on the beach together and having plenty of alone time. I envision Rick in his board shorts and no shirt, and me in my bikini snuggled into the crook of his arm. Both of us getting a tropical tan as we nap together on our lanai. The ultimate relaxing vacation and somehow I get to enjoy it with my not-a-fantasy-anymore-baseball-boyfriend.

I feel Rick's warm hand on me and I reach up to put my arms around him. "Hey, baby," I start talking sleepily.

"I'm just letting you know I'm home." I open my eyes and look at him. Happy to see him, not happy to be home and not on the beach in Hawaii. "Sounds like Hawaii is going to be perfect." He has a dirty grin on his face and who knows what I said. Well, he does and he probably won't tell me.

Rick takes off for a quick shower before the game and I attempt to get some more work done, but in reality all I do is turn on the pregame and check the lineup. Rick gets out of the shower and I call out, "Saben is catching today." That should make this an easier game to watch than last night. There are only three more games including today until Rick is back in the clubhouse.

Rick joins me on the couch to watch the game and this time I'll actually be watching the game, so he'll experience what it's really like to watch a game with me. The game starts and Rick's picking everything apart.

"Saben doesn't have the skills that Stray has." Rick starts in, analyzing everything.

"Not near, but Stray is a righty like you and Saben is a lefty." Rick turns and looks at me, as if he's waiting for more. "You have a more determined attitude on the field than either one of them. Saben always feels more laid back, but Stray is definitely trying to prove himself—but, he's still a baby. Also, you're catlike behind the plate and instinctual. Saben isn't. Stray's getting ahead of himself, he'll probably be great in a year or so."

"Anything else, my baseball queen?" He grins and laughs, but doesn't disagree with me.

"Actually yes, pay attention to Rhett. I bet he can be an ace if he's given the right support." Rick shakes his head and we continue to watch the game. No action yet, and the team has been defending well.

I've intrigued my king with my baseball opinions, "What else do you see when you're watching the team?"

I look at him unsure and not wanting to say something I

shouldn't, but spill it anyway, "I'm starting with a disclaimer. I love my team. Cross should be in centerfield every game, he has the range and isn't afraid to dive for it. Mason feels better to me when he's in left and I'd love to see him get tried at shortstop. Rock belongs in right field, he's solid, he's senior, and he's earned it. Bubbles needs to get benched and used strictly as a designated hitter, he doesn't care about the game as much as he does other things any more. Martin is as good at first base as you are at catcher and it'll be years before somebody takes that spot from him, nothing matters more to him than the game when he's on the field. Lucky's good wherever he gets played and I know that's his job as a utility player, but he'd be a bigger benefit for the team if he played the same position every game and I like him best at third base. Second base is a revolving door, nobody is sticking there and we need somebody new there. The back-up outfielders are what they are and do fine when they're needed, but I can never even remember the guy's name who's been playing third. He isn't impressive at all. The relievers have been doing a great job, but not getting as many innings of work this year. The starters are strong and going deep into games." I stop my ramble and watch Rick processing.

"I get a different view from my vantage point behind home plate. But, I'm going to watch for what you're seeing."

"I'm not playing. I'm not paying attention to signs, balls and bats getting thrown all around me or players running toward me ready to knock me out of their way to score. I envision it more as a big puzzle with moving pieces. I'm sure you have a better idea than I do, I'm just a fan." I smile at him, happy to have a real baseball conversation.

Rick leans in, "You're much more than a fan to me." He presses his lips to mine, sending his electricity through my body and pulls me over to sit against him with his arm around me while we watch the game. He gets an odd look on his face, "I've never sat like this and watched a game with a woman before." I pull my feet up onto the couch and snuggle into him, enjoying the moment and the game.

Time for the seventh inning stretch, so I get up and toss a bag of microwave popcorn in to pop and run for a bathroom break before the popcorn burns. I grab the hot bag from the microwave and a couple sodas, then back to my spot on the couch. The score is 4-1 Seals and those rookies in the outfield have been killing it, generating all four RBIs. The rest of the game isn't very eventful and my king seems to be more interested in me. Who am I to argue?

Rick starts to rub my arm and hold me tighter to him. I catch him looking at me and not his usual glare while he shakes his head thinking I'm off the deep end or intense when he's serious. He's just looking at me. He pushes my hair out of my face, running his fingers through it and cups my head bringing my lips to his. He releases me, "You make me so happy." His eyes tell me that he loves me and wants me. "I have a couple errands to take care of and I'll be back to get you at 6pm for our date night, okay my queen?"

"I'll be ready." I smile at him, happy to have time to get ready. It's a jeans night not a fancy night and those are my favorite, more my style and I can play with my outfit. I already know it's going to be a fun night. Rick disappears into the bedroom for a few minutes and returns wearing his perfect fitting jeans, a black T-shirt that's stretched enticingly across his chest and tennis shoes. He grabs me, kissing me passionately before he winks at me and walks out the door. That man drives me crazy! I want to look good for him tonight, but not be overdressed so I follow his example and pull out my best jeans. I look through my shoes for my cutest tennis shoes and my red metallic Chucks jump out at me. I know exactly what I want to wear! I turn on some music and listen to my *Fun* playlist while I get ready, it starts off with

The Go-Go's "We Got the Beat." I strip down to nothing and start over with red satin panties and a matching push-up bra. I pull on my jeans and my sparkly Chucks. I want to wear my black sleeveless deep V-neck that says POP STAR in red foil letters across my breasts. Before I pull it on, I brush my hair out and try a few different things, finally taking my curling iron to it and going fluffy. I have time to get it all curled and it'll make me feel like I'm dressed for a date even though I'm basically wearing jeans and a T-shirt. I pull my shirt on and look in the mirror as "One Way or Another" by Blondie comes on. I put on smoky silver eye shadow, black eyeliner, black mascara, a touch of blush and cherry flavored fire engine red lip gloss. I look in the mirror again and I love all of the red. I'm pumped up, dancing around the house and singing to "Lola" by the Kinks with the volume turned up.

I scream out startled when someone touches me. Rick got back and I didn't hear him come in. "Sorry, my queen. I knocked because it's date night, but you couldn't hear me over the music." He looks me up and down, "Those are some red lips."

"They're cherry flavored just for you." His body reacts, he wants to taste.

"I can't kiss you. I'll mess you up before we ever get out of the house."

I giggle, "It's just lip gloss and I have more."

"Before you distract me, I want to take you out tomorrow for a late night picnic. Interested?" He waits to see how I respond and he has a bag in his hand.

"Anything with you, my king." I smile wondering what he's up to.

"I thought you could put together the food, seems right up your alley." He pulls a backpack out of the bag, "Everything we need will have to fit in here and I'm driving, so no alcohol. Think midnight snack or something like that."

The backpack is made for picnics. It has a section that keeps things cold, a place for a blanket, and everything else you might need. I see a trip to the public market on my to do list for tomorrow. "Challenge accepted!"

He puts his arms around my waist and pulls me in for a taste of my cherry lips. "The cherry is fun, but you taste sweet all by yourself." Enjoying my playfulness and making sure I know he loves me the way I am, without anything extra added.

"We're walking tonight. Are you ready to go?" I put on my moto jacket, adding my ID and lip gloss to the pocket. I smile at him and he takes my hand as we walk out the door.

We casually stroll and talk on our way to wherever we're going. "I've really enjoyed having more time with you the last few days. I've been rewarded, not suspended." His words make me warm all over because I feel the same way. At first I felt guilty because it never would've happened if I wasn't there, or I simply managed to keep my mouth to myself. But, getting to help him with things like getting his hand to stop bleeding and reducing his pain, well, somehow it burrowed him deeper into my heart and brought us closer together. The effects of real life, pushing us together rather than pulling us apart like they do to so many people. I'm thankful his injuries weren't worse and the last few days of his suspension have been time for us.

We walk up to the Locale and Rick opens the door for me, "I thought it would be fun to go back to where it started." He guides me through the door with his hand on the small of my back and gets a nod from the hostess. This has obviously been set up ahead of time. Rick leads me to the table in the back corner where I found him that night a couple months ago and I slide into the corner with him next to me. There's a bouquet of tropical flowers on the table and a small white gift box with a purple bow stuck on top of it. I look at him and he nods at me to open the box. There's a long gold beaded style necklace with a key pendant on it engraved with "You have the key to my heart" on one side and R+S on the other.

"I love it!" I kiss him leaving a lip print on his cheek and he blushes. I wrap the chain around my neck three times and wear it like a choker, arranging the key to hang down a couple inches in the center front. I hug him and whisper in his ear, "I don't know how I got so lucky. I don't deserve you. I'll always be yours, my king." His arm pulls me closer to him, sitting hip to hip.

"You deserve everything, my queen." He smiles at me. "How about dinner and then we actually play some pool?" We order drinks and dinner and more drinks. This is one of the rare times he drinks while we're out, probably because we could walk. We laugh together and talk the whole evening. We even play pool after he shows me how to handle the stick, which turned a bit dirty. We had to take a break in the parking lot after he was rubbing up against me from behind. The juke box was playing and when the music stopped, Rick went over and got it playing again. The first song he plays is "Oh Sherrie" by Steve Perry. Then he's at my ear, "Oh Sherry, I'm in love." He's got the lyrics wrong, but that's typical for this song and I appreciate his effort. His version is better. We continue to play pool sloppily and I dance around to the music playing. "Thinking Out Loud" comes on and he grabs me, holding me close and dancing with me. It's a special moment when I feel his heart beat with mine, our eyes connect and he whispers the last line of the song in my ear, "We found love..." I've never heard anything more sincere.

We keep tossing back the drinks, I order shots to challenge him. I'm having so much fun and Rick is, too. Touching each other. Kissing each other. In a happy haze together. Teasing him by swaying my hips, shaking my butt in front of him when I bend over to shoot, and making sure he has a view down my top when I lean over the table. Rubbing against him at every opportunity. To say we're buzzed is an understatement. We aren't paying attention to anyone around us. We don't care. We're just out having fun together. I walk up to him and put my hands on his chest. His shirt pulled snug across his pecks has had my attention all evening, I finally give in and touch with both hands, fingers spread. He draws my lips to his and I move my hands, now gripping his fine ass. He pushes against me, telling me how much he wants me. We dance around together playfully, comfortable together. Our server keeps bringing us shots of Jack. I gaze into his eyes and claim his mouth right there, climbing him and wrapping my legs around him. His hands hot on my back and the need in his pants evident, hard against me. Rick walks to our table, I pick up my flowers and he walks home in the late night with me wrapped around him, kissing him everywhere I can reach.

It's a short walk and we're home, Rick steps into the elevator and I can't help myself, "We're in the elevator."

"I know, baby. That's not what I want. I don't want to be a bonehead caveman. I want to love you." We get home and Rick locks the door behind us. He slides me down his body, and I put my flowers in water while he puts on some music. Apparently, he has a few playlists as well and starts his *Lovin' Time* playlist. It starts with "Thinking Out Loud" and he puts his arms around me to dance around our place. He leads me to bed and I pull his T-shirt off over his head, focused on his chest that's had my attention all night long. I can't help myself, I kiss his chest all over, dragging my tongue and nibbling a bit as I go. He's so fucking sexy. I run my hands up and down his upper arms, exploring his muscles. I kick my shoes off and he pulls my shirt off, finding my red push up bra. He kisses the tops of my breasts and unbuttons my jeans while I unbutton his. He's not wasting any time. He hooks his fingers on my panties and pulls them off with my jeans. His jeans disappear and he leans over me kissing me as he slides into home, "I love you, my queen. I'll always love you. Tell me you want to be mine."

Rick's unbelievable sliding in and out of me slowly, methodically. "I'm already yours, my king. I want to give you everything I can, to show you how much I love you. It'll always be you. I want nothing more than to be yours forever. You're my only man, my only love." He holds me tight, claiming my mouth with his while he continues to push and pull, driving me out of my mind with his lips on me and his hard love inside me. His heart beating strong, his pulse racing, his breathing goes ragged and uneven, enjoying the weight of his body on mine. I feel how much he loves me and I give myself to him completely.

He strokes into me deliciously and repeatedly, bringing me to climax multiple times. Each time telling me, "I love you, my queen. I'm only for you, Sherry. You're my happiness."

CHAPTER FOURTEEN

I wake up early Thursday morning with Rick holding me possessively and our legs entangled. My alarm hasn't buzzed yet. I don't smell coffee brewing. It's early, I'm awake, the playlist from last night is still playing on repeat and I'm in bed naked with my man. I'm a happy girl. "Won't Stop" by OneRepublic is playing and it hits me that he made this playlist for me. I didn't pick up on it in my drunken state last night, but I should've since it started with our song. Its like he made me a mix tape.

I'm anxious for our late night picnic and lay in bed considering options for the backpack. I want to bake something. I want something sweet and something savory. Maybe a cheese sampling, fruit, crackers, and some dry deli meat. I need to inspect the backpack and see exactly how much room I have. I also need non-alcoholic beverages. I admit I'm curious about where we're going, but the anticipation makes it fun and I have no idea what he has in mind.

I roll over and snuggle into Rick's chest, wrapping my arms around him, running my hands up and down his back, and kissing his chest after having flashbacks of last night. The vision of him in that tight T-shirt is permanently imprinted on my brain, and did I mention he's sexy as fuck? But, the way he loved me last night—He made me shake with pleasure and emotion, and I know he was showing me our future. It's almost as if this strong man feels like he needs to prove himself to me. He doesn't need to, but I'm not complaining.

Rick runs his hands down my body and rolls me underneath him. "I may not need to, but I want to and I'm going to again," he says as he pushes into me. He moves slowly and doesn't seem completely awake. He gets a big grin and groans in pleasure as he moves, "So, you think I'm sexy as fuck, huh?"

Damn it! I was talking out loud again! I can play this. "Yes! Have you looked in the mirror?"

"You're my version of sexy, my queen. Everything about you is perfect. The way you make me feel—oh fuck me." He strokes into me harder and faster, with need taking him over. He grabs my nipple with his teeth and sucks my breast into his mouth, tugging at me like a direct line to my orgasm. Everything crashes in on me at once and I scream out his name as he pushes me head first over the edge and goes with me, releasing his pleasure with a manly guttural groan. Can I start everyday this way? Rick lays his head down on the pillow next to mine and I fall back to sleep in his arms.

The alarm wakes me a couple hours later and I smell the coffee brewing. I stretch and Rick whispers in my ear, "Good morning, Sherry. I love you, my queen."

I turn to him and kiss him, "There's no one else like you, my king. I love you, Rick. I'll always be yours." I say this looking straight into his eyes, so he knows I'm awake and not just saying sleepy things. He hugs me tight and I feel his happiness radiate off of him.

"Do I get any other details on our late night picnic?" I'm curious.

"You need to wear long pants, preferably good jeans, and good closed toed shoes. We'll be outside, so don't worry about your hair and make-up —I like you without it."

Interesting. "Okay, then I have a few errands to run today before work."

"I need to run and work out, so I'm ready for the field on Saturday. Game is at 7:05 tonight. Afternoon nap between my work out and the game. We'll take off on our adventure after the game. Okay, my queen?"

"I can't wait." I kiss him and get up quickly, my mind racing with ideas for the backpack. I hear Rick on the phone with Chase, planning to go work out together. I pour coffee for both of us and peruse the refrigerator and pantry.

"I'm going to breakfast with Cross and we're going to work out. He's picking me up and I'll be back later, my queen." He disappears into the shower quickly and there's a knock at the door before he comes back out. I check the peep hole and see Chase looking back at me.

I open the door, "Good morning, honey!"

Chase hugs me, "Hey, sweetheart."

"Come on in. He's still in the shower. Want some coffee?" I offer up being a good hostess.

"No thanks. Got any cookies?"

I pull the reserve from my last batch from the freezer and pop them in the microwave for thirty seconds. I hand them over to Chase with a glass of milk.

His eyes get big, he's such a big kid. "Thank you," and he's a happy camper.

Rick comes out ready to go. He shakes his head when he finds me hanging out with a cookie eating Cross. He kisses me, leaving me punch drunk and drags Cross off on their work out. I happily eat the last two cookies with my coffee and get my day started.

I go to my closet and pull out my good pair of old school regular jeans and tennis shoes that are good for hiking, not just looking cute. I thumb through my closet in search of a top that's better than a plain T-shirt, something to add some style to my jeans. I find a fitted ribbed black long-sleeved shirt with laces at the chest and immediately trade my tennis shoes for my black combat boots.

I find where Rick left the backpack and realize he already had it stored somewhere. I wonder what else he has hiding. The backpack has a pouch for a blanket at the bottom, two tube shaped spots for wine bottles, an area that can be kept cool and open space for room temperature food, utensils, napkins, etc. It has quite a bit of room, considering it's not very big. I decide to make my chocolate chip banana bread and baseball sugar cookies for my sweet. I've been considering my savory options and I keep changing my mind. Maybe I'll make up some Italian Sandwiches on Focaccia, and maybe some grapes or sliced up fruit, possibly some popcorn. I toss my beach blanket into the wash, and go to the store.

I wander the store picking up bananas that are a little over ripe, a tube of red icing, a fresh loaf of Focaccia, a variety of Italian meats and cheeses from the deli, a bunch of grapes and a take and bake pizza. I pick up some throw away plastic containers, so it'll be easy to pack and nothing will get squished.

I get home and immediately mix up my sugar cookie dough. It needs time to chill before I slice it up and bake it. I turn the oven on to preheat. I mash up my bananas and mix up my banana bread batter, adding the chocolate chips last and pour it into a buttered loaf pan. I put the chocolate chip banana bread in the oven and wash the grapes, putting them in a container ready for the backpack. I move my beach blanket to the dryer and cut the Focaccia, seasoning the inside with garlic salt, basil, oregano, black pepper, and a drizzle of olive oil on both sides. I cover the bottom with provolone cheese, followed by layers of thinly sliced ham, pepperoni, and hot capicola. Then I top it with another layer of cheese and put the top on. I cut the sandwich into finger sandwiches and load them into plasticware. I really want something salty and I'm inspired to make some popcorn. I get a pot with a lid, put it on the flame and add some popcorn kernels along with some butter and olive oil. I put the lid on it and swirl it around until it starts to pop. I keep shaking it around and listen for the popping to stop, hoping I don't burn it. I turn off the stove, and I give it a peek and a taste. I add some more olive oil, salt, some fine crushed red chili flakes and some grated parmesan cheese. I put the lid back on and give it a good shake, trying to get everything coated evenly. I give it a taste and I'm satisfied, so I package it up for the backpack. I check on my banana bread and it's almost done, it needs a few more minutes. I get my sugar cookie dough out and slice thin round medallions, dip them in sugar and arrange them on my parchment lined baking sheet. I pull my banana bread out of the oven and slide my cookies in. I take the bread out of the pan to cool and it smells delicious, so I have a piece. I need to get some work done before Rick gets back. I can't neglect my work because I'm having fun playing house with Rick Seno.

Interesting. Am I playing house with Rick Seno? Sometimes reality just slaps you in the face. First of all, I'm dating, no, I'm living with Rick Seno. Holy hell! I've gone from having a fantasy baseball boyfriend and dirty dreams to Rick Seno living with me and in my bed every night. Not only that, but he takes me out on date nights. We have fun together, the sex is amazing and he says he loves me. I know it's true. I don't understand why. He must be off his rocker. I worry that my unique brand of crazy will send him running away, but he's broken, too. That might be what keeps him with me. Honestly, after the last few days I believe he really does need me. Before I thought he'd move on and date a woman his own age or maybe one of those hotties who are always hanging around the field. Somebody who would succumb to his desire to take care of them and pay their way. Not any more. He needs someone who can stand up to him and be his equal, it's why he wants to take care of me and pay my way. We're learning to be a team. Though, I admit, the beginning of this week was probably the hardest day of my life. I'm embracing my girliness, and even though I don't want him to take care of me—I need him and I need him to be okay. I'd never felt things, said things, considered things that ran through my head on replay. Hearing my own voice and knowing it was me, I was the worried girlfriend. I don't do those things! I'm independent! I'm self-sufficient! I don't need a man or anyone else to take care of me. And I still don't, but I want one. Only one. Only Rick Seno. The funny thing, or maybe not so funny thing is that I'm not playing. This is my life. This is what I want. It's what Rick wants right now and I hope it stays that way. He's my soul mate.

Distracted by my own thoughts, I suddenly smell cookies and pull them out just in time. I move the cookies to the cooling rack and let them cool completely before the next step. I slice up some thick pieces of the chocolate chip banana bread and put it in plasticware, ready for the backpack.

I move on to my work, checking my email and social media. I reply to a few emails, but not much going on really. So, I take the opportunity to write up my proposal for Carter and the Seals. Illustrating how it will save them money by freeing up time for Carter to do other things. I put together a portfolio of group trips I've planned to use as a resume accompanying my proposal. I go over it multiple times, trying to make it perfect. I'm ready, and I plan to drop in on him at his office when I bring in cookies for the whole clubhouse.

I fold up my dry beach blanket and pack it in the backpack along with the popcorn, banana bread, and napkins. I put a couple bottles of water in the freezer and move on to my baseball cookies. I knead the tube of red icing and snip off the tip, then I carefully pipe baseball stitching onto my cookies. I love them!

I have some free time and take advantage. I change into my bikini and lie out on my lounge chair to enjoy some sun on my private balcony, face down with no top. It's a warm, lazy afternoon and I'm falling asleep, so I go inside and lay down on my bed... The warmth of the sand and the breeze as it blows over my body are relaxing, leaving me to focus on the sound of the ocean and the tender touch of a hand and lips on my body. The palm trees swaying and the sea turtles surfing. The tropical sun zapping all of my energy, I sleep while my man's hands protect me... I'm dreaming, but those hands are real. Rick whispers in my ear, "I'm home, my queen," and his hands wander my body, exploring me like he needs to have me. He moves his hands from my belly to my breasts to my ass and finally my hips, and he rocks against me. "I love you, my queen. I missed you. I need to have you."

I roll to him and gaze into his eyes, "I love you, too." He was only gone part of the day and I missed him, too. It's getting worse. I'm fucked. "I missed you, too, my king." I kiss him and he pulls me on top of him, straddling him while I kiss him. His need reaching for me, I slide back onto his hard cock, dragging my kisses from his mouth down his neck to his strong chest. His chest is solid muscle and I want to touch it, lick it, kiss it, bite it, suck on it—I want to leave a mark with my teeth. He grabs my ass appreciatively and strokes into me deep, taking control and driving me to call out his name. Sometimes his touch is all it takes to drive me out of control.

He rolls us over, taking me underneath him and I whimper as he pushes into me all the way, holding his solid length there while he talks to me, "I need you. I need this. We fit perfect together. I only want you. I only love you." I feel his heat. I reach around his neck and pull my mouth to his, claiming him while he strokes into me. He feels amazing and I know this isn't going to be a marathon because he's already breathing unevenly. This is him needing to have me. This is one of those times he needs to know I'm here and I'm his. It's part of how he's broken, what other women have done to him. I hate that they've made him feel like this, but I'm happy to be the one he needs. I cry out at his every stroke and it adds to his drive. He tries to pull back, but I don't let him. I hold his head and kiss his neck, sucking and nibbling, driving his intensity and pushing him closer to release. He pulls away and takes my mouth with his quickly, roughly, letting me know I'm his. As he pulls away I kiss his chest and bite there, sucking as he strokes into me hard, sending me farther over the edge than before and I cry out into his chest as I bite him and bring him with me.

I wake up to Rick worshiping between my legs a few hours later. It has to be the best way to get woken up. Better than breakfast in bed. Once he knows I'm awake he slides two fingers into me while he licks at my sensitive nub and sets me off almost instantly. Fuck me. He takes me in his arms as he climbs me and slides into me deliciously. He kisses me and he has something else in mind. He pulls out and drags me to the edge of the bed where he takes me from behind, slamming into me hard. I may be his playground this afternoon. I'm not complaining. He leans over me and nibbles at the back of my neck while he circles my magic button. I scream out at the connection and he pushes it farther. "Tell me you want all of me. Tell me you always want me in you." His voice raspy and giving away that he's on the edge.

"I want all of you that I can get. Every inch of you. I always want you inside me. Nobody makes me feel like you do. Nobody else can ever have me."

"Fuck me fuck me fuck me." His release is hard and pulsating. He pushes into me hard and takes me with him.

A few minutes later he pulls out and I roll over. He has a huge grin on his face and kisses me. He wraps his arms around me and picks me up. I put my legs around his waist and he slides right back into me, like it's where he belongs. He carries me to the bathroom and turns on the shower. Kissing me and holding us under the warm shower spray.

CHAPTER FIFTEEN

Rick and I miss the pregame, ending up in front of the TV in time for the second inning to start. I preheat the oven and put the take and bake pizza in to bake between innings. We're comfy in sweats and T-shirts, snuggled together on the couch to watch the game. Stray is behind the plate tonight with Tommy pitching. There's no score after the third inning, but in the bottom of the fourth Cross hits a home run with Mason and Tommy on base. Martin hits a double. Stray hits a double, bringing Martin around. Lucky gets a single, pushing Stray to third. Rock hits a home run bringing in Stray and Lucky Lucine. We could do no wrong in the fourth inning, it was a continuous line of hitters taking turns getting hits and RBIs. The end of the fourth inning and the score is 9-0 Seals. I worry about games like this because of the false sense of security. There are still five innings left and anything can happen. Nobody scored in the fifth inning. Nobody scored in the sixth inning. Top of the seventh and Houston had a run like our fourth, scoring eight and taking the score to 9-8 Seals. Bottom of the seventh and the Seals respond with thunder, Martin hits a grand slam and

Rock hits a double bringing in Stray. Lucine gets tagged out at home and Tommy hits into a double play. Score at the end of seven 14-8 Seals. It's insane! We never play high scoring games! Top of the eighth, Houston scores two more. Bottom of the eighth, bases loaded and we can't score to save our life. Top of the ninth, bases loaded and Houston gets a grand slam. The game is tied at 14 and we go to the bottom of the ninth hoping for a walk off win. It doesn't happen. The game goes into extra innings and as much as I love baseball, let me be clear, I'm anxious for our late night picnic adventure and we aren't going until the game is over. This game needs to hurry up already! The game is still tied at 14 and going into the fourteenth inning, current game time is 4 hours 50 minutes and it's almost midnight. The players are tired, the silly mistakes start to happen and I hope Houston loses it first. Bottom of the fourteenth inning, Kris Martin hits a solo homer off Houston's seventh pitcher of the game and we get the walk off win 15-14 Seals. I cheer out loud and Rick shakes his head.

"Should we get ready for our picnic adventure?" I ask ready to find out what he has planned.

"It's later than I thought. We can do it another night." He sees my frown, "Actually later might make it better. Go get ready."

"Yay!" I smile and start a fresh pot of coffee to put in the backpack. I take off for the bedroom to get ready. I change into my jeans and put on my black combat boots with thick socks. I brush out my hair and put a hair tie around my wrist. I pull on my long sleeved black top that laces up at the neckline and leave the laces loose. I look in the mirror and I'm happy. I pour the coffee into a thermos and pack it in the backpack. I pack the sandwiches and grapes, and package up the baseball cookies. Everything fits into the backpack easily and I pull the frozen water bottles from the freezer, dropping them into the wine bottle spot in the backpack. Rick walks out, ready to go. He's wearing jeans, black combat boots and a black long sleeve waffle-knit shirt that's stretched deliciously across his chest. We kinda match. I hand Rick the backpack, proud of the spread I've put together.

"Are you ready to go, my queen?"

"Yes, I just need to grab my jacket."

"You don't need a jacket. I've got that covered."

"Okay." I glare at him funny, pretty sure I'm going to freeze my ass off.

"Just you, you don't need money or keys or anything else." He smiles and now I really want to know what we're doing. Rick locks the door and we walk out to his car. He pops open the trunk, but rather than putting the backpack in the trunk he starts pulling things out. He pulls out a lime green leather jacket with a black stripe and white reflective trim and he hands it to me. "Put this on." He pulls out another jacket that's exactly the same, but larger from the trunk and puts it on. It fits him like a glove. He reaches for me and zips mine up, it's snug in all the right places. "So, have you ever been on a motorcycle?" He hands me a matte black helmet with custom lime green paint on the back at the neck that reads "My Queen". I look around and see there's a motorcycle parked in front of Rick's Challenger, sharing the parking space. It's a cool looking matte gray Yamaha motorcycle with lime green wheels. It looks fast.

"Yes. I rode dirt bikes when I was a kid and I've ridden with friends before."

"Are you up for this adventure?"

"Anything with you, my king." I smile at him knowing he has a plan. "Um, how many women have you called your queen?"

Rick laughs, "Only you, Sherry. I bought the helmet and had it done custom for you. I had it linked to mine, so we can talk and listen to the same music while we're riding." He shows me his helmet matches and has custom lime green paint just like mine, but his says "Catch Me".

I smile at him, custom car, probably custom bike, custom matching helmets and matching leather jackets. I'm his queen. "My queen. I love being your queen." How was I not aware my fantasy baseball player boyfriend rode a motorcycle? This seems like something I would've heard about on an interview or something. Then again, it's Rick Seno and he's one of the most private players there is. Well, until he started carrying me through lobbies and dragging me into dugouts and kissing me at the field wall and holding my hand at the net. "So, do you have any other secrets?"

He looks at me caught off guard. "This isn't a secret. I have a garage I rent to keep my bike, sporting goods, accessories and stuff like that I use, but takes up too much space. Mostly, it belongs in a garage and not inside."

"What else should I know about you?"

"That I'll do anything for you. I'll never hurt you. And, I want to make all of your dreams come true." Rick leans in and kisses me with intent. "Are you ready?"

I nod with enthusiasm and he pulls his bike out into the open. I put on my helmet and he straps it on tight, making sure it fits right. He puts on his helmet, fastens the strap and starts talking to me through the helmet. "Can you hear me? I haven't tested this yet."

Cool! "Yes. Can you hear me?"

"Yes. Let's try the music." He turns on music and it's old school Metallica "Seek and Destroy," his walk up song.

"Bike ride appropriate. I love the old Metallica." Helmets appear to be functioning correctly. We're wearing our matching jackets and helmets. Time to get on the road. Rick puts the backpack on backwards, wearing it on his front and climbs on the bike. He starts it up and stands over it, letting it warm up. He offers me his hand for help on and I hop on the back like it's nothing.

"Put your arms around me, my queen. Hold on tight." I reach around him and slide my hand into the front of his jeans. "How about not on your first ride?"

"Oh, my hand was cold." I laugh trying to pretend I wasn't getting into his pants. I'm giddy on the back of his bike with my arms wrapped around him, plastered to his back and the bike rumbling between my legs.

"Ready?"

"Yes! Let's go!" He slowly takes us through the complex to the street, cruising the surface streets to Shelter Island and sticking close to the shoreline. It's a nice ride with a beautiful view, but nothing crazy. He takes Harbor past the airport, around the curve and past the Maritime Museum. He takes us out to the roundabout at the Embarcadero North and then over to the Coronado Bridge where he picks up speed and I remember what I love about motorcycles. He has control of everything. I knew he would, he doesn't do anything without being the best at it and knowing everything about it. He takes us up and down the Silver Strand a few times, truly a breathtaking view and it's high tide.

He pulls off into the parking lot at Glorietta Bay, (now I know when to find parking) turns off the bike, and I hop off. He gets off the bike and sets the backpack on it. We take our helmets off. He unzips both of our jackets and pulls me close. He gives me a quick kiss. "What do you think, my queen? Are you having fun?" He's happy, relaxed, and all smiles.

"I like it. It's fun." Very matter of fact.

"Okay. What else? I can see you have more to say."

"Um." I don't want to lead him to trouble. "Faster would be better. Forget the view, I want speed." He basically attacks me, tongue in my mouth, fingers digging into my body. He pulls back and a glint shines in his eyes. I have a feeling it's time to experience how he really rides.

"Promise to tell me if I go too fast?" He searches my eyes for my answer.

"You can't go too fast. Show me what you got." I know better than to taunt him, but I can't help myself. I kiss him, rubbing my body against his, and put my helmet back on.

He grins, zips me back up, and looks at me in a way that tells me this night is going to end well. I hope I don't have anything I need to do on Friday. Fuck it! Even if I do, it's my last day with Rick on suspension. He gets ready and climbs back on his bike, starting it up, and I hop on. I wrap my arms around him, "I'm ready for take off, my king."

"Hold on tight." "Caught Up In You" by .38 Special starts to play as we take off on the Silver Strand at a faster speed. The music is loud and upbeat, perfect for a ride. We get to the freeway and Rick takes us Northbound on the 5 to the 15, the freeway with the highest speed limit. "The Stroke" by Billy Squier comes on. He kicks it into a higher gear and when he hits sixth we're blowing past the other cars on the freeway like they're standing still. He takes us into the fast lane, there aren't many cars on the freeway once we get out of downtown. I hold on tight, loving the adrenaline as we fly up the 15. The music gets louder as we go faster. "Fell in Love With a Girl" by The White Stripes fills my helmet and I totally love that song. This is obviously Rick's riding playlist, fast, pushing, loud. I sing along to myself in my helmet and the music stops suddenly, "Are you okay? Did you say some-thing?" So, apparently he could hear me singing along.

"I'm fine. I was singing along. Love the playlist." I spread my hands and fingers across his abs in appreciation.

"Are you staying warm?"

"Yes, my king. I'm fine."

"Do you need anything?"

"I have you in my arms. I don't need anything else."

"You're so fucking perfect. I love you." I can hear his grin.

I lean my head against his back and The White Stripes come back. He cuts West into a canyon near San Marcos, leaning into the curves and I squeal with joy. "Blow Me Away" by Breaking Benjamin comes on and the driving force in the music keeps going throughout the playlist. He makes a couple of turns and we're at the East end of Batiquitos Lagoon.

The music stops, "Freeway or coast?"

"It's your adventure. I'm along for the ride." I couldn't decide. I love the view of the beach, but not much beats the adrenaline from the speed. He takes us back onto the freeway at La Costa and we're Southbound on the 5 at full speed in no time with Foreigner blaring "Feels Like the First Time." He takes us from the 5 to the 805 to the 163 and off the freeway at downtown. We ride around the stadium and out to the Embarcadero South, stopping at the end of the parking lot.

He turns off the bike and holds it steady for my dismount. I take my helmet off as he gets off the bike and takes off the backpack. He takes his helmet off and claims my lips with his immediately, sending a warmth through my body. My hands go to his waist possessively, standing there and kissing him. He locks the helmets to the bike, gets the backpack and leads me to a grassy area near the bay. We take the blanket out of the backpack and lay it out on the dewy grass. We stretch out next to each other and I lean on him affectionately. The lights from Coronado reflect on the bay romantically, like Van Gogh's Starlight Over the Rhone. The sound of the bay lapping against the rocks is relaxing. The night sky is dark and glittered with stars sparkling like faceted diamonds. There's nobody out here, but us. There's no place I'd rather be.

I have no idea what time it is and it's refreshing to be out with no phone or anything. I'm wondering why this was a late night adventure. Maybe Rick likes to ride at night? Or when there are less cars on the road? Embarcadero South has kind of become a significant place for us, so I get the picnic location and besides you can't get a better view. I feel so close to him, I don't want to forget this moment. "Do you have your phone?"

"Yes." He responds with a questioning tone.

"Be the selfie master and take pictures of us here together." I look at him imploringly. He pulls out his phone and starts taking photos of me, making me laugh and continuing to take more pictures. "No, I mean of us together."

"I know what you meant. I want some of you." My heart is lost completely to this man. He pulls me close and clicks away, kissing me, making faces, putting up bunny ears, kissing me more, gazing at me, lost in each others' eyes and claiming me completely. He drops his phone and focuses on me, like he doesn't have a choice. His lips worship mine. His hands on my back, hold me to him. He stops and looks at me like he wants to say something, but doesn't.

"Are you okay?"

In his low raspy voice, "I'm better than okay."

"Me, too." I'm done letting my head get in the way of my heart. I press my lips to his, nibbling and sucking on his lower lip. I want him so bad right now, I rub my hand against his crotch and his change in breathing tells me he wants me, too. I push my luck and slide my hand into his pants, waiting for him to make me stop. He doesn't, instead he pushes me further with his greedy kisses. I wrap my hand around his cock and stroke him while we kiss, but I want more and I unbutton his jeans. There's nobody out here, right? It's the wee hours of the morning.

"You can't do that, baby." Obviously wanting it and trying to control the situation. Rick doesn't do anything to make me stop, yet keeps kissing me and sucking on my tongue.

"I know you don't want me to stop." He responds by flexing his hips. I lay my head in his lap and unzip him. Rick pulls the blanket up around us and I find him with my mouth, licking him and sucking him in.

"We're in the park, my queen."

I respond with a positive, "Mmmmhhmmm," with my lips wrapped around him. Again, he does nothing to make me stop and encourages me with his actions as he runs his fingers through my hair, feeling my head move as I pleasure him.

"Fuck me. We can't do this." He's so hard I couldn't put him away if I wanted to, and I don't want to. "My queen. Fuck."

"I'm not stopping, my king. I'm taking care of you."

"I need you, Sherry. I love you. I, you fuckin' make me crazy." He's still in his head and not saying words that want to come out, but at least I have his other head in control of the moment. I continue licking and sucking on him. "Need you, Sherry. In you." I stroke him with my lips, truly loving on him and worshiping him. "Please. Please. In you." He begs with need and I glance at him to find his eyes are closed, he's lost in the moment. I take control of the blanket and wriggle my pants off of one leg. Blanket wrapped around us, I straddle him and take just his tip inside me.

"You want this?"

"Yes."

"You want this now, here, in the park."

"Yes." He gets a hit of reality trying to sneak through. "Oh, fuck me. I'm so fucked." He puts his arms around me and holds me while he pushes into me with need. He's hard and fills me instantly. I take his mouth with mine and lose control at the heat of our connection.

I wrap my legs around him and whisper in his ear, "Better, my king?"

"Yes, my love. Everything is better when I'm in you." He loses his words and gets absorbed in the moment. He starts rambling and he isn't with me... "I need her. She needs to be mine. She needs to be mine always. I can't control myself around her. She's so fucking perfect. I need to make her mine. I need her to say yes. I need her to love me forever. Fuck me! I can't keep being a caveman. Shit!"

I'm not sure if I should say something or let it go. He isn't talking to me, but I hope he's talking about me. He can't be talking about another girl. Can he? No, there's no way. Don't even go there, Sherry. No backwards slides. "I'll always say yes to anything you want that's legal, and apparently sometimes things that are illegal." I say as I consider the charges for indecent exposure and fornicating in public. "We should go home."

"No. It's not time yet. I want to watch the sunrise with you." That's why it was a late night adventure!

"I was just thinking if we go home, we might not get arrested."

Something in his eyes change, "Why did you say you'll always say yes?"

"Seemed like the thing to say. It's the truth." His face changes. "I guess the 'her' you referred to could've been someone else."

"I was talking?"

"Yes."

"What did I say?"

"First, am I the 'her' and 'she' you kept talking about?"

"I don't know what I said."

"Then I think it was private and just for me." I laugh, enjoying the opportunity to use his own words against him. "How many 'hers' and 'shes' are you thinking about in there?"

Rick rubs his hand over his face in frustration. "You, Sam and my Mom, in that order. What did I say?"

"Something about wanting me to say yes and needing me. Nothing big." I kiss him before he can get out of hand. "Now, how about we finish this when we get home and enjoy our picnic?" I smile at him, he always wants food. He nods at me, still lost in his head. I stand up quickly and get my pants back on while I wonder what's going on in his head. I've learned my head needs to stay out of it when it comes to us. I sit back down next to him with the blanket wrapped around us and his jeans are still undone. I unpack the backpack, setting out the different containers and opening them. I pull out the thermos of coffee and bottles of water, realizing I didn't bring cups for the coffee and that's okay because we can share. "Okay, my king. We have Italian Sandwiches, seasoned popcorn, grapes, chocolate chip banana nut bread, baseball sugar cookies, coffee, and water." I take a drink of the coffee and it's still warm. We sit together grazing and talking for a long time. Our conversation flows organically and he likes everything I brought to eat.

Sometimes I catch myself staring at Rick and trying to determine if I'm dreaming. I've dreamt about him so many times. Even the first time I woke with him, it felt like a dream. If this is a dream, I don't want to wake up.

I look up and Rick's smiling at me, "I'm real. This isn't a dream." Damn it! I did it again. I must be getting tired.

I wonder if this is a way for him to make sure we spend time together without having sex. If it is, it didn't work. He gets the weirdest ideas sometimes. I get it. We need to have more between us than physical attraction, even if the physical attraction is off the charts and so far off the charts it's in a completely different galaxy. We're growing everyday. Becoming a team, true partners. Honestly, I don't think our need to be close and our physical connection could be nearly as strong as it is if it was just sex. I know it's been fast and a lot has happened, but I wouldn't change it. I can honestly say I would do anything for him.

"I want to spend time with you. I want to do everything with you. Everything is better with you." His words melt me.

The stars start to fade and the lights on the Coronado Bridge shut off as daylight breaks. Rick holds me close, "I wanted to watch the sunrise with you. You brought me back to the living and you show me you love me everyday. Your heart, your love is everything to me." Tears fall down my cheeks as he holds me tight and I listen to his words. We sit quietly and watch the sunrise.

I've never watched the sunrise. Sunsets many times, but this is different. The way the sunlight outlines the white fluffy clouds, giving them a glow. The fresh light making everything new. The dandelions and wild flowers opening to greet the sun, like they've been woken up and need to stretch. The cottontails sitting still like statues observing the beginning of the new day and casting shadows before they hop off into the bushes. The trees that were somewhat ominous, now filtering the light and allowing it to speckle the ground. Everything gets to try again, hope has been granted by the new day.

I have a new strength and I'm not afraid of the love in my heart. I grab ahold of Rick's hand, squeezing and entangling our fingers. I think about the desperation he's been hiding in his head and how I never want to play games with his heart. The warmth of the sunlight reaches my face and I caress his cheek with my thumb as I lean in to kiss him tenderly. I pull back and gaze into his eyes, unable to control my happiness. "It's only been a short time and you might think I'm crazy, but I'm already yours." I giggle and a tear rolls down my face. "There will never be anyone else. I promise you, I'll say yes. And, for the record, I love your caveman moves." I smile at the shine in his eyes, "Now, please get out of your head because that's not what we're about, with us it's all heart."

"How about I get into you?"

"Yes, but not until we get home."

"Do you have any plans today?"

"Yes."

"What are they?"

"I'm spending the day in bed with you."

"I like those plans. When does that start?"

"As soon as you take me home."

Rick claims my mouth and I shiver at his touch. "Home it is." We quickly toss everything into the backpack and shove the blanket back into the pouch. We zip up and Rick gets our helmets off the bike. He gets on the bike and starts it up, holding it steady for me to climb on. "Hold onto me for a second before you put your helmet on." I happily wrap my arms around him and reach to kiss his neck. He has his phone out and he's taking selfies of us on his motorcycle together. I reach around and stroke his beard. We put our helmets on and he's still doing his selfie thing. He starts some music and slides his phone back into his pocket. We take off for home as "Kashmir" by Led Zeppelin plays.

We get home and strip as we walk through the door, leaving a trail of boots, jeans, jackets, helmets, shirts, and undergarments on the way to our bedroom. We climb into bed together and nestle in under the warm blankets. Rick holds me close to him, our bodies against each other and his lips on mine with need. Lying on our sides and facing each other, I wrap my upper leg around him and invite him in. "Please, my king."

He slides into me with desire. "Is this for me, my queen?" He groans in pleasure.

"Only for you." We lie together making out while we move slowly, knowing we have all day to ourselves.

CHAPTER SIXTEEN

I t's Friday, the last day of Rick's suspension. I wake up in the middle of the afternoon with his left arm around my waist, his right arm under my pillow and his warm breath at my neck. He's completely out and I'm wide awake. I move his left arm and attempt to get out of bed without waking him, but my attempt is unsuccessful.

Rick wraps his arms around me, pulls me to him and says, "No," without ever opening his eyes. This would've been really sweet and made me giddy, if I didn't have to pee.

I try again, this time whispering, "I gotta pee," before I make quick action. He still doesn't open his eyes, but he must've got the message. I run to the bathroom and close the door behind me.

I don't live by myself anymore. There's a man's razor and deodorant on my bathroom counter next to my tropical soaps and personal items. The mosaic sea glass cup that holds my tooth-brush, now holds two. He moved in with me. Makes sense, since I asked him to. We've spent most of the last week together, most of it here at home. But, somehow seeing his razor and toothbrush—

he lives here with me! I wonder what other people think when they see me making choices, committing to things and then realizing what I did a week later. I asked him to live with me. I put his books on my shelf. I made space for him in the closet. I've been cooking for two. I gave him a key. What have I done? I start to freak out and wander through my, no, our home in search of other signs he lives here and the sight of our riding gear strewn across the house smacks me in the face with memories of our late night adventure. The blanket that has taken up residence on my love seat, where we use it to snuggle and picnic in front of the TV when we watch the game. The small picture frame with the crowns on it sparkles in the sunlight, featuring our photo from Rick's first selfie session and reminding me we're here together. I catch my reflection in the mirror and I look different. My face is thinner. My skin is glowing. My eyes are shining. I have a bounce in my step. I look up to discover Rick standing there looking at me and my smile lights up. I stare at him through the reflection in the mirror, "Did you know your toothbrush is in the cup with mine, and your razor and stuff is on the bathroom counter? You live here now." I say it and it's more for my benefit than for his. I turn to him. Freaking the fuck out. I sink into his eyes and feel his arms wrap around me. My freak-out instantly fades away and my heart wins.

"Yes, this is home. A king usually lives with his queen, sharing their castle together." He is all it takes to make everything right. "I thought you were coming right back to bed, but it's been over an hour. Everything okay?"

I lost an hour catching up with my own life? Or, I guess it's our life. How is that possible? "I'm fine now. I was just looking around. We made a mess. I don't remember this place ever looking so lived in." I glance around me. "I don't know where the hour went, I was going back to be with you and I ended up here with you behind me. Did you know you live here now?"

Rick strokes my hair and hugs his cheek to my head, helping me calm down. "It's a big step for us. We made it a whole week, and we were tested this week with my suspension, my injury, and my temper. I love how you took care of me when I needed it and didn't take my shit. What would I have done if I weren't here with you?" Rick pulls back to search my eyes and smiles, "I live with you. Where doesn't matter as long as we're together."

I was freaking out and maybe I blacked out or something from the emotional trauma. "You make everything better."

Rick kisses me sweetly on the forehead and holds me to him, "Good, because I'm not letting you go." I feel his worry in the way he holds me. He means it when he says he's not letting me go. He doesn't want me to leave him again.

I lead Rick to the love seat and wrap the blanket around us. "I was freaking out, but that doesn't mean I'm leaving. My head is catching up with my heart. You have your own version of it. You start to say something and then stop or edit your words before they come out. You tell me more with your touch and kiss than words could ever say. I know what you want. I know how you feel about me. I know your dreams." I take his face in my hands and lock eyes with him, "I want everything you want and I only want to have it all with you. I've never wanted any of it before, never even thought about it."

"You left me in LA. You packed your stuff and left me, ran from me. I know you were hurt. You pulled away from me and wouldn't listen to what I was saying. You hid from me and wouldn't answer my texts when I couldn't find you. You wouldn't even respond to Sam. You didn't come home for days and when you did, you packed and disappeared for weeks. We can't do that, we need to go to each other for answers—not run. When you freak out, it makes me worry that you'll do it again. I'm not leaving you alone. Now I know that asshole was after you, when you were weak and needing me, but wouldn't admit it. I did my best not to get pissed about you dating Adam, and I still hate it. Sherry, we need each other. Stupid shit happens, but together we make it okay. I don't blame you. I know what it looked like. You're what's important to me, none of the rest matters. Honestly, I suck at the rest without you."

"We can't be together every minute of every day. You have to trust me."

"Stop! I do trust you. But, you have these moments like today when something clicks in your head about me living here and I don't want a moment to make your flight instinct kick in. Shit! With you, you could be on a plane in thirty minutes and on your way to Hawaii."

"That's not going to happen. I'm not going anywhere without you." Rick shakes his head unsure. "You have to trust me. Stop letting your head get in the way, believe in your heart." I take a deep breath, "Do you want me to tell you the crazy thing I've been thinking about doing? I guess I may have already told you in my sleep. What can I do to help you understand and believe I'm with you, never leaving you?"

Rick stares at me, his wheels turning.

"You know I have days where I'm waiting for you to take off with one of the young baseball hotties, right? I'm older than you. You can have any of those girls you want. I know they're perkier and tighter all over. They'd be easier, do whatever you want and let you take care of them. Not insist on paying their own way, not difficult in any way. You have girls waiting in your room on road trips! Damn it! I'm already 35. You want a family. I've never worried about any biological clock before, but I have limited time to give you the family you want and your mother already thinks I'm too old for you. Fuck! And, that crazy doesn't even include the crazy thing I've been thinking about doing! So, we might as well put all our insecurities and crazy out there."

Fuck! Fuck! Fuck! The tears start rolling down my face. My tone turned to yelling as I ranted insanely. He's already concerned about me having moments that could make me want to run away and I'm showing him how fucking crazy insecure I am about him.

"I only want you. You want me for me. None of those girls out there care who I am. They all want a baseball player. I don't care how old you are. I love being with you and if it's always just me and you, well I'd rather have you than anyone else." He closes his eyes, "Tell me the crazy thing you've been thinking about doing. Might as well get it out there."

I'm quiet for a few minutes while my thoughts twirl about. I can't tell him what I'm thinking about doing. I just need to do it, crazy or not. I don't know why I want to give him everything and maybe it will make some of our insecurities disappear. I gaze at him with a quivering smile and take his hand. "I'm done thinking about it. I know what I want. I'm ready to stop taking my daily pill for you. You tell me when. I promise this isn't a trap. I want to give you everything and I'm not pressuring you. I'll keep taking my pill until you say when." We've talked about someday, but I made someday real.

Rick's whole attitude changes, his body language loosens up. "Do you mean that?"

"I wouldn't say it if I didn't mean it. I'll never hurt you intentionally and I know it's a soft spot for you."

His smile reaches his eyes and his cheeks, "I love you. I don't want to rush it. I want us to have time together. Please don't take this the wrong way, because I want it with you more than you know." He stops. "Maybe when we get back from Hawaii," he says quietly.

I need him, I turn to him with sexy eyes, "Is there anything else I can do to help eliminate your worries?"

"Please book your air travel for all the away games for the rest of the season and use my credit card. I want to know you're going to be with me."

"I'll do that right now." It's a little thing to help make him happy. "The game is on soon."

"I only want to be with you tonight. No game. I'll be back at the stadium tomorrow." His eyes are shiny, "Sherry, you make me happier than I've ever been. Nobody has ever offered me anything that means so much to me. We'll talk about it together closer to the right time. Joint effort, my queen. We're a team." He holds me close and I feel his heart beating.

I turn on the radio and open my laptop to schedule my flights. The sexy sultry sound of "Let's Hurt Tonight" by OneRepublic fills the room and Rick's at my back watching me schedule my air travel. He's listening to the music and wraps his arms around me as he kisses my neck. The lyrics are on the nose for the conversation we're having.

"Let's stay in tonight," he whispers in my ear.

I can't think of anything better, "Perfect." I smile at him. "I'll make dinner."

"No, let's order in. I want you and no distractions tonight. I need to be at the stadium early tomorrow. It's the last night."

"It's not the last night, my king. I'll be with you every night, wherever you are, baseball or not. I can't wait to get out there and cheer for you tomorrow. I'll drop you off and come back early for batting practice in your car, so I'll be in the garage waiting for you to drive me home after the game."

"How are you so perfect?" He keeps kissing my neck.

I giggle, "I'm excited to get to go to the different stadiums. We're going to be on an adventure together."

"It's work for me."

"I know you have to be at practice and work out and play games, but maybe I can make it more fun."

"It'll definitely be better with you. I like quiet time between games, holding you will make that better."

"I was thinking about all the elevators." I bite my lower lip and grin deviously. "I'm going to start a travel diary with a map, so I can keep track of the elevators you pull the stop on and the elevators we have sex on and the elevators that don't see any action. Maybe a special section for sex outdoors. You know, on the beach or in the park."

Rick's gaze is heated, "...and in the car."

"Maybe we should start a selfie collection. Pictures of us together in every city we visit or in the shower of every hotel room we stay in, or maybe the bed." I grin at him suggestively.

"Are you done booking your flights?"

"Yes. Emailing you my confirmations, so you have my flight info." I turn to him and he's looking at his phone. "Are you checking my work? Did I spend too much?"

Rick rolls his eyes, "I'm not looking at my email. I don't care how much you spent." He seems distracted. "I'm looking at the selfies from this morning."

"Oh! Send them all to me, selfie master."

"All of them? I took quite a few."

"All of them." My phone starts vibrating with pictures coming in. I hear it buzzing wherever I left it last night and go searching for it, following the sound. I find my phone and it finally stops vibrating with messages.

"Check out this video I have." Rick calls out to me.

I find him sitting on the love seat and stand behind him to watch over his shoulder. He plays the video of him kissing me at the first base wall the day I went to tell him I love him, but it's so much more. Somebody has edited it together with me on the big screen when he sent me his bag with his glove and him watching me, him kissing me when it was on the big screen in Colorado when Hannah was interviewing him, him pointing at me from the field a handful of times, him carrying me through the hotel lobby, us holding hands through the net, us kissing in the dugout, us walking across the field to the bull pen holding hands—all set to "Thinking Out Loud." It's absolutely perfect. Rick looks back at me, "Are you okay? Come here, baby." I realize I'm crying as I sit in his lap and he embraces me.

"I'm fine," I say as I wipe my tears away. "Its perfect." I'll do a test in the morning to check because I'm so emotional, I think to myself as I hear Sam in my head. "Who made that?"

"I don't know. Cross sent it to me. He's missing me this week." Rick chuckles and kisses my cheek. "He might be jealous."

"Tough luck for him because he can't have you!" I laugh and claim Rick's mouth as I change my position and press my naked breasts against him, straddling his lap. Rick groans appreciatively and takes control, lifting me with him as he stands. I wrap my legs around him while he kisses me. "I need you, my king."

"I need you, too. We're in the same place and want the same things, so no more freaking out, okay?" He puts his forehead to mine and gazes into my eyes, while he carries me to the bedroom.

"I can't promise to not freak out, but I can promise not to leave." I say, knowing I have no control.

"I'll take it." Rick takes a deep breath, "How about we keep everything the way it is right now until the end of the season? I need to work on keeping my head straight and not getting suspended. Me and you in a monogamous relationship, living together, spending time together, traveling together, and sharing expenses until you let me pay for everything. Big decisions and next steps all on hold. Two months or so of status quo."

"Okay," I kind of smile.

He looks at me as if he's reading my mind, "Don't go getting in your head and reading anything into it. You know I want more.

I want the same things as you and I want them with you. I need to manage to get through the season and bring my stats up."

"I understand. You might need to remind me that I want my team to win and that means you need to be behind the plate." I grin happily, laughing at myself.

I wrap my arms around him and he takes the bed on all fours with me hanging on him. He puts my head on the pillow and rests his body on mine, sharing the pillow with me and pulling the blankets up over us. His hands touch me tenderly with desire. He kisses my lips softly, sweetly, tasting me. He moves his mouth to my neck where I feel his hot breath and he whispers, "I love you, baby," in my ear as he pushes into me. His whisper so sincere, I feel how much he loves me. He moves slowly and he's in another world, needing to love me. He moves, making noises under his breath with every slow stroke.

I wrap my legs around him tight and my whole body needs him, more of him. "I love you, my king. Please give me more. Not harder. Not faster. All of you, deeper." He sits back on his knees and pushes all the way into me, and I cry out in need. My cry pushes him forward and he hooks my knees with his arms as he comes back down to me. Pressing his lips to mine, his tongue dancing with mine as he pushes into me further and holds my knees spread at my chest. Pushing in more with each slow stroke until he's all the way in and driving me crazy with need. "Oh, Rick. I need you, baby."

"I'm right here, baby. You're so tight, I don't want to go too fast." He stops moving and leans into my ear, "That's me buried all the way in you, Sherry. Do you remember how big I am? Do you remember watching me slide in and out of you? Do you remember how far I can slide out and still be in you? Do you remember how thick and hard I was, when you were watching me stretch your tight hole? That's what you have again right now.

All of me, baby. All of me and only for you. Nobody else will ever have me. You're the only lock for my key." He grinds against me while he remains buried deep and I cry out his name. He does it again and I scream out. "How about some more." He says more as a statement than a question and keeps grinding against me at our connection. My heat builds instantly and I can't help but squeeze him. "Fuck me. Sherry, tell me you want more. Tell me to take you. Give me permission. Something. Oh fuck. Please Sherry. Please. You're so fucking tight, I..."

"Take me, my king. However you want. I'm yours." I know he wants it hard and fast. I know he wants to pound into me in this position. He doesn't move. "I need you to slam into me hard and fast, and I need you to not stop. I need you to spread my legs wide and hold my feet at my ears. I need you as deep as you can get, hard on every stroke and I need you now. You can still love me, while you send us over the edge." He smiles and does what I ask. He didn't need permission, he needed to know he was still loving me. "That's perfect. I love you, baby." He's amazing and it doesn't take much to send us both into ecstasy together, as we cry out in unison and reach for each other, needing to hold each other close while we come down. Our physical and emotional connection together are crazy. He claims my mouth, kissing me while we keep our connection and I'm in heaven.

I wake up starving at around 4am and go to the kitchen to find food. I make an Italian Sandwich, and I grab the leftover cookies and banana bread. I take it all back to bed with me, he'll be hungry and awake when I get back to bed.

"Where'd you go, baby?" He says sleepily.

"Grabbed us something to eat. I know you're hungry."

Rick sits up groggily, "How are you so perfect, my queen?"

Happily inhaling part of the sandwich. He's not fully awake and that's okay. I close up the banana bread and cookies, leaving them sitting on the floor at my bedside. I lie back down in bed and Rick immediately rolls me underneath him as he slides back into me, stroking in and out slowly until he has a smile on his face.

I wake up to the smell of coffee brewing. It's Saturday morning. Rick is off suspension and back to playing baseball today. Right now he has me lying on top of him and his arm holding me there. "Good morning, my king. It's a 5:40 game day, what time do you want to be at the stadium? Do you want breakfast? Shower?"

Rick groans at the thought of morning, "Earlier is better today. How long to make breakfast?"

"I can have an omelette and coffee ready for you in less than fifteen minutes."

"Okay. Breakfast, please. I'll shower and be ready to eat in under fifteen." He sits up with his eyes still closed and I pull the blankets away to find his naked cock in need.

I lean down and kiss him on his tip. "Do you have an extra five minutes for me?" I ask as I slide my lips over his cock, licking and sucking.

"Oh, yeah." He doesn't have anymore words.

He gets harder in my mouth as I stroke him with my hand and my mouth. He's in the moment and half asleep, so this isn't going to take long. I suck and lick as I pull him with my lips. He grabs me, pulling me on top of him and I slide on to his hard length, drawing a growl from him. He flips us over and pushes into me hard and fast, setting me on edge and pushing me over rubbing my magic button. I fall hard and crashing, pulling him with me uncontrollably.

"I love you, my king." The alarm clock goes off and it's almost 9am.

"One snooze and then we get up, my queen." I hit the snooze button and enjoy Rick wrapped around me for nine more minutes before the real world invades our private world once again.

CHAPTER SEVENTEEN

The alarm goes off. I want to support him and make the rest of the season as easy as I can. I'll be at every game for the remainder of the season and I'll be cheering for him like nobody else can. I jump out of bed and get dressed quickly, pulling on some black bikinis, denim shorts, a black bra, and a black strapped camisole tank with lace edging. I put a fresh towel in the bathroom and turn on the shower for Rick. I turn on some music and go with my *Good Morning* Playlist. I hit shuffle and "Shape of You" by Ed Sheeran comes on making me want to dance, so I set it on repeat and hear Rick get in the shower as I make my way to the kitchen. I quickly gather what I need for breakfast and switch up my normal omelette a bit, using provolone, my leftover Italian sandwich meat, mushrooms, basil, thyme, and a shake of garlic salt. I toast up the last couple pieces of bread to go with the eggs and meet Rick at the table as he walks out in his gym shorts, running shoes and "Property of the Seals" T-shirt. I grab my phone and take a picture of him because he's fucking hot.

"Really?"

"Shouldn't you be more appreciative of a woman who woke you with a blow job and made you breakfast?" I say jokingly, I want him in a good mood.

He smiles and shakes his head, "Take as many photos as you like." He laughs and sits down to eat his omelette. "This is really good. Italian style?"

"Sure. Using up the leftovers, since there wasn't enough left for another sandwich. You can put the eggs on the toast and make it a sandwich if you want." I clean up the kitchen real quick while he's eating and make sure I have everything for making cookie bars. I pour coffee into two travel cups and package up a few baseball cookies with a piece of chocolate chip banana bread for Chase. I give Rick one of the coffees and start to nurse the other. "When do you want to leave for the stadium?"

"Cross is picking me up in a few minutes. Thought it would make it easier on you since he's going early today, too."

"I'm happy either way. Tell him to come up and get you because I have something for him." A few minutes later Chase is knocking on the door. I open the door and hug him, "Good morning, sweetheart." Rick gives me the eye.

"Hey lovey, heard you have something for me and I'm hoping its chocolate chip."

I hand him the bag of baked goods and tell him what they are. "Let me know what you think."

"You two don't need to talk. Remember, my woman." Rick grabs me and claims me excessively before he walks out the door, leaving me boneless and needing to recover before I can continue.

Chase smiles at me, "Thank you." He laughs and follows Rick out the door.

I have things to get done today and a limited amount of time.

Text from Sam - Good morning! My bro is back playing
today, right?

The message from Sam reminds me the first thing I need to
do is pee on a stick. I decide to include Sam because I need moral
support. I don't want to be sad, I need to keep it together and be
happy to support Rick through the season. No freaking out.

Text to Sam - Yes. He just left for the stadium. I know he was
on suspension, but I had the most wonderful week with him.

Text to Sam - Really emotional again last night and missing
him like crazy even though he just left. Doing a test. Cross
your fingers.

Text from Sam - Cross my fingers?

Text from Sam - Uummm... Do we want it to be positive or
negative?

Text to Sam - I don't want to talk about that.

Text from Sam - You should definitely pee on a stick. Go now.
Send me the results.

I work myself up on the short walk to the bathroom and pee
on a stick with intentions of walking away from it and getting
some work done, but that doesn't happen. I stand there and
watch it for ten minutes. Confused and freaking out with tears
running down my face. This makes no sense at all.

Text from Sam - Remember a negative isn't bad, it means not
yet and you have time to practice. ;)

What the fuck is wrong with me? Sam's right. I'm on the pill and that means it should be negative. I look back to the test and sure enough, negative. I send Sam a picture of the test.

Text from Sam - It's okay. Probably better not to come up positive during the season anyway. You know how possessive he is, who knows how that would affect him.

Text to Sam – True.

Text from Sam - I know how you really feel, trying to find the silver lining. It just means not right now.

Text to Sam - I know.

Text from Sam - Get rid of that test, so you don't have to see it and nobody else does.

Text to Sam – Okay.

I toss the evidence down the trash chute and clean up a bit. I start some laundry and mix together a huge batch of chocolate chip cookie dough. I set it aside to rest in the refrigerator and turn the oven on to preheat, while I sort out a couple more loads of laundry. I sit down to drink my coffee, check email, and social media. I missed a text from Rick, crap.

Text from Rick - I miss you.

Text from Rick - BP is at 2:30.

Text from Rick - ?

Text to Rick - Sorry, hands were in cookie dough.

Text to Rick - I've been thinking about you ever since you left.

Text from Rick - What are you thinking?

Text to Rick - How I can't wait to be in your arms with you inside me...

Text to Rick - Is that bad?

Text from Rick - I want to be close to you, too.

Text from Rick - Maybe you can get here early and we can steal a few minutes somewhere before BP.

Text from Rick - I need a mid-day visit. I feel like I'm addicted and went cold turkey.

I laugh at the mere idea that a professional athlete could be addicted to me, but get warm all over at how much my king needs me.

Text to Rick - I'll be there before batting practice.

Text to Rick - I love you, my king.

Text from Rick - :)

Text from Rick - I don't remember what it was like without you. I love you, too.

He can make my heart thump with a text. I pick up my pace,

so I can get to the stadium early. I take my cookie dough out of the refrigerator and press it into three cookie sheets. I put them all in the oven and set the timer.

I want to be sexy for Rick, and appropriate for Carter, when I get to the stadium with cookies and my proposal to assist with travel plans. I peruse my closet for the right thing to wear that'll easily change over to game attire. It's a warm day and a 5:40 game, great day for a skirt. I toss my denim mini skirt on the bed and put my Seals leggings in my game bag. I pull the jersey for today's game from the closet, it's the navy with white jersey. I hate wearing white tops, so I search my closet for navy blue options. I get the matching hoodie and cap, adding those to my game bag. I go with my navy sleeveless V-neck that gathers on the sides and then change my mind, choosing a basic navy camisole. I brush out my hair and smell cookies baking, so I check on them and the timer goes off as I open the oven. They're perfect, so I take them out of the oven and let them cool before I cut them into squares. I turn the shower on to warm up and tie my hair up in a tight bun. I bring up my playlists, wanting something different than my normal *Steamy* playlist and see a playlist I don't remember *Sherry*. I go for it and hit shuffle. "Oh Sherrie" by Steve Perry starts playing as I make my way to the shower. I stand in the shower with the hot water beating down on me, taking a few minutes to relax and let everything go. "If I Lose Myself" by OneRepublic comes on next. Tears start falling and I wonder what's wrong with me. When did I become a girl who cries for no apparent reason? There must be a reason. Maybe it's the big changes. I'm living with my fantasy baseball boyfriend, he's real, and my life has definitely changed. Shit! What I want in life has changed. I turn to the water and close my eyes, feeling the water on my face. I focus and finish my shower, so I can go see my man. I dry off, then cut up and package the chocolate chip cookie bars before I get dressed. I let my hair down and give it a shake, hoping for a bit of wave. I get dressed, get my things together, and check the mirror. I put on my baseball bracelet and my key necklace. I text Rick on my way to his car.

Text to Rick - Leaving for the stadium now :) See you soon!

I get in the Challenger and start her up. The muscle car reminds me of the man she belongs to—powerful, rumbling, sexy, and fast.

I arrive at the stadium in no time and park in the player's garage. I take the cookies and my proposal, and I make my way to Carter's office. I knock on his open door and Carter smiles at me, inviting me in.

"Hey Sherry, what are you doing here?"

"I'd like to talk to you for a minute and I brought you some cookies." I hand him the smaller bag of chocolate chip cookie bars and wait for his response.

"Thank you." He looks at them and feels they're still warm. "What's up?"

I hand him my proposal. "You mentioned that you don't like dealing with the travel arrangements and you may not know this, but I'm a travel agent. Planning travel is what I do and I enjoy it. So, I'm offering you my services."

Carter stares at me unsure, "I don't have a budget to pay you with. It's part of my job."

"I understand. I've done the research and I believe I can take the duty from you with the cost staying the same. Allowing you to have more time for other things, essentially adding to your value with the organization and saving the organization money with whatever extra duty you take on—and I'll make a profit." I stop because I don't want to go too far and I don't want to be pushy. "This proposal gives you some of my background and illustrates why you should have me handle travel. It makes sense." I smile and shut up.

"This isn't my call, but I'll review it and run it by my supervisor. I'm not sure about this and Seno."

"This has nothing to do with Seno. This is all me. Let me help you handle the part of your job you don't like to do."

"I'll check it out."

"Thank you." I turn to get out of his office. "Do you happen to know where Seno is?"

Carter under his breath, "Stray is catching tonight."

"So, where does he go when he wants to be a dick?"

"He's probably running the warning track. Hold on..." He calls out, "Seno?"

Of course, he would be running somewhere. That's what he does when he gets pissed and pouty.

"Not in here." I recognize the voice.

"Chase?" I call out and he comes walking in.

"Hey lovey, twice in one day!" He smiles while he talks to me.

I hand him the cookie bars, "Rick said you wanted more of these and asked me to make enough for the whole clubhouse. Please share and they're compliments of Seno. Do you know where he is?"

"Nope." I send him on his way.

Text to Rick - Elevator?

"Thank you, Carter. I'll get out of your way."

I walk out to the concourse looking for him on the field while I wait for his reply. I see him look at his phone and reply.

Text from Rick - Been working out hard. I'm not in the lineup.

Text to Rick - I know. That's why I suggested the elevator and not your car. Did I mention I'm wearing a short skirt and no panties?

Okay fine, I lied. But, he needed to be persuaded and I can take them off before I get to him.

Text to Rick - I bet you're all hot and sweaty. You're not starting, why not have some of me?

Text from Rick - You're a bad girl.

Text to Rick - I'm your bad girl.

Text from Rick - Elevator

Yes! Fuck! I'm as bad as him! I quickly run into the ladies room and pull off my panties, shoving them into my purse. I go to the elevator and he's there waiting for me when the door opens. Rick presses the button for the top floor and pulls the stop before we get there.

"Nice skirt." The only words that come out of his mouth before he presses me up against the elevator wall, passionately claiming me with his lips. He runs his hands all over my body, feeling for the edge of my skirt and reaching under it to find out if I'm going commando. He finds my wet folds and slides a finger into me, groaning appreciatively at how wet I am. He strokes me while he continues to kiss me, and slides a second finger in. He drops to his catcher's crouch and pushes my skirt up around my hips as he licks and sucks at my wet sex. His tongue is fucking amazing as it glides along my wet heat and dips into me. His big warm hands on my bare ass, holding me to him. He goes back to stroking me with his fingers and moves his mouth to my clit, sucking on me hard. He can feel me start to go over the edge...

"No. Don't come. No yet, my queen."

"But... Please... I can't help it..."

"No. Bad girls have to wait."

I whine uncontrollably and he squeezes my ass. Rick stands up and turns me away from him, bending me over in front of him with his hands spread across my hips and ass. I can't help myself and I shake my ass in front of him. He slides into me hard, fast, and deep, all at once and his body mashed up against mine.

"Fuck me. You can come now, baby." He says as he pounds into me repeatedly. He reaches around me and circles my sensitive nub, feeling how wet and ready I am. "You want it harder?"

"Yes. Bad girls deserve to get fucked hard."

"Yea, and you're my bad girl. Do bad girls deserve to get spanked?"

"Bad girls have to do whatever their man wants them to." I say breathlessly.

"Oh, fuck me. Then you have to watch." He bends me over further, so I can see him fucking me and holds me up with his arm around my waist. "Do you like that?"

"I like whatever you want, my king."

"Fuck! Fuck! Fuck!" He grabs my hips hard and pulls me back onto him, using my body to stroke himself. Sliding me on and off of his hard cock, harder and harder, faster and faster. He sends me soaring and doesn't stop. "A few more strokes, baby." He groans and I feel his pulsating release. He pulls me back upright and leans me against him where he talks in my ear from behind me, "You make me fucking insane."

"You're a baseball player for me, right?" I say out of breath.

"Yes, my queen."

"I'm going to be there to watch batting practice and I want you to knock it out of the park. I want you to get yourself in the game today. You work Skip and you make it a win for me. Can you do that?"

"I'll work it, my queen."

"My team can't win without you. They need you behind the plate. I'll be cheering for you and I'll be in your car waiting for you after the game. You look like a warrior going into battle when you step behind the plate and it's the hottest thing I've ever seen." His eyes start to heat up again.

"I love you, baby. I'm taking this elevator down to the clubhouse before I need to have you again. I'll see you at BP." He turns me to him and kisses me until the elevator doors open and he leaves me there without another word.

CHAPTER EIGHTEEN

I was early getting to the stadium and have some extra time before batting practice. I wander out of the stadium and across the street to sit at the bar and have some carne asada fries. How can you go wrong with fries made up like nachos?

I keep track of the time and get situated behind the home dugout before its time for batting practice to start. It feels good being back in the stadium after missing a week. It's my happy place, especially on a sunny day like today with a clear blue sky and a high of 75 degrees. I take my jersey off, put my cap on and slather myself in sunscreen. The coconut scent makes me happier. A cool breeze blows through and I realize I should've put my panties back on, but there's no time for that right now. The team is starting to wander out onto the field and the field is set up for practice. The seating bowl isn't open yet, so I'm the only one sitting in the stands. I see the new catcher, Stray, as well as Mason, Lucky, Kris, Rock and Chase with bats in their hands. Cross looks up, noticing me in the stands as he swings a bat and heads my direction.

Cross walks up to me in the stands in his happy-go-lucky way, "What did you do to Seno?"

"What do you mean? Is he okay?" Elevator injury?

"He's not hurt. He was happy to be back this morning. Then he was pissed when he found out Stray is catching today, and I was avoiding him because he was being so pissy. Now he's walking around with his chest puffed out, like he's the king again and he won't leave Skip alone. He says he needs to play today."

Yes! I look straight at Chase, "He's going to put on a hitting display during BP, too."

"I believe it because you said it. Those cookie bars were still warm, and delicious by the way."

"They should be. I made them fresh this morning. Did you like the stuff I gave you this morning?"

"The baseball cookies were cute and good. The banana bread was yummy, you should add nuts."

"I'll remember that for next time. So, where is Seno?"

"He's probably still working Skip."

He needs to get his ass out here and show off his bat. "Seno!" I yell out, thinking I might get a response. I know, not only did I give him instructions, I want it done my way. Damn! I'm bossy today. Maybe he just needs it today to get through.

"You still didn't tell me what you did to him." Cross stares directly at me.

"Let's just say it was the cookies," I smile innocently.

My Rick comes walking out of the dugout, he looks up at me in the stands and smiles. He quickly makes his way to me. He glares at Cross, "My woman, go."

Chase mutters as he walks back to the field, "Shit dude, you've got it bad. I'm the one who found her."

Rick pulls me out of my seat, puts his arms around me and dips me while he kisses me, getting catcalls from the team. He's in a much better mood. He brings me back up and makes close eye contact with me. "You give me strength and point me in the right direction when I've lost my focus. That's proof we're more than physical." He gets a big smile, "I'm not starting, but Skip says he'll put me in."

I clap loudly, "Go show me your bat, big boy!" I swat him on the ass as he turns back to the field. Both of us laughing as he gets to work.

The team as a whole is hitting well today. My Rick gets his first turn to hit and sends the second ball to the Right Field Upper Deck, home run. The third ball straight out and over the wall in Center Field. He broke his bat on the fourth ball, sending a grounder up the first base line. He walks to the dugout for a new bat and looks at me for affirmation. I blow him a kiss and yell, "Perfect, baby!" He continues to hit them out of the park on each turn at batting practice.

Text to Rick - You have an awesome bat.

Text to Rick - Yes, I'm referring to both kinds of wood ;)

Text to Rick - Since I'm already here, should I scout the other team for you?

Text from Rick - I'm glad you like my wood. I'll give you a demonstration with it later.

Text from Rick - Stay behind the home dugout while you're scouting and be quiet. Very interested in what you see.

Text to Rick - Yes, sir!

Text from Rick - You are the baseball queen.

Wow! There's no way he values my baseball opinion. He does this for a living and I'm merely a spectator. Though he didn't argue with me when I gave him my views during the games. His suspension was a gift. When would we ever have been able to sit and watch a game together? Baseball is something we have in common. Rick has obviously been thinking about that, trying to find proof we're solid together and not just sex. It was a glimpse into spending the off-season together.

The visiting team comes out for batting practice and I don't even pay attention to who we're playing. We're playing LA and that means the stadium is going to get rowdy. LA is a rival team and the fans flood the stadium whenever they play here. They aren't obnoxious like the Sissy's and their fans though. I check their website to see who they have on their current roster and who is on the lineup for tonight's game. I figure out who is in the outfield catching balls, and who is hitting. I watch for anomalies, unsure footing, bad hitting, anything odd and see if it repeats.

Text to Rick - Their lead off hitter can't connect with the ball to save his life

Text to Rick - Check out Kragen when you come out. Lineup says he's hitting fourth and playing Left Field. I think he's favoring his right leg. See what you think.

Text from Rick - Are you serious?

Text to Rick - Yes! This is baseball!

Text from Rick - Anything else?

Text to Rick - I'm still watching. Outfielders aren't paying attention, but that's probably because it's BP. There are a couple of them out there in a deep conversation. Can't see who they are.

Text from Rick - Any observations from Seals BP?

Interesting that he'd ask.

Text to Rick - Stray seems a bit full of himself for a guy who's been up less than a week. Probably makes him a liability behind the plate.

Text to Rick - Mason, Cross and Martin are on point. Rock looks tired. Bravo is favoring his hip. Nothing else stood out to me except your big bat.

Anybody who watches batting practice can see these things. You'd think somebody from the team would be watching everyday.

Text from Rick - Thanks. Tell me if you notice anything else.

Text from Rick - My bat and I miss you.

Text to Rick - I'll show you how to handle your bat later.

Text to Rick - Did everybody like the cookies?

Text from Rick - Mason requested peanut butter cookies, Martin requested brownies, and Rock said more please and thank you.

Text from Rick - I thought I owed you a batting lesson.

Text to Rick - Either way I get to touch your bat.

Batting practice is over, so I check my phone to find out which seat I'm in tonight and I'm behind home plate where Rick wants me to be. I check the schedule, Monday is an off day and we're in Seattle on Tuesday. I need to do laundry. I've been too busy or I should be honest—I've been neglecting household chores and opting to spend time with my Rick. Like there's really any choice to consider, it's a no-brainer. I run up to the bathroom and pull on my panties, as well as my leggings. I stop by the member lounge to pick up $5 beer and free popcorn on my way back to my seat, and I'm a happy girl.

The pregame hoopla gets started and since Rick isn't starting, he catches the ceremonial first pitches. Which is nice because I get a glimpse of my favorite view and he's not wearing full catcher's gear. He turns to me and smiles before he heads back into the dugout. He's focused and ready to play.

Stray gets set behind the plate and I wonder about his name as I read his jersey. Stray like a stray cat? Stray because he's not loyal? He doesn't follow rules? A wanderer maybe? It doesn't matter, probably just his name and means nothing.

The game is moving slowly, like it always does when Rick isn't behind the plate. It's the top of the fourth inning, there's no score, and Skip hasn't put my Rick in to catch yet. Young catchers always keep a slower paced game and that's bad because a) it bores me out of my mind, so I eat or drink more and most likely end up wasted and b) everything becomes transparent to the opposing team when you don't keep them on their toes. I don't know why I have an urge to numb my brain when I'm already bored, like putting myself out of my misery I guess.

I text Rick, knowing he probably can't see it.

Text to Rick - Stray needs to pick up the pace. LA can see right through him and he's boring me.

Text to Rick - I'll be sleeping in your car or possibly passed out from the quantity of alcohol I'm going to require to get through this slow ass game.

Text to Rick - I know you won't see these during the game.

Middle of the fourth inning and I need time to make two beer runs if I'm going to make it through this game. I stand up and stretch. I turn to walk up to the concessions stand and hear, "Hey, blondie! Where do you think you're going?" It's my favorite voice. I turn around and my Rick is standing in the on deck circle swinging his bat. His grin burns through me and I go back to my seat.

I yell at the top of my lungs, "Let's Go Seno! Wooooooooooooo!" There's a new electricity in the stadium, at least there is for me.

Rick's replacing Stray in the seven spot, so he'll be catching the rest of the game. First pitch is outside. Second pitch is low. 2-o count, and the third pitch is on fire straight down the middle. Rick connects and let's the fastball do all the work, launching it over the Center Field wall. The horn sounds and the fireworks fly. Home run. Rick runs the bases at a quick pace and he makes eye contact with me as he approaches home plate. He kisses two of his fingers and points them at me as he steps on the plate. "Yeah, baby! Wooooo! Seno!" I yell for him and he can hear me. The next hitter pops out and the pitcher is up in the nine spot. Tommy is pitching tonight and he's not a great hitter. He sees an opportunity to bunt and ends up half hitting it down the third base line, somehow legging it out and making it to first base safe. Mason is in the lead off spot and hacks at the first pitch, sending the ball over the first basemen's head into the Right Field corner. Mason safe at first and Tommy on second. Cross is hitting second, "Wooooo! Cross! Smack it!" 2-2 count and he breaks his bat, knocking the ball straight up the center of the field and sending wood shards toward the pitcher and short stop. The ball choppers through the infield and right over the short stop's head. Bases are loaded for Kris Martin and he's swinging his bat like it's the at bat he's been waiting for his whole life. First pitch, hit foul into the stands off first base. Second pitch, smacked hard foul and only a few feet from being a home run in Right Field. Third pitch, 0-2 count, is a ball high and outside—they're trying to get him to chase, but Kris isn't falling for it. 1-2 count, and the fourth pitch is outside away again. 2-2, fifth pitch is hit foul into the Seals dugout. Sixth pitch and I hear a clean ringing noise, I stand up and watch to see if it has the distance. The ball hits the outfield wall, missing a grand slam by about 9 inches. Tommy scores, Mason scores on his heels and so does Cross only a few feet behind him. Kris is safe at second base. Score is 4-0 Seals, still the bottom of the fourth and one out. Lucky hits a ground ruled double, bringing in Kris. Rock steps up to the plate and gets walked intentionally. Bravo covering third base tonight, steps up to the plate and hits into a double play. Of course, running slow with his hip obviously bothering him is pretty much a give away for LA. Ending the fourth inning at 5-0 Seals.

The team comes running out of the dugout to their positions for the fifth inning and the last one out is my Rick dressed in all of his catcher's gear, ready for war and sexy as hell. "Looking damn sexy, Seno! Wooo!" I stop myself and reset, "Take these guys out! 1, 2, 3, Tommy!" Rick turns to me and shakes his head.

The next few innings are quick and all three outs in a row except Cross getting a double and knocked in during the seventh inning. My Rick catching makes all the difference in the world. Okay, I may be biased, but the game is going quicker and I no longer feel the need to kill anyone or be intoxicated. Seno always keeps the game on track and in motion.

Top of the ninth inning and the score is 6-0 Seals. Tommy's still pitching and LA comes out ready to eat him alive. Four consecutive solo home runs, taking the score to 6-4 Seals. Skip pulls Tommy and brings in Houck since it's now a save situation. I watch Houck throw a few to Rick and something's off. This doesn't look like Houck's normal stuff. Rick's catching him fine and they're in sync. I can't place what's different. No outs and nobody on base. Houck throws and it's away, and I mean away like I could've caught that pitch if I was still sitting at the bar across the street. Seno manages to grab it and not let it get by him, arm straight out to reach it. Next pitch is away, but not as far. Third pitch is just outside and high. At least he's getting closer, but the count is 3-0 and it might as well be a lead off walk— always a bad thing. Houck manages to get some control and takes the count to 3-2, and ends up walking him anyway. The tying run is at the plate and I'm on the edge of my seat, "Get this guy out!" The pitch isn't where Rick is set up, I knew Houck was off! I hear the bat connect, "Oh fuck!" The ball is out of the park and it's a tied game. Skip pulls Houck and Rhett comes running in from the bull pen. Interesting move. I watch him toss to Rick a few times and he's on point. Rick claps a few times and makes eye contact around the field, I can almost hear him saying "Let's do this!" It's a whole new game. We need to get three outs and then come up to bat and score. Rhett fires in three in a row and strikes out the next hitter before he knew what hit him. Next hitter is their DH. Rhett and Rick are playing a game with him, each pitch located at a different spot around the plate, they almost circle it. The hitter gets a piece of a few of the pitches and pops out. The lead off guy is up and Rick glances back at me, then turns back to Rhett. I told him he couldn't connect to save his life and he hasn't connected all night. They literally play catch with him at the plate, pitches at about 78 miles per hour. Rick didn't even get all the way down into his crouch—strike three and the third out. That was a bit of a ballsy thing to do. Doesn't matter, on to the bottom of the ninth.

Bottom of the ninth inning and we're starting with Chase. Cross hits a double. Martin strikes out, caught looking. One out and one on when Lucky walks, taking the empty space at first base. Rock gets a base hit and everybody moves up one. Bases loaded and we only need one to win. Bravo is at the plate and Seno is swinging a bat in the on deck circle. Bravo strikes out swinging. Rick turns to me and grins. "All we need is a base hit! Let's finish this, baby!" He nods and walks to the plate, pointing at me before he turns his attention to the ball. "Go Seno!" The coaches are flashing signs, and Rick has made eye contact with his teammates on base. I don't think they're going to stick to the script. I hope they don't get crazy, we need Cross to score. The first pitch is low and inside. The second pitch is a fastball straight down the pipe. Rick swings and connects. It's beautiful and almost an exact copy of his home run from his first at bat in the game, except this time it's a grand slam! The horn blows. The fireworks go crazy. The big screen is my Rick running the bases with comic book word bubbles, pow, pop, wow, boom, wham, smack, bursting around him. Cross scores, Lucky scores, Rock scores and Rick slows as he approaches the plate, jumping on home plate as his team mobs him. I'm out of my seat, jumping up and down, clapping and dancing like a wild woman. "That's my man! Wooooo!" Walk off win, 10-6 Seals. The celebration on the field is insane and Gatorade is flying everywhere.

Hannah grabs Cross and nods to Rick for an interview. She starts with Cross and Rick walks over to the net, "The team wants to go out and celebrate, but I want to celebrate with you."

"We can celebrate together later. I'll be waiting for you."

Rick nods, "Or, you could go with us."

What? I can go celebrate with the team? Oh, I mean, I can go celebrate with the team! "I don't want to impose on your fun time with the guys."

"It'll be better with you there. My girl sitting on my lap will just make me happier." He smiles at me and takes off to do his interview with Hannah. I watch the interview, he's absolutely beaming and as always not taking credit for anything.

Hannah focuses on him, "This was a great return from your five day suspension. The days away didn't hurt your game at all. Do you regret your actions on the field last Sunday?" Uh oh.

Rick stops before he speaks, "I regret that I didn't have enough self-control to keep it off the field. It was evident they were throwing at me intentionally. I allowed them to get under my skin, personally, and that won't happen again." A reasonable and politically correct answer for the fan base. He looks at me and the truth is he'd do it again in a second. He'll always protect me and defend me.

Text from Sam - Bullshit! He'd do it again in a heartbeat. Guys shouldn't fuck with you if they want to live.

Text to Sam - Ha ha! I was just thinking he'd do it again in a second!

Text to Sam - He's taking me out to celebrate with the team tonight.

Text from Sam - That's new. Remember he needs to be the man around the team and have fun!

Sam's right, I need to make sure I don't embarrass him around the team.

Text from Rick - Let's meet up with the team, but not stay too long. I want some alone time and tomorrow is an early game.

Text to Rick - Alone = naked with me?

Text from Rick - YES

My body shivers in anticipation. You'd think we didn't spend most of the last week together and we haven't been naked at every opportunity we've had. It doesn't get old. I always want more. I always want to be with him. I can't believe it's only been a couple months. It feels like it's always been this way, it's how it's supposed to be.

Text to Rick - I can't wait.

Text from Rick - Meet me at the clubhouse level elevator and we can walk over to the Batter Up together. I'll be there in 15 minutes.

I take the elevator down to the garage and drop off my bag in the Challenger, keeping my ID in my pocket. I walk back to the elevator as Rick is walking up to it.

"Did I tell you how amazing you were tonight?" I throw my arms around his neck and he lifts me, so I wrap my legs around him. "I love that you're only a baseball player for me. Let's go celebrate with the guys, so we can go home and talk about your big bat." I kiss him, sucking on his lower lip while I run my fingers through his hair, rubbing his head.

"Maybe we should skip it and go home." His eyes hooded with serious sexual need.

"You should hang out with the team. You're just back from suspension."

Rick agrees with me and we walk to the Batter Up. We find the guys at the table in the back where they always hang out. Rick walks around the table shaking hands and offering high-fives. He has me in tow and introduces me to the guys I haven't met yet. Chase gives me a hug and gets reminded I'm Rick's woman. I get Kris to pose for me and text the picture to Sam. We get settled at the end of the table where there's enough room for me to be planted on his lap, and he holds me there possessively with his arm around my waist.

Mike with the Mic walks up, "Sherry? I'm about to start open mic night. How about you get us started tonight instead of my tired Bon Jovi tune?"

I look at Rick and he nods. "I'd love to!" I kiss Rick on the cheek, hop off his lap and walk across the bar with Mike. "What am I singing?"

"I was thinking Pat Benatar "Shadows of the Night" or Elle King "Ex's and Oh's." You rock both of those. You can do both."

"Let's do both." I smile and Mike goes to the stage.

"Welcome to the Batter Up! I'm Mike with the Mic and it's time for karaoke! We have a special treat tonight! Our contest winner, Sherry, will be opening for us tonight with a couple of her best." He hands me the mic and gets the music queued up, starting with Elle King. I love to sing this one and its even more fun when I'm not competing. I'm not dressed the part, but I still have the strut and attitude in my voice. Rick's watching me and there's a crowd of women that have swarmed the table. A couple of them standing by my Rick and taking pictures with him in the background, but he doesn't even know they're there. The crowd claps while Mike starts the next song, the wrong song. Instead of "Shadows of the Night," "We Belong" starts to play. I'd be irritated if it was any other song, but this one has invaded my head over the last week and there must be a reason. Mike looks at me and mouths "oops," giving me a self-deprecating smile. I give him an accepting nod and let it rip. I'm trying not to watch the team's table while I sing the lyrics off the screen. I know Rick isn't interested in that drama. I finish the song and there's cheering from the crowd, but I honestly don't even remember singing.

I walk back to the table slowly, watching the team interact and the swarm try to infiltrate. The women touching them and, for the most part, not being acknowledged. Just as I'm walking up to the table a woman walks up to Rick and puts her hand on his shoulder, smiling at him like she's offering him everything. I pick her hand up off of my man and stare at her directly in the eyes with a look that could kill, "He's taken, honey. Hands off."

"I don't see a ring." She says glibly and puts her hand back on Rick. Chase is watching, suspecting there could be blood. Why is he letting her touch him!

I turn to Rick for direction because I keep hearing Sam say not to embarrass him with the guys. "I'm so taken. I'm fuckin' addicted to you, my queen." Rick's eyes are heated and focused on me. He pulls me into his lap and I put my arms around his neck, ignoring the player chaser as he claims my mouth with his. I wanted to flip her the bird as she walked away, but my hands were busy in Rick's hair and that's more important. Rick moves to whisper in my ear, "How about we get rings to wear, so we can avoid this crap?"

I'm not sure what to think, but I don't want a ring that doesn't mean anything. I don't care if I ever get a ring, as long as I have him. I whisper in his ear, "I'm not after a ring, my king. Just you."

He whispers back to me quietly, "You have me. What if I want you to have a ring? A pretty one with diamonds that means I love you and I want to be with you for the rest of my life."

Tears are building at the thought and I'm struck with the reality of never wanting this until now. Never wanting to get married, but Rick makes me want things. What happened to keeping things the way they are and not talking about taking things further until the season is over? I kiss him passionately and speak breathlessly, "I'll never say no to you."

Rick stands and picks me up with him, throwing me over his shoulder. "Good game today, guys. Have a good night, gentlemen. I'm going to leave you now to handle some personal business." I wave as we leave and he carries me all the way back to the stadium parking garage. I can't wait to see this on the internet.

CHAPTER NINETEEN

I snuggle up to Rick for the drive home and he wakes me up taking me out of the car. I admit I'm tired and it's been a long day, following an emotional week. My head is spinning at a different speed than the world around me. I need to pack for away games, make sure work is caught up, and all kinds of other things, but all I can think about is the player chaser at the bar and a ring with diamonds that means he loves me. I'm tired. My brain isn't functioning. I nestle against Rick's strong chest and hold on with my arms around his neck, letting him carry me in. He kisses my forehead while we ride up on the elevator, "You're being quiet and that worries me. What's going on in there?"

"I didn't like that girl touching you."

"I know, you took her hand off of me and claimed me like a cavewoman." Rick chuckles.

"But, when she did it again then I didn't know what to do. I didn't want to overstep my boundaries, especially with the guys there."

"What did you want to do?" Rick unlocks the door, and takes us to the bedroom where we continue our conversation.

Tell her to get the fuck away from my man and knock her on her ass, oh wait, I can't say that. "I don't know. It made me possessive and I wondered why you were letting her touch you." Which is also true.

"Its like that a lot. I pretend they aren't there and they usually go away."

"Usually?"

"If I don't give them any attention they move on to another player. I'm only interested in you, my queen."

"What happened to keeping things the way they are until the season is over? Not making any relationship decisions."

"As soon as I suggested rings, I knew it came out wrong. I heard myself say it and thought 'what an asshole,' rings aren't to make chicks stay away. One special ring is for the one special woman in my life, because I love her and only her forever." Rick stops, "Don't worry about the team being there, just be you. It makes me happy you won't say no."

I grin at him and roll my eyes, feeling like a fool.

"It's late, come here my queen." He holds me and we fall asleep in each others' arms.

Early in the morning, Rick whispers in my ear, "Come here, baby. I need to have you." He pulls me up on top of him and pulls my panties off while he kisses me, needing me. I don't know where this comes from in the middle of the night, but I'll never get tired of it. It's hot, needy, and quick while we're half asleep. He holds me on top of him. I sleep there with my head resting on his chest, and his cock still inside me. I'm his home.

The alarm goes off and I smell the coffee brewing. I'm still lying on him. "Good morning, my king."

"I love you, my queen. I'm so happy you're going on the road with me. I hate empty hotel rooms and every hotel room without you in it is empty. I hug his chest as I appreciate his words and I don't want to get up, I want to stay right here.

CHAPTER TWENTY

I must've known my world was about to become a whirlwind. I should've stayed in bed longer. In fact, I should've stayed right there on my Rick's chest for as long as I could.

Suddenly, I find myself living the life of a professional baseball player. Well, that runs a travel business, too. From the moment I step foot out of the house on Sunday morning, the world only seems to stop when I'm *alone* with Rick. If we're home, I'm doing laundry, cleaning, baking (because I need cookies on the road), or at the game. If we're away, I'm working, trying to find time to explore, sleeping, or at the game. Either way, my nights and some of my mornings are spent with my man. My he-used-to-be-just-a-fantasy-baseball-boyfriend that turned out to be better than I could've ever imagined, real life, breathing, hot and sexy, we need each other more than air, professional athlete who worships me. I'm still not sure I deserve him, us.

The Seals have been playing well. The trade rumors have been hard, especially since the team kept Stray up a week longer than they needed to cover Seno. But, he didn't talk about it and we made it through the trade deadline without getting traded. In fact, the Seals have made it clear they intend to offer him a long-term contract, but that's something that'll get handled in the off-season.

I've made a point of making Rick get out to see the places we travel to for away games, even if it's only one thing and not always the tourist spot associated with the location.

In Seattle, we had a late night dinner at the top of the Space Needle. That's over 600 feet up in an elevator. I know, totally touristy, but the elevator sealed the deal and it had to happen. It was pitch black out and the lights across the city shone with a haze from the marine layer. On our free morning we explored Pike's Place Market, enjoying breakfast together with a beautiful view of the Puget Sound. Seattle's elevator action was unparalleled. We had a late night reservation and I made sure we'd have the elevator to ourselves for the ride up. We lost the series 2-1, but they didn't sweep us and Rick was a double hitting machine with two in each game. Unfortunately, none of his teammates were able to bring him around to score even once.

Chicago was crazy! We were on a pizza-testing mission. Every day we tried pizza from a different place, including Chicago style—which we agreed was good, but not what we want from pizza. Pizza shouldn't require a fork, there should be no cornmeal and the toppings are called toppings because they belong on top. The stadium there is in the middle of a neighborhood with no parking. It was interesting to see everybody come out of the woodwork, watch from their rooftops and fill the old stadium, maintaining traditions. We won the series, taking two of the three games. Cross was on point for the whole series, hitting two home runs and making a diving catch that had the internet world photoshopping a cape on his back like a superhero. Rick was a single shy of a cycle in game three, but we all agree that we'd much rather have the two homers he hit that pushed three of his teammates across home plate to score.

LA was hard. First, we got swept. Second, it resurrected bad memories. I could see and feel Rick watching me, almost waiting for me to leave him there. He took me back to the Hawaiian Themed restaurant in Malibu, this time he insisted we start with dessert. We spent all of our time at the hotel, and when I say he needed me, I mean I required help to stand at one point and nearly missed a game due to soreness. It was because we were in LA. Every insecurity we have was right there in front of us, taunting us, and we didn't say a word about it. There weren't many words between us at all, LA was more about not having anything between us. I'm not sure if I've ever felt how much he loves me like when we were in LA. I hate to say it, but Rick was distracted and it was reflected in his game. He didn't call the games with the same confident positivity. The whole team combined only got six hits total over the three games, scoring only once.

San Francisco was a fun trip. Rick got me a ticket in the friends and family section, so I was sitting with the wives. He didn't want me to be alone in the stands and he didn't want to worry about the Sissy's pulling crap like they did the last time they were in San Diego. The truth is, he didn't want Adam to know I was there. He was hiding me in the crowd. I understood, and knew he still thought about Adam touching me. He hates him, luckily he wasn't in the lineup. I don't know if he got sent back to the minors, or if he's still on the DL and it doesn't matter either way. He's not in the stadium and that's a good thing. The players' wives were mostly welcoming. I cheered louder and made sure Rick could hear me. I don't understand the friends and family box. They clap and occasionally call out, but there isn't much excitement or cheering really. I felt slightly judged for my decibel level, but continued anyway. I haven't heard any comments from their dugout and Rick keeps looking for me behind home plate even though he knows I'm not there. It's a habit at this point. We wandered the wharf one morning, checking out the sea life and taking in the scenery. I managed to find a chocolate shop where I bought my weight in high end flavored chocolates, and wandered a jewelry store that only had items from estates, so nothing new and trendy, only cool pieces and some one of a kinds. We took the series 2-1 and made the hitting slump a thing of the past with ten hits or more in each of the three games. The outfielders were really working for it and held it together until game three when the Sissy's took the win. Rick hit a grand slam in game two and a homer in game three, but it wasn't enough.

The freeway series against the Orange County Characters was only two games and was bookended by off days, so Rick indulged me and took me to Disneyland. Walking through the amusement park while holding hands with my guy, having his arms around me on the rides, buying silly hats and matching T-shirts that point at each other with a character's cartoon hand saying "I'm with her" and "I'm with him"—I was in heaven. We split the series, and the whirlwind continued.

The home games were refreshing. I missed my stadium. I missed our private penthouse. I missed my bed and my kitchen. None of it mattered or even came close to how important it was for me to be with him wherever he was playing. Not just for him, but for us.

CHAPTER TWENTY-ONE

I t's September and we're finally home for more than a week. I finally have time to get the laundry caught up, change the bed sheets, clean out the refrigerator, and catch up on some email I've been putting off. Mike with the Mic has emailed me numerous times for different things. He wants me to host karaoke at the Batter Up, so he can add another location to his list and still get a day off. He wants me to cover him, so he can go on vacation. He wants me to judge the qualifying round for the next competition. He wants me to lead eighth inning karaoke for the Seals. What? Hold on, I better read that one...

From: MikeMic

I got a special request from the San Diego Seals. Are you interested in going on field and leading eighth inning karaoke? They want to feature you because you won the contest and they'd like to do it this Saturday night. They said something about it being part of fan appreciation week. Let me know ASAP!

Mike with the Mic

I turn to Rick and show him the email. "That's cool! You should do it and invite your Mom. Show all your baseball peeps and your Mom how good you are."

I think about it for a few minutes. It's an opportunity to show my Mom my "singing thing" and a chance to sing on the field. It could lead to singing the National Anthem. That's it. I'm doing it! I send a message back to Mike.

To: MikeMic

I'm in. What song am I leading? Since I'll be on field, is my baseball jersey acceptable?

So cool!

Thank you,
Sherry

From: MikeMic

Baseball attire is preferred as long as it's Seals. They're going to let the fans vote on which song you sing, but will only give them choices from the songs you sang in the finals and semi-finals. I have already sent them a list of those songs. Will call has a ticket waiting for you.

Mike with the Mic

To: MikeMic

I already have a ticket to the game. I'm sitting behind home plate if you need to find me.

Sherry

I check the schedule and the game starts at 5:40 on Saturday. Today is an off day and it's nice to have a day at home *alone* together. Rick turns on the music and his arms are around me instantly. He's holding me close and we're dancing to "Thinking Out Loud." There is nowhere I'd rather be and nothing else matters, it can all wait. Twenty minutes later we're still dancing and he has the song on repeat. We aren't talking. We aren't kissing. He's holding me close while we move together. He pulls back and gazes into my eyes. I don't know what he sees, but it makes him happy and I feel a change in his body. No words pass between us. He turns the volume up loud, picks me up, and takes me to bed in the middle of the afternoon. He's different this afternoon, its good different and I didn't think that was possible. I mean, how could he possibly get better? We lie on the bed together and he starts to kiss me tenderly. He rolls me underneath him and kisses my neck. He cups my head, holding me where he wants to kiss me and slowly pushes into me, burying himself a little at a time. He feels amazing.

He gazes into my eyes as he strokes into me deeply and deliberately. "Do you know how much I love you, my queen?" He already has me rendered speechless with his movements. "I love you more than anyone else in the world. I truly would do anything for you. I want to make you happy and I want to make your life easy. I want to be with you every minute of every day. I want to give you everything. I can't imagine my life without you in it, and I don't want to." Still moving at a steady, even pace, and driving me out of my mind. "When I look at you, I see forever."

I whimper as tears roll down my face and I'm unable to put

words together. I pull his face to mine, so I can kiss him because it's the only way I can respond to his words right now. I rub his head and play with his hair lovingly. I do my best to convey my feelings for him without words and he gets it. His heart is pounding and it's not from exertion, since he continues his slow deliberate pace. The friction building is driving me out of my mind. Our connection is strong and growing as we become more familiar. It's only been a few months, but it feels like it's always been us together, somehow, and the world would end if we were torn apart. Well, the world might not end, but my world would end. When he loves me its special, I feel it in every bone and in every muscle. I wrap my legs around him, encouraging him for more. He strokes just a little harder and a little faster, but I suddenly feel like I've been hit by a truck, slammed into a brick wall. My body tenses up and he comes hard, "I love you, baby. Always you, Sherry." He holds me tight against him. "Are you okay?" Concern in his voice as he goes back to his slow, steady strokes. I can't answer him. He kisses me and reaches to play with my magic button. I simply keep eye contact with him and when he sends me over the edge I cry out his name in ecstasy. His eyes lock on mine, reading me and seeing it's more than usual. He stops moving and lays down next to me, pulling me back to him so he can hold me and comfort me. "I've got you, my queen. I'll never let you go."

CHAPTER TWENTY-TWO

I t's Thursday and it's an off day, which usually means date night. But, it's already late in the afternoon and Rick hasn't said a word. "Since we're home, how about I make dinner for you tonight?"

"I was thinking it should be date night, but I just want to stay home and have a romantic evening with you." I totally get it. All of the travel during the season wears on you and I only did it for half of the season. I've never heard him say the word romantic, I'm intrigued.

"Romantic, huh?" I giggle.

"Yep. I'm going to romance your socks off you."

I look at my feet, "I'm already barefoot." The words come out and I immediately hear "and pregnant" in my head, which I'm not. I see his grin and know he's thinking we can practice for the "and pregnant" part.

His bright blue eyes soften. He reaches for my hand, bringing it to his lips and he kisses every knuckle of every finger. Tenderly spending time with each one. "You're beautiful, inside and out. Nobody has ever made me feel as loved as you do. I know you love me completely." He leans his forehead to mine while he holds my hands in his, "I hope I'm worthy of you. I hope you feel how much I love you. I promise I'll always love you and I'll never hurt you." His voice goes raspy. "I promise to give you everything you want. You're my happiness. You're my forever." I lean into his chest and he holds me as I absorb his words.

Rick wraps his arms around me and holds me tightly to his chest, "I know we said no relationship stuff until after the season is over, but the season is almost over and you're in my head." He kisses the top of my head and regroups before he continues. "I'll be the happiest man alive whenever it happens and I only want it with you." He stops again, taking a deep breath, "But, I don't want to try to make it happen yet. I want you all to myself longer, maybe another season." I feel his heart beat while he's talking.

"I'm not rushing you. You tell me when, my king." A lone girlie tear falls and I'm afraid I'm going to start bawling. I worry that maybe I'm too old for him, but try to hide the thought away. "I just want you to know I'm willing. Anything for you." Rick tries to pull back, but I don't let him. I don't want him to see the crazy girl that's trying to come out. He cups my head, running his fingers through my hair and holds me there in silence.

"I changed my mind, let's get out of the house for a bit."

"Okay. I need to get ready." I probably have a tear stained face, the shorts I'm wearing have a hole in them, and I never got anything on my top half beyond the bikini top I'm wearing.

"No, you're fine." He pulls a T-shirt on and scoops me up off the love seat, carrying me out the door. I giggle uncontrollably. "That's what I want to hear. Happy woman."

We get in his car and he drives us toward the beach, parking near dog beach and, my favorite, lifeguard stand five. He takes my hand and we walk out onto the sand. It's almost sunset and the tide is higher than normal. The wind is blowing at the tips of the waves, sending misty breezes toward the shore. Rick sits down at the top of the berm and pulls me down with him. He puts his right arm around me and I lean into him. He pulls me into his lap and we sit together watching the sunset as the waves crash and sizzle. The sky is mostly clear, the few clouds in the far off distance turning dark purple as the sun lowers. The sun blankets the sky with golden yellow hues and surfers turn to dark silhouettes on the horizon. My happy place, sitting in his lap with my back to him and his warm breath at my neck, watching the sunset. I melt into him and he kisses my cheek, "I love you, my queen." The sun disappears, the golden sky turns rusty, and the breeze turns colder. Rick stands and pulls me up with him leading me back to his car.

Rick looks at his phone, "The guys are at the Locale playing pool. Do you want to go?"

"No. But, you should. You need some time with the team. I have some baking I want to do and I'll be home when you get there." I smile at him.

"Are you sure?"

"Yes, you can continue the romance when you get home." He drives over to the Locale and parks in the lot.

He takes my face in his hands and kisses me, sliding his tongue across my lips before claiming me completely. It's one of his don't-forget-me-kisses and so much more. I slide behind the wheel as he takes off across the parking lot. I pick up take out from the deli at my favorite Mexican Food place on my way home and consider my baking options.

Text from Rick - Cross wants to know what you're baking.

Text to Rick - I haven't started yet. Picked up tamales for later on my way home.

Text to Rick - Do you or Chase have any baking requests?

Text from Rick - Cross wants you to save some for him and
says he likes it when it's still warm.

Of course he does.

Text to Rick - What about you?

Text from Rick - I'm a fan of cake and whipped cream.

My body reacts to his response, low in my belly and I'm
going to make a cake. I need to check the whipped cream
supply.

Text to Rick - I have a couple 12 packs hiding in the
cupboard if you want to bring the guys by. I'll bake up some
good stuff, save the cake for us later. ;)

Text from Rick - Chill the beer just in case. You're perfect.

First thing, I put the beer into chill. I look through my pantry
trying to decide what I want to make and I decide on PB&J
Thumbprints, butter cookies, brownies and, of course, cake. I mix
up a batch of my butter cookie dough and a batch of my peanut
butter cookie dough, putting them both in the refrigerator to chill.
I turn on the oven to get it preheating and mix up some brownie
batter, adding chopped walnuts and toffee bits. I butter my
brownie pan, pour the brownie batter into it and slide it straight
into the oven. I clean up the kitchen and get a bowl for my cake
batter, but I can't decide what flavor I want to make. I pull the
butter cookie dough from the refrigerator, portion out the dough
onto two cookie sheets, and put them in the oven. I get the peanut
butter cookie dough and portion them out evenly over two cookie
sheets. I press my thumb into the middle of each one and pull the

brownies out of the oven, replacing them with the peanut butter thumbprints.

Text to Rick - What kind of cake would you like? I made brownies with walnuts and toffee bits, I have my PB&J Thumbprints baking and butter cookies are about to come out and get dipped.

It takes a few minutes for him to answer, but I finally get a response.

Text from Rick - Be creative. I like it when you make stuff up.

Text from Rick - Now Cross is rushing us because the brownies are warm.

Text from Cross - Seno hit me because I want brownies and they're warm

Text to Cross - They'll be warm for awhile. The cookies aren't done yet. Play another game of pool.

Text from Rick - Is Cross texting you?

Text to Rick - Yes. Lol.

Text from Rick - Looks like the guys are going to come home with me. Since Cross can't shut up about brownies now.

Text to Rick - He's such a sweet kid.

Text from Rick - You really don't need to talk to him.

Text to Rick - Gotta go, baking!

I pull the butter cookies from the oven and let them cool. I search my kitchen for something creative to do with cake. I see the leftover coffee from this morning, s'mores flavored instant pudding mix, and marshmallow fluff. Coffee makes everything better, especially chocolate. I pull the peanut butter cookies out to cool and move the butter cookies to the cooling rack. I mix up my cake batter starting with a box of yellow cake mix and start adding things to make it delicious. I replace the water with my leftover coffee and add the instant pudding mix. I add about a cup of milk and debate with myself about adding the marshmallow fluff in place of the eggs or dropping spoonfuls on top, so they get toasted like at a campfire and go with toasty. I add eggs and stir it up, adding some melted butter instead of the oil and more milk until I get to the right batter consistency. Baking is a science, but it's never been a problem for me to doctor stuff up and make it better. I taste the batter and now I can't decide if I want to cover it with mini marshmallows instead of pools of fluff. Sometimes it's hard to be me, but when baking decisions are the hardest thing you deal with—I guess I shouldn't complain. I can swirl the fluff through the cake. I can mix the marshmallows into the cake. That's it, I add mini marshmallows to my cake batter and pour the batter into my buttered cake pan. Then I drop spoonfuls of marshmallow fluff all over the cake and kind of swirl it through, which doesn't work very well and I go with it anyway. I slide the cake into the oven and cross my fingers. I melt some chocolate and chop up some pecans, and proceed to dip my butter cookies using the chocolate as the glue for the pecans. I get the grape jam from the cupboard and put a few big spoonfuls into a small bowl with a small amount of water and microwave it, stirring it repeatedly until it's the consistency I'm looking for. I move the peanut butter cookies to the cooling tray and fill my thumbprint with the grape jam mix. Both cookies are done. Brownies are done. Cake is baking. Not bad for a couple of hours. I clean up the rest of my mess, making sure I lick all of the utensils and don't let any batter go to waste. Just as I'm licking the batter off the last spatula, I hear the door open and throw the spatula into the sink quickly.

"It smells amazing in here. Where are the brownies?" I hear Chase before anybody else.

"Dude, chill." I know Rick is shaking his head at the rookie even though I can't see him. Rick calls out to me, "I'm home and the guys are with me. I walk out of the kitchen and Rick grins at me as he walks toward me. I prepare to be attacked with the team standing right there, but Rick simply laughs and licks my nose. "That's chocolate with something?"

I turn red and wonder where else I have batter on me. "That's your cake. You'll have to wait and see."

"Are you toasting marshmallows?" Chase, of course.

"Kind of, its Rick's cake." I say trying not to give away what I'm making because it's for me and Rick, it goes with the whipped cream. "My king, you want to get the guys drinks while I plate up some sweets?"

Rick walks past me in the kitchen, making sure to rub against me on his way by and kiss me on the neck. I cut up the brownies and stack them pyramid-like on a plate. I make a plate of PB&J Thumbprints and a plate of chocolate dipped butter cookies. "Chase sweetie, will you help me?" Before I finished talking he was there at my side, eyes wide. "Will you get the two plates of cookies, please?" He picks them up and follows me out to the guys in my living room.

For the record, I'm getting used to being around the team. However, when I step foot into my living room and my leading man along with Chase, Jones, Kris, Rhett, Tommy and Lucky have all made themselves at home—stretched out all over the furniture and the floor, basically filling my living room while they talk about what movie to put on or if they should play video games—I about lose it. It's too much for a fan to take. I knew Rick was bringing the guys back with him, but seven professional baseball players in my living room sets the testosterone levels in here to emergency overload.

I walk directly to my Rick and announce what I've baked, "Okay, so these are PB&J's, these are dipped butter cookies, and these are walnut and toffee brownies. Let me know what you think, so I know which ones to make for you again," I say as I look into Rick's clear blue eyes.

"Sure thing," Chase chimes in.

I laugh, "That's fine, but I was mostly talking to Rick. My man gets what he wants." I realize how it sounds after it comes out of my mouth, but decide it's true and I don't care who knows it.

"You got it, baby." Rick smiles at me and I leave them alone to their guy things.

The plates get passed around and they've come looking for more beer. Well, except Chase, and he wanted milk. Once I have a chance to absorb it, I like having them all around. The team is family. Rick is home and hanging out with the guys. I can hang with them or do my own thing, and they like my baking. Rick finds me periodically, to kiss me or touch me or whisper in my ear. I know he's buzzed, but the promises he whispers in my ear— well, fuck me. I discreetly take a picture of my living room and another of Kris, texting both of them to Sam.

Text to Sam - So, this is my living room tonight.

Text from Sam - OMG! Are you handling that okay?

Text to Sam - Yes. I like it. I freaked out a bit internally when I first saw them all, but I got over it. I'm good now.

Text from Sam - Tell Kris hi for me.

At about midnight, a couple of the guys had left and I find Rick kicking the rest out, "Game is at 7:05 tomorrow night. Go get your rest and be ready."

I heard varying responses.

"Whatever. You just want to get laid."

"Okay. Porn king."

"Can I have another brownie to go?"

"Make sure you treat that girl right."

"Thanks for the beer."

Sudden silence followed by the sound of the door latch locking, romantic music starting to play, and Rick's hands on my hips. His body against my back and rocking against me.

"Do you want to try the cake and whipped cream?"

"Will it still be good after the game tomorrow?

"Yes."

"Then, I'd rather have you right now," Rick says as he picks me up and carries me off to the bedroom. I wrap my legs around his waist and my arms around his neck. "I feel like I've been away for days and I was only out playing pool for a couple of hours." Rick strips me naked quickly and makes himself comfortable between my legs putting his mouth on me. Licking and sucking at my tender folds and clit, he slides a finger in and strokes me.

"I want all of you, my king. I want you inside me. Please make love to me, Rick." His whole tone changes and he loses his clothes. He pushes into me and grinds against me. He pulls out and strokes in with purpose, repeatedly until he comes. He slows and claims my mouth with his, sucking on my lower lip. He holds me to him while he kisses me and goes back to stroking into me with intent repeatedly until he comes again on a growl. He keeps going, pounding into me harder now. Wanting more. I lift my legs for him, trying to give him better access and he catches them with his arms, bringing my feet to my ears and spreading me open for his pleasure. He buries himself as deep as he can get and leans in to kiss me while he grinds against me. His grinding action rubs against my sensitive nub and I want more. I grind back and squeeze him, feeling how deep he is. I rock my hips and he growls as he slams into me once, and again and again and again and again until we both crash together and fall asleep in each others' arms, unable to recover.

CHAPTER TWENTY-THREE

Friday morning I wake up before the alarm and before the coffee. Rick is wrapped around me and has his hard length snugly between my thighs. "Are you awake, my queen? You were saying sweet things to me and suddenly stopped."

"I don't know. What did I say?" I respond sleepily on a yawn.

I feel him smile, "You told me how amazing I was last night and then you woke up." Sounds right. I probably said more than that and he isn't telling me. I'm beginning to wonder if there's more to why he doesn't tell me, but I guess it doesn't matter. We have no secrets and the personal things between us are out there. There's nothing to hide.

"That's true. I think you had different things running through your head last night." Rick rolls me over to face him and I feel his gaze on my face.

"Maybe I did."

"Do you want to talk about it?"

"We already did."

I wonder if I was awake for that conversation because I'm obviously not going to get any clues.

"Let's walk over to the Yolk for an early breakfast. Cross is going to pick me up early to go work out." He kisses me on each eyelid and then my lips. I can't argue with that.

It's a beautiful San Diego morning with no marine layer hindering the sun's rays and I love the warmth on my skin as we walk to breakfast. Rick holds my hand, rubbing his thumb on my hand and across my fingers while we walk the four blocks to the Yolk. I love to walk with him at my side, when he holds my hand he makes me feel like his queen.

He leads me into the Yolk and they immediately seat us in a back corner booth where he slides in next to me and puts his arm around me. The waitress doesn't even ask if we want coffee anymore, she just brings it and knows I like the flavored creamers. We sit together happily and enjoy breakfast while we pick at each other's plates. We laugh as he steals the chicken from my waffles and I eat most of his hash browns. He always has his arm around me or his hand on my thigh. I love how he's always touching me. I love the way he looks at me and I find him watching me lick the maple syrup off of my fingers. He takes my hand and sucks on my fingers, licking off the sweet syrup with his blue eyes focused on me, watching me as he's driving me crazy. I reach for his leg under the table and somehow end up with my hand around him inside his shorts. I have no idea how that could've happened.

Rick looks down and then back at me. "I thought you wanted breakfast."

"Turn about is fair play, finger sucker." Oops, where did that come from? I know better. It's a game day. I review our surroundings. We are facing the wall and nobody has a line of sight to under our table unless the waitress wanders by. I stroke him a few times. He stiffens in more ways than one. I'm being bad, but I can't help myself.

"You know it's a game day and we're sitting in a restaurant we like to go to?"

"Yes."

"You know you'll have me walking home with a raging hard-on?"

Playing innocent, "Oh, I'm sorry. Let me out so I can go wash my hands, they're all sticky. Your hands might be sticky, too. Do you need to wash up?" He slides out of the booth and I get up, glancing back at him as I walk to the bathroom swaying my hips at him.

I walk into the bathroom and look in the mirror to see I'm red, warm to the touch and my breathing is irregular with hope he'll come find me. If I stay in here long enough, he'll have to. I turn on the water to wash my hands and hear the door open, close, and lock. I see Rick's reflection in the mirror and his eyes meet mine. He walks up behind me, unties the back of my halter top freeing my breasts and slowly pours warm maple syrup all over my breasts and nipples as I watch in the mirror. He turns me and lifts me up, setting me on the edge of the counter. He pushes my short skirt up and groans in pleasure as he finds me going commando, shoving into me hard as he licks and sucks at my breasts. His mouth and tongue all over me, cleaning up the maple syrup. No words. He sucks at my nipples while he fucks me and the combination makes me want to scream out. He can feel where I'm at and claims my mouth with his to quiet me while he strokes into me as deep as he can with every pass. I shake and shudder without warning as Rick slams into me, filling me completely with his rock hard cock. I pull him with me and he pushes us through, while he kisses me roughly. He smiles at me with a dirty glint, ties the back of my halter top, pulls his shorts up, washes his hands, puts my feet back on the ground, and leaves the bathroom.

Still no words. I turn back to the mirror and see the red blotches all over my chest and neck. There's no other way to say it, I look thoroughly fucked.

I do my best to quickly put myself back together and go back to the table, where Rick lets me slide into the booth to finish breakfast nonchalantly.

"You okay, my queen? You were gone for awhile." Like he doesn't know what he did.

"I'm better than okay. I'm energized for the day."

"Why is that?" He asks smugly.

I'm still feeling playful, "The hand soap scent in the bathroom is invigorating."

"Is that all?"

I lean in and kiss him, refusing to comment.

CHAPTER TWENTY-FOUR

We walk home quickly and Cross is already there waiting for Rick to go work out. I bribe him with brownies, so Rick has a few minutes to clean up.

Rick gives me a kiss on his way out the door and grins at me, unsure of the situations we can get into. "Are you going to be early for batting practice?"

"Yes, sir!"

"I'll look forward to your scouting report. Love you, my queen." He walks out the door with Chase in tow and looking at Rick like he's lost his marbles.

I'm home alone and I have hours before I need to be anywhere. This is an uncommon occurrence in my life of a professional baseball player. I have tons to do. Work to get done. Groceries to shop for. Cleaning to put off. Since I'm making bad decisions today, I run with it. I open all the windows to let the breeze and the sunshine in. I turn my music on random shuffle and kick up the volume, ready to dance around or do nothing or whatever I want. Except for one problem. I don't want to be alone, unless it's me and Rick alone.

Dancing around isn't fun without him holding me close and randomly twirling me around or dipping me. Nothing is great, when he's with me. What I want is to be with Rick. I switch gears and work as quickly as I can to get everything done, so I have more time to be with him. I shower using my good scrub and the conditioner that makes my hair shine. I make sure I smell fabulous and look radiant. I take the time to blow dry and curl my hair. I even put on mascara and lip gloss. I'm getting ready to go to the game, so I take a hair tie just in case and pull on my skinny jeans with my Seno V-neck T-shirt. I shove my cap and jersey into my bag and grab my hoodie on the way out the door.

I hop into Rick's Challenger to drive to the stadium. Guys are usually protective of their cars. Their cars are their babies and they don't let their girl drive them even if the car is crappy, or maybe because the car is crappy and I'm missing the point. Rick didn't even flinch. In fact, he told me to drive and handed me the keys to his custom car with the extra power built in under the hood and the 6-speed stick-shift. He doesn't worry about his car. He wants me riding home with him and he doesn't want me on the trolley. The car doesn't matter, I do.

I pull into the player's garage with a wave from the parking attendant and find a seat to watch batting practice.

Text to Rick - Just letting you know I'm here for BP :)

Text from Rick - :)

Carter steps out of the dugout and sees me sitting in the stands. He looks at me twice and then comes up to see me. "You look gorgeous today and I mean more than usual, you're always pretty. I had to take a second look to make sure it was you." My extra effort is going to be noticed!

"Thank you. It's nice to be home and have some time to relax."

"You're here early."

"It's becoming a habit. Rick likes me here for BP and I don't always manage BP at the away games, its easier here. Let me know if I'm in the way. I don't want to be a problem."

"No, you're fine. It makes him happy and the guys get a kick out of their tough as iron catcher being crazy over a beautiful blonde that yells at the game, bakes, sings, and from what I hear—knows her baseball. We expected to see you more when he came in and told me to get you set up with your access card. The guys don't do that if the girl's a gold digger or baseball skank, well unless they're whipped. No offense. We all know that's not you. Especially, Seno. I was surprised when he came in to request an access card for a woman."

I smile, unexpectedly flattered. "I have a pretty good understanding of the game."

"Well, you keep up the good work. Those cookies were great, by the way. I liked your proposal and I passed it on to my supervisor, but I suspect it's sitting somewhere and won't be discussed until they start talking about plans for next season." He smiles as he turns and makes his way back to the field.

I look out to see the field had been set up for batting practice while we were chatting and the team has started to make their way out to the field. My Rick comes out with a bat in his hand. I yell out, "Looking good, baby!" Cross, Martin, and Bravo all turn to look at me and start to move in my direction. They don't wave or yell hi back. No, they don't recognize me? Do I look that shitty when I come to the game or what? I edit my shout out, "Looking good, Seno!" Seno looks at me and smiles, as he notices the other three turning back away.

Rick runs up to me, "You're fucking beautiful. Glowing. Are you sure you're mine?"

"Only yours, my king." I smile uncontrollably.

"You cleaned up all nice like this for me?"

"You're the only reason I want to look good. Part of it could be the maple syrup." I giggle like a teenager and he kisses me before he runs back to the field. "Knock it out, Seno!"

I watch the guys as they wander the field, hang out around the backstop and hit, with my eyes on irregularities. I find myself concentrating on my Rick, not because he's doing anything odd. Something about the way he holds himself on the field, I can't help myself. It's always been that way for me. It's why he was my fantasy. Bravo is still favoring his hip. Mason might be limping. Rock keeps rubbing his right arm. These things are to be expected as we get close to the end of the season. 162 games is a long time to stay healthy. The roster was recently expanded and some of the minor leaguers have been invited up to the big league club. I don't know who they are yet, but I see them waiting for their turn to hit. The newbs are rambunctious, but I guess it's to be expected. Every time my Rick connects to the ball it's out of the park and I cheer him on every time, reminding him that he's the king—or at least my king.

Text from Rick - Scouting Report?

Text to Rick - Bravo is still favoring his hip, Mason looks like he might be limping, Rock's right arm is bugging him.

Text to Rick - The newbs are a little out of control. They need to be knocked down a notch or they're going to hurt someone.

Text from Rick - Interesting

Text from Rick - Has anyone ever told you that you're the most beautiful baseball scout of all time?

Text to Rick - Stop!

Text from Rick - Well, if anyone told you that they were wrong.

What? Where is he going with this?

Text from Rick - You're the most beautiful woman anywhere. <3

Huh, my extra effort really was noticed. That makes it all worth it. Since I can't help myself...

Text to Rick - You're biased because I have sex with you and cook for you.

Text from Rick - I can only tell you what I see from my eyes and my heart. Anybody that doesn't agree is blind and stupid. Cross, Martin and Bravo were going to hit on you and didn't even recognize you today. You're in demand, my queen.

Text to Rick - Exactly... Your queen.

Text to Rick - Go get ready for the game. I'll send you the visiting scout report after their BP.

Text from Rick - I love you... My queen.

I check the lineup and we're playing Colorado this weekend.

They have some of the new guys brought up for their expanded roster on the lineup tonight, including a first time starting pitcher, a second baseman, and two outfielders all making their debut. I wonder if it's because they need to give their everyday guys a break due to soreness and injury, because that's not a bad idea when you're not in the running for postseason anyway.

I watch Colorado's batting practice and about halfway through a couple of their players are looking at me. I sink down into my seat, hoping they'll ignore me. "Hey sweetheart! Are you a baseball fan?"

I ignore them, seeing a flashback of Rick getting hit by a pitch and dislocating the jaw of the Sissy's first baseman, Adam.

"This is my first time in San Diego. Do you think you could give me a personal tour? I'll give you a tour of the visitor's clubhouse and a night you'll never forget." The veteran player high-fives the rookie for going for it.

Anything I say, can and will be used against me. I know this. I learned this the hard way. I need to keep ignoring them. Or, I could play a game with him and his game will go to shit. No, don't do it. Rick will get pissed. Observe and keep your mouth shut.

Text to Rick - I learned to keep my mouth shut, but I need to cheer for the whole team equally tonight or these guys will target you like the Sissy's. Keep your eye on 15 at third base and 77 in the outfield. The veteran was pushing the rookie to go for it and they're paying close attention to me, yelling at me from the field. Maybe I should sit in my old seat for this series?

Text to Rick - Also their centerfielder is limping, they have four players debuting tonight, starting pitcher, second base and corner outfielders. Outfield is probably weak, center-fielder won't be able to help cover as much territory.

Text from Rick - Good intel. I trust your judgment, but I'd rather have you behind home plate and cheering louder for me. Give me a minute.

A few minutes later Carter sits down next to me. "I happen to have the seat next to you for the game tonight. Mind if I hang out with you for the game?"

Sure you do. "Wow! Really? How long have you had it?" I look at him and he knows I'm not stupid.

"It's my solution to keep Seno happy and everybody off the DL. I'll handle any potential disasters and you can cheer the way you want. I'll call them out if they pull anything."

"I'm too much trouble for you, Carter."

"I never get to watch the game from the stands and most likely you've heard all you're going to hear about it."

"So, basically you're my babysitter?"

"No, let's say personal security."

"No, thank you. I don't need a keeper."

Text to Rick - Seriously? You sent Carter to watch me? I don't need a keeper.

Text to Rick - How about I do what I did last time and you manage your temper? I can handle myself.

Text to Rick - Damn it! I didn't get hurt last time... You did and I don't want you hurt again. I don't want you to get hurt worse or...

I'm about to lose it when I have an idea. "Carter, when you magically got the seat next to me, how many seats next to me were available?"

Text from Rick - My first instinct is to protect you, baby. Don't be mad.

"Four or five."
"Can you get them all for me? And include yours?"
"Absolutely."
"Thanks. Then I have this handled." It is Friday night after all and all my girls are here.

Text to Rick - Don't worry. Found my own solution. I will be behind home plate cheering for you and it will be more than normal. Hope you like it!

Text to Rick - I may have added some seats to your account for tonight. Hope you don't mind.

I run up to the member's lounge and catch all my girls in line for beer. I tell them about the problem and how I need help, so I'm not singled out causing a problem for Seno on the field. I don't want him on the DL or suspended again. We all leave the member's lounge with two beers each and head down to the seats behind home plate. We haven't talked in so long, it's a nice departure from watching the game and cheering by myself. I catch them all up on traveling to the away games and of course that Seno now lives with me and I show them my access card. They all tell me how good I look and that the changes are definitely agreeing with me. It's great having Meli, Dina, Sandy's wife Shan and a couple of the part-timer's, Jenn and Rona hanging together and cheering as a team. Carter checked on us to make sure we got seated and brought down bags of peanuts, buckets of popcorn and some hot dogs.

Rick was already out in the bullpen warming up our starting pitcher, Grace the Ace, by the time we got to or seats. I hope I didn't screw up his game. The girls and I make a plan, so we will all yell and clap together. The beer may be making it more fun than it really is, but what the hell! Why not have fun at the game?

Rick walks across the field from the bullpen with Corey and looks straight at me. He gets a weird expression on his face and walks all the way to the net in front of me without stopping. "Do I want to know?" Rick asks unsure.

"Probably not. There are six of me tonight." I smile at him and I'm already buzzed.

"It's hard enough to handle one of you, my queen. And, you're all buzzing already. This is going to be a fun game."

"Hey, whatever you do, you have to do for all of us or to all of us, or this plan won't work. So, if you want to kiss me through the net, make it on the cheek and be prepared to kiss each of us on the cheek. Get it?"

"I love you, all." Rick shakes his head, turns and walks away.

We all yell in unison, "Make it a win!"

Rick turns back and looks at us, unable to keep the smile off his face.

Jenn and Rona hadn't met my Rick before, "He's really cute up close," Rona drools.

"You should check out Chase Cross. Total sweetheart, better age for you, available, and easily controlled by baked goods." I suggest as I look at her and think they'd make a cute couple.

"You mean the centerfielder?" Rona confirms.

"Yes."

No action in the top of the first inning. Chase is leading off for the Seals and walks into the on deck circle, swinging his bat with time to spare. "Chase!"

Chase looks up and walks over to the net, "How are you today my lovey? And, who are all these women?"

I smile, "There are six of me today, just avoiding a problem with the visiting team." I run through everybody introducing Chase and then I get to Rona, "And this is Rona, she gets my stamp of approval. Get it?" she smiles with a shy expression on her face.

"I get it. Do you bake, too?" Chase asks Rona. She nods and Chase gets to work.

"I don't know why I nodded. The only baking I've done is pre-made cookie dough." Rona laughs.

"I can teach you if you end up needing to learn." I laugh mostly because I probably don't need more beer, but also at the young girl that went flush talking to Chase. Kids!

We all cheer for Chase together and for Martin and of course louder for my Rick. But the game is pretty tame until the beginning of the third inning when 77 comes out on deck ready to lead off the inning and walks up to the net.

"So, do you ignore all the players or just me? Give me a chance and go out with me tonight. I promise you won't regret it."

In unison, "Sorry, you're on the wrong team. Bye-bye!" Loudly and of course Rick heard it. He hangs his head and laughs.

The game picked up after that. We may have relieved Rick of his worry so he could focus on the game. Carter shows up during the next inning with a dozen beers and he has apparently been enjoying the show.

No score and it's the top of the fifth, 15 is leading off for Colorado and walks over to us at the net, "Why are you ladies stuck on the Seals?"

In unison, "Colorado sucks!"

"You should let me show you how good I am at sucking. You'll never forget me and you'll want me again."

225

In unison, "Fuck off, asshole!" 15 walks up to the plate and we plot against him. As soon as he's ready to hit, we chant, "Suck, suck, suck, suck!" and laugh uncontrollably. 15 strikes out looking and Rick looks back at us giving us a thumbs up. I love that my girls are able to see what games with Rick are like for me, well sort of.

Bottom of the sixth inning, still no score. One out, Martin on second and a newb running for Mason at third base. My Rick is swinging his bat in the on deck circle and making faces at us because we're loud obnoxious drunks. As he walks up to the plate, "We love you, Rick! Knock it out, baby!" In slightly slurred unison. And he does just that on the first pitch. We all jump up and scream different, finally coming together with, "That's my man! Go Seno!" The newb scores with Martin on his heels. Rick comes around and focuses on me as he's ready to step on the plate, but plays along blowing all of us kisses as he scores. It's perfect, all of us flailing about like teenage girls and fanning each other. It was the highlight of the game, final score 3-0 Seals.

Hannah grabs Rick for her post-game interview, but he insists she talk with the newbs first. She interviews each of the newbs while Rick comes over to the net, "Thank you, ladies. I appreciate you all for going along with Sherry tonight. Sherry, are you ready to go home or are you going out with these wonderful ladies?"

I do a quick census, "We're all pretty much done. We drank enough. Good game, baby." I laugh and eat some more popcorn.

"I'll meet you at the car in about twenty." He leans in and kisses me on the cheek, and then he did the same for each of my baseball girls, winking at me as he goes to Hannah for his interview.

"All 3 runs tonight came from your bat. You've been hitting well as of late. Are you doing anything different?" Hannah questions.

"The bat feels really good when I'm swinging. I'm not doing

anything different. I always put my all into the game." I like seeing him on the big screen.

"You've had your own personal cheering section behind home plate for a few months now. I think we're all aware of that. Tonight that seemed to grow. Have you been recruiting fans?"

Rick smiles and laughs under his breath, "That was all my personal cheering section. She's my only."

Hannah hangs her head to the side as if she's saying how sweet, "I heard a rumor she'll be on the field tomorrow night. Do you know anything about that?"

Rick looks at me and I nod, "Yes, she'll be leading eighth inning karaoke tomorrow night from the field. Not my doing. That's all her and her winning the Batter Up karaoke competition. She's great, everybody is going to love her." Rick smiles proudly.

My girls are still here and I hadn't told them about that. They're all excited for me and going to try to come to the game. I thank my ladies and say my goodbyes, taking a bucket of popcorn with me to Rick's car as I try to dry up my stomach.

Rick finds me sleeping on his front seat, "Again?" He shakes his head and slides into the car.

I sit up and snuggle up against him for the ride home. "It was a special party night. You have to admit my plan worked."

"What about tomorrow and Sunday?"

"Those guys have already forgotten about it and I'll try not to look so good, so they aren't interested." Rick laughs and puts his arm around me for the drive home.

We get home and Rick holds my hand as we walk into the building and get in the elevator. As the elevator doors close, he presses me up against the wall and claims my mouth while he rocks against me, causing me to rock my hips and a low groan to escape him. His hands on my hips, he nibbles at my neck, ear, and collarbone until the doors open.

I sit down on the bed to change, before I get the cake and whipped cream—and fall asleep.

After midnight, "Cake and whipped cream is no fun without, my queen. I did taste the cake and it reminds me of a campfire. Does it somehow have s'mores and coffee?" Rick's warm breath in my ear has me half awake.

"What, baby? Do you need something?" I turn to him and touch whatever part of him I can reach.

"I need you, my queen. I need you to feed me cake and whipped cream. I need to cover you in whipped cream and lick it all off. I need you wrapped around me, so I can be whole." His voice low and raspy.

I sit up and Rick sits behind me, holding me. He has the cake and whipped cream with him. He gives me a piece of the cake and fills my mouth with whipped cream so he can take it from me. The cake is delicious, but right now it's in the way. I put the cake pan on the floor, take the few remaining pieces of clothes I have on off and look at Rick, already naked and I didn't even notice. I cover his cock in whipped cream and enjoy my dirty dessert. Rick spreads my legs and covers me in whipped cream, the cold sensation intensifies with the heat of his mouth on me. We kiss, suck, and lick each other clean while we drive each other toward orgasm. Rick is close and I work him with my tongue and lips, I want to make him come for me. I want to taste him in my mouth and feel how hard he comes. "Sherry, please. I need in you. I only come in you."

"Whatever you want, my king." How do you deny a request like that? I climb on top of him and slide onto his hard cock drawing a shiver from Rick. "Is this what you want, my king?"

"Yes, my queen. Always need to be in you. Tell me you'll always be here for me."

"I belong to you. It will always be us, my love. I promise I'll never leave." He gets harder and I grind against him. I lean forward and kiss him on the lips softly, sucking on his lower lip. His hands on my hips guide me to what he wants and he takes control, wrapping his arms around me and rolling me underneath him.

"I need you, Sherry." He strokes in and out, needing me desperately even though we're one.

"I'm here, baby. I'm right here." I run my fingers through his hair and pull his lips to mine. "I love you, Rick." I lick his lips and slide my tongue into his mouth to dance with his. I suck on his tongue and he moves faster. "You're so hard right now, you feel amazing. Come hard for me, baby. It's okay." He needs to be loved and taken care of. I don't know why. It's the first time he's shown any insecurity about us in weeks. I hold him tight and whisper in his ear, "You're my forever. Nobody compares to you. I want to give you everything. Nobody makes me feel like you do." I whimper and I don't know where it comes from. Rick is completely in control and I'm simply his. He sucks on my lips, nibbling at me, and needing more of me. I feel him get harder and our bodies tense up, we hit our release together as we cry out. He tightens his grip and pounds into me harder and faster, needing more. He pulls my legs up to my chest, and slams into me deeper until he releases a low guttural groan.

"Oh, baby. You drive me crazy, my queen. Everything is perfect when I'm in you. I need you to love me."

I hold him tight and rest my head on his chest. "Always, my Rick. I'll always love you."

CHAPTER TWENTY-FIVE

S aturday morning I'm woken up by the smell of coffee brewing and find cake on the floor in the bedroom with a can of whipped cream sitting next to it. I don't feel Rick anywhere and I don't like it. "Rick?" I call out hoping he got up to use the facilities. He walks into the bedroom doorway, looking tired. "What's wrong? You didn't sleep?"

"I couldn't sleep."

"What time do you need to be at the stadium today?"

"Cross is coming to get me to go work out."

"I think you should get some sleep. Come here." Rick walks over to the bed and crawls in next to me. I pull the blankets up and wrap my arms around him, snuggling into him. "Try to relax, my king. Whatever it is that's bugging you, it'll be fine. The season is almost over and then it'll be you and me, nobody else. We can stay home, hide out, and order food delivery for weeks and never go outside if you want. I'm not going anywhere. I'm happy as long as I have you."

"Really? I'm enough to make you happy? Enough to keep you happy?"

Now we're getting somewhere. "You're more than I ever wished for. More than I thought was even possible. You make me happy everyday. I only want you." I get a smile. "I'll do anything to make you happy and keep you that way. I can't wait to nap on the beach with you and share a lounge chair every afternoon in the sun while we're in Hawaii. I want to show you my favorite places. I want to share everything with you. Nothing means as much if you're not part of it." I mean every word I say and have been driven to tears by my own words. I'm such a fuckin' girl! I can't maintain myself even when I need to, but then I see Rick's face and realize what my tears mean to him. They prove how much he means to me, that all of my words are real and not empty, meaningless words to console him. "Hold me, my king, so I can start the day with you happy." Rick holds me tightly until the alarm goes off and we agree to snooze a couple of times.

Eighteen minutes later, "I want to stay in bed with you and hold you."

"I don't know how you do this every year. The season is so long for you, yet too short for the fans. It's almost over. I can't wait to have you all to myself." I say softly and gaze into his eyes. He squeezes me and doesn't let go until the alarm goes off again. "Do you want coffee?"

"All I want is you." He presses his lips to mine and slides his tongue between my lips to dance with mine. His large hands glide down my body, stopping at my hips and I rock against him pulling a low groan from his lips. Rick sits up against the wall and pulls me with him, leaving me straddling him. He squeezes my hips while he leans in to kiss me passionately. I feel his need for me and see how desperate he is. I reach for his cock to find him huge and solid. I rise up on my knees and work myself down onto him until he fills me completely. I see the pleasure on his face as he holds me, breasts pressed to his bare chest while I rock my hips. His chest is wide and muscular, but not hard. Rick wraps his arms around my shoulders tightly, "I want to keep you right here, like this. I love you, Sherry." He gazes at me and I see things in his eyes I've never seen before, or maybe I've never looked. It's not only my reflection. It's our reflection together. The story of our life together and ready to unfold. I can see us together years from now. I can see our family. Our happiness. How much I mean to him and how my love for him effects him. His head has insecurities and is uncertain, but not his heart. He's afraid I'll leave with someone else, like I'm worried he'll realize I'm old and difficult, and go with a younger girl that does what he wants. We're both crazy, worried about the same thing. I want to comfort him and take away his fear. What if I'm wrong? What if I'm seeing what I want and not how Rick feels at all? I'd rather be wrong than have him torturing himself with worry.

"Do you know in your heart that I only want to be with you? Do you believe I love you?" I search his eyes.

"I know you love me. I can feel it every moment that I'm with you." Rick replies quietly.

"It's only been you for me, even in my dreams. It's only been you for years. That's never going to change. I'll always give you everything you want from me." I search his eyes for something, relief maybe. "I've never felt this way with anyone else. I've never told another man that I love them. It's only you, my king." His eyes relax as my heart tries to beat out of my own chest at my admission.

Rick whispers in my ear with his sexy voice, "I love you, baby. I love how you take care of me and I wish you'd let me take care of you." I realize I haven't given in on anything real, I've only offered him more.

"You take care of me. Paying my way has nothing to do with loving me." I hear the words as they come out of my mouth and it's the truth.

Rick's eyes light up as he claims my mouth with his and rolls me underneath him. "I have other ways of taking care of you." He says as he strokes into me deeply, taking control and, yes, taking care of me. His hands on me both soothe and excite me. "We're sticky, my queen." He pulls me up to his chest, "Hold on." He carries me off to the shower and turns it on, blocking me from the cold water while it heats up. He kisses me and turns around, pressing me to the shower wall while he pushes into me.

I call out his name and he's in complete control of me. I'm on the edge and he pulls out of me. I whimper at the emptiness and he slides down my body, licking and sucking at my breasts on his way down to his catcher's crouch. His large hands move to my ass and hold me where he wants me, while he licks and sucks at my sex. My legs are shaky and he leans me against the wall, "It's okay. I've got you, my queen." I cry out instantly, flying over the edge at the flick of his tongue to my clit and he grabs me around the waist to keep me from falling to the floor. I worship his cat-like catcher's skills, even more when he's catching me. He lifts me back to his chest and slides into me deliciously. He strokes into me quickly and hard. "I love you and I'll always take care of you in any way you'll let me," he whispers in my ear as we come together and he leans against the wall, pulling my head to his shoulder.

We hear a knock at the door and Rick's body tenses. "That's probably Cross." He grabs a towel and wraps it around his waist on his way to peek through the peep hole. Rick unlocks the door, "Come in and help yourself to some coffee in the kitchen. I'll be right out."

"Dude, why aren't you ready?" Cross irritatedly questions.

Rick runs back into the bathroom and slams the door behind him as he loses his towel and gets back into the shower with me. I giggle uncontrollably and scream out as Rick wraps his arms around me, holding me under the spray of the shower and kissing me silly. He's obviously feeling better, and so am I. He turns the water off, "I need to go work out with Cross, baby. I'll see you at the stadium. I know you'll rock it tonight leading karaoke." He smiles at me as he quickly gets ready and grabs his things. I dry off and stay out of sight since Chase is here.

"Dude, seriously? Tell me you didn't have sex while I was getting coffee." Cross complains, but more likely is jealous.

I yell from the bedroom, "No, we were already done. Just finishing up the actual showering portion of the shower."

"How about I go have sex again and make you wait longer?" Rick being a smart ass looks to Cross for a response as he walks out with his gym bag, ready for their work out. Rick yells back to me in the bedroom, "I love you, my queen."

Cross yells out, "I love you, too, sweetness." Rick chastises Cross and gets laughed at in the process as they leave, locking the door behind them.

Tonight is the night I lead eighth inning karaoke at the stadium. I'm excited and anxious, only a tiny bit nervous because I don't know what song I'm going to be leading. But, it'll be a song I know well. It's at the game, so I need to wear my Seals gear. It's a 5:40pm game and it's a warm September Saturday. I'll be out in the stands early for batting practice and I decide to wear my denim mini skirt with a tank top, bringing my jersey and cap with me. I blow dry my hair and curl it, then put on a touch of make-up.

I'm concerned about the visiting team giving me a hard time again, but not as concerned as I am that I look good for the game and karaoke. I refuse to go out on the field and probably be on the big screen looking like crap.

I take a few minutes to myself to enjoy my coffee and eat some of the leftover cake, while I check my email, social media, and messages. Nothing new or crazy going on, so I have some free time for a change. I handle an important errand and restock the kitchen, making sure not to forget the whipped cream. Huh, I'm not sure what part I like best—The whipped cream on me, the whipped cream on him, or the shower. I lose more of my day considering this question in a daydream than I should probably admit, and find myself eating more cake.

> Text from Sam - I feel like it's been days since I've talk to you or my bro. Oh wait... that's because it has been!

I read Sam's text and call her. "It's about time!" Sam exclaims.

"Hi, Sam. I'm home alone right now."

"How's things? No drama? My bro is doing okay?"

"Everything is fine. Rick is great. I'm happy it's near the end of the season."

"It's a lot of baseball, isn't it?"

"I love the baseball. Honestly, I'll probably miss it when the season is over. But, we're definitely looking forward to some time together that's not regulated by his schedule."

"What was with the women sitting with you last night? I've never seen that before."

"Those are my friends from the section my season ticket is in. The visiting team noticed me in the stands during BP and yelled at me, and I mean asking me for a personal tour of the area and offering me a night I wouldn't forget. Anyway, it was my idea to have six of me and that would avoid anyone getting suspended or having their jaw dislocated."

Sam laughs, "Seriously? I guess it worked."

"Yea, and the girls and I got toasted. It was fun, but your bro was slightly irritated with me when he found me sleeping on the front seat of his car after the game. I may have been more inebriated than I thought." I laugh remembering the time with the girls, all of us cheering together, and yelling at the jerks on the other team.

"I'm sure he got over it quick."

I wonder if it's what triggered him not to sleep. "He was amazing this morning and happy when he left to work out."

"Don't tell me my bro was amazing. I don't need to hear that."

I try again as I giggle, "Rick was fine when he left this morning, better?"

"Much."

"He's been out of the house early the last couple of days. Chase has been picking him up to work out."

"He's looking good behind he plate, especially considering how deep into the season it is." The proud sister tone in her voice shining through.

"Yeah, but I think he's in his head about me." I'm not sure I should be sharing, but Sam has been there for me since the second I met her.

"Why do you think that?"

"He couldn't sleep last night. He told me I've been in his head. We had decided no relationship stuff until after the season, but he brought it up anyway."

"And, no positive tests?"

"No, I'm still taking my pill."

"You still believe the pill can guard you from the super sperm of a professional baseball player?" Sam jokes with me, I think.

"I don't know. So far it has. I told him I'd quit taking it whenever he wants me to." F'ing DOTM!

"You what?" Sam's voice hits a higher pitch than I've ever heard.

"What?" Play dumb Sherry, maybe it will go away.

"Did you say you offered to quit taking the pill?"

"Yes."

"But, you're still taking it, right?"

"Yes. He basically said not yet and it made him happy that I offered."

"I know my bro. I'm sure it made his chest puff out and he strutted around. You can't play games with him like that. You know how much he wants it."

"I only play board games with him, and some flirty teasing sometimes."

"You know what I meant."

"Yes, I do. Don't tell him, but I was sad that he didn't want me to quit taking it."

"Sherry, it's only been a few months."

"I know and the things I want—Fuck! I've never wanted them before and it makes me crazy, Sam. I'm doing my best to keep my head straight and to support him."

"I knew you two were combustible together, but you really do love him. I've been worried."

"We belong together." I hear my voice and my heart beats faster. "I'll do better at staying in touch. I've got to get to the stadium."

"It's kind of early, don't you think?"

"Rick likes me there for BP. I've been scouting intel for him pre-game." I laugh at the thought of it.

"Okay, I'll be watching as always."

"I'm leading karaoke on the field tonight. Don't know if you'll be able to see that. Talk soon!" And I hang up as I grab my things and run out the door for the stadium.

CHAPTER TWENTY-SIX

I pull into the player's garage to park and Carter catches me walking into the stadium. "Do you have your jersey for being on field later?"

"Yes, sir! I'm ready!"

"I could get use to your new look, gorgeous." I made an effort, but I have no idea what he's talking about. Big deal! I curled my hair. "Contact me if you have any issues with the visitors. All of these guys need to be professional."

Text from Carter - Text me if you need to be discreet.

Text to Carter - Thank you, sir.

"I'll tell Seno I saw you walking into the stadium. I don't know what you do to that man, but I know I've never seen him as happy as he is when he sees you." Carter walks away into the depths of the stadium leaving me with a warm heart and a bright smile that I couldn't hide if I wanted to. Who would want to hide a Rick Seno smile anyway?

I sit behind the Seals dugout and slather on my sunscreen.

Text to Rick - Behind the dugout. Ready to watch you swing your bat. ;)

No response. I check the lineup to make sure my Rick is starting and he is. The lineup is normal.

The field gets set up for batting practice and the team starts to show up on the field. Most of the guys stretching and loosening up. Some running sprints and throwing a ball around in the outfield. No Seno. I look around to see who's out and there's no Chase. Okay, that's interesting. The rest of the team goes on about their business, nothing out of the ordinary. Kris and Mason wave at me. I observe and keep an eye out for Rick and Chase. They finally join the team about halfway through batting practice and they're all smiles, joking together. Rick runs up to see me between his turns at bat, kissing me like I'm his life source. His bat is on fire today. The knock of the ball against his bat is perfect every time. It's almost as if the ball and bat are being pulled together by a magnetic force, they can't miss each other. Bravo isn't taking batting practice today, since Skip put him on the DL. Mason is showing no sign of limping. All of the Seals look good, except Rick and he looks like a super hero.

Chase visits me after batting practice, "What did you do to him? His bat is on point and he's been picking on me all day."

"Nothing that's not normal. He didn't eat breakfast before he left with you because we chose to stay in bed a bit longer."

Chase looks at me funny, "He said he already ate this morning."

I blush as I remember him eating me this morning in the shower and make a quick recovery, "We did have cake early this morning."

Chase nods, "I think I need a woman. I want to be getting it whenever I want and have a woman that wants to do sweet things for me, like you do for Rick."

I wonder what Rick has told him, "You might not be ready for that. You're so young still."

"What about your friend that you introduced me to last night?"

"Rona? She's nice and she's not a player chaser. But, she needs to get settled a bit. She'd be fine for dating, I think you should wait and see what happens. The season is almost over and you're going to want to go home, not the best thing when you start dating someone who lives here."

"You're probably right. I need to think about it over the off-season. Will you keep baking for me?"

"I will bake for you even when you have a girlfriend. You basically introduced me to Rick, I've got your back." I owe him everything and he's such a good kid. Chase smiles and gives me a hug, before disappearing into the dugout.

Colorado is already out doing their batting practice, so I watch for any tells and try to stay low-key. I don't want any special attention from any of the players. I don't want any trouble tonight. No extra drama. I want to stay calm and not get nervous before going on the field to lead karaoke in front of thousands of people. I'm watching Colorado and they have even more newbs brought up for the expanded roster. Carter's hanging out behind the backstop. Why do I feel like Carter has taken on the job of regulator? I guess it makes sense for the team to avoid trouble, he's not just looking out for me. Shit! He wouldn't be doing this if I wasn't here. Get out of your head, Sherry! Get back to baseball. Don't worry about Carter. I check Colorado's lineup and their shortstop is making his debut tonight, with the newb second baseman that debuted last night. Hmmmm... Lots of focus on one of the players.

Text to Rick - Colorado short stop is debuting tonight and 2B is the same guy that debuted last night. They came from different farm teams.

Text to Rick - Trainer has been paying too much attention to Martinez that's in the lineup to play 3B. Looks like his neck is stiff.

Text to Rick - Same lead off as last night, still not hitting well. But—he did actually connect to a ball.

Text to Rick - Hope Carter isn't out here watching because of me. I'm not here to cause a problem.

Carter finds me after BP, "So, tell me what you saw."

"What do you mean?"

"Seno says you're feeding him info you see at BP. What did you see today?" I share the info with Carter that I shared with Rick. "Interesting. What about the Seals?"

"They all looked good. Nobody hurting or anything that's in the lineup. Seno's bat is above average, even for him—I know I'm biased, but this has nothing to do with that. He's going to kill it tonight. Seno and Cross have been working out more and I think they're determined to end the season strong."

Carter quirks his head, "I was out here to see if I saw the same things you see. I do for the Seals, but not for the visitors and I'm not saying your wrong. I don't have your eye. Enjoy the game." Carter heads off into the dugout and I indulge in a $5 beer from the member lounge. Just one.

CHAPTER TWENTY-SEVEN

S itting behind home plate is where I belong now. It's not just about the game, hanging out with my section peeps, gazing down upon the serene green expanse of field, and supporting my team. In fact, most importantly it's about Rick Seno. Yes, I've been following his career and yelling louder for everything he does for years. This is different. This is about the smile he flashes me when he's crouched behind home plate and a heavy hitter strikes out. This is about him pointing at me and blowing me a kiss when he steps on home plate generated by his own home run hit. This is about the way he hangs his head and laughs when he hears me yelling at the other team. This is about the way I feel his eyes pierce me when I defend him by yelling at the pitcher that's throwing at him when he's at bat. Nothing is the same without him with me. It makes him happy when he can see me here with him. Maybe nothing is the same without me.

I look up and my Rick is standing at the netting looking at me. "You okay?"

I jump up to meet him at the net, "Now I am."

"Are you ready to blow this place away in the eighth?" He says as he smiles at me.

"I'm always ready for karaoke." I give him attitude. "Just like I'm always ready for you, my king." I gaze into his eyes, willing him to know how much he means to me and my own eyes fill up with tears.

His voice drops and he reaches for my fingers at the net, "I love you, Sherry."

I smile, unable to speak and when he turns to walk out to the bull pen and warm up our pitcher I yell, "I love you, Rick!" He runs back to me and gives me a quick kiss through the net, before he kicks it into high gear and full baseball mode.

The ceremonial pregame hoopla starts and they announce I'm leading karaoke in the eighth inning. It sends a shock through me and a rush of adrenaline. I'm excited and can't wait to find out what I'm singing. The big screen says:

Vote until the end of the sixth inning for the eighth inning
karaoke song on social media using
#sealskaraoke and your pick
#LoveRunsOut #ComeHome
#ThinkingOutLoud #TheWarrior

I love it! Now I know what the options are. Which one do I want? I should vote! Leading karaoke on the field. I performed all of them in the competition. Don't freak out. I have to wait and see what the social media world decides. I wonder who votes and how that'll impact the results.

Rick is walking toward the plate and yells at me, "Get out of your head, my queen! You got this." He does that thing where he points two fingers at his eyes and then at me a couple of times, like he's telling me to focus because we got this.

"Woooooo! Make it a win, babe!"

He smiles and nods at me as the game gets underway. I knew Rick was on point with the bat, but he's also right there calling the game and moving like a cat behind the plate. Nothing will stop him tonight. He's in control of the whole game and it's moving quickly, the top half of the first done in less than five minutes. Three strike outs in a row. I should be giving some of the credit to Rhett Clay, he has come far since his debut and his arm is a live wire. Bottom of the first, Cross leads off with a double. Mason walks. Martin strikes out. Seno is hitting fourth and connects on the second pitch. The ball bounces off the right field wall and the rookie in right field can't come up with it, Rick turns it into a triple sending Cross and Mason home. 2-0 Seals. Lucky gets a single. Rock hits into a double play and onto the next inning. The next few innings are uneventful. Rick hits a ground ruled double, the ball bounced over the wall, but nobody brought him home. Colorado is still scoreless in the fifth, and the Seals are giving a hitting demonstration. The bases are loaded and they keep pushing each other around the bases with singles and doubles. Rick starts the inning with a single and I get a shiver, he's a home run away from hitting for a cycle. When he runs across home plate and smiles at me, I yell, "Get a Homer!" He glares at me funny and continues into the dugout. The merry-go-round on the bases and with two out, my Rick is back in the batter's box with bases loaded. Colorado brings in a new pitcher. Rick chokes up on his bat, turns to me and smiles before he focuses on the pitch. Strike, Rick swings and misses. Strike, right down the middle of the plate. The third pitch and I hear it smack, I jump out of my seat screaming because I know he hit it out of the park. Rick watches the ball fly out of the park as he drops his bat and turns to me as he pounds his fist into the air and runs the bases. 10-0 Seals. Lucky strikes out ending the inning.

Top of the sixth, the big screen is showing the current voting results with a few minutes left to vote for the karaoke song. It looks like the two OneRepublic songs have split their share of the vote and the other two are running close with "Thinking Out Loud" ahead by a small margin. I run up to use the ladies room before the seventh inning stretch, so I don't have to pee when I'm on field. Mike with the Mic catches me on the concourse and tells me that I'm singing "Thinking Out Loud."

Text from Rick - With you singing in the eighth, the win is a lock!

One out in the bottom of the seventh, no score change and a Seals representative escorts me from my seat to the field gate. We wait there for a few minutes and I watch Rock hit a solo home run. Houston goes down one, two, three in the top of the eighth inning and I'm rushed onto the field near home plate as I hear Mike with the Mic over the PA, "Ladies and gentlemen, please welcome the Batter Up Karaoke competition winner Sherry to lead your eighth inning karaoke tonight. You voted on the song and chose her wild card song, the final song she sang in competition. Please sing along to 'Thinking Out Loud!'" I hear cheering from the Seals dugout and watch the karaoke start up on the big screen. I'm looking around to see where Rick is because I've never sung this song without him. I hear the crowd cheering me on from the section behind home plate and it makes me think of him, what he hears when I cheer for him. I'm singing the song and happy with myself for not freezing in front of this huge number of people. The baseball park has always been my happy place and I'm relaxed here. Rick is walking toward home plate in full gear about halfway through the song and I figure they're going to cut the song short because of the game timing. But, none of the other players are on the field. As soon as I see him, my emotions flow and I hear the song get better. My heart gets happier. I let it rip. At the last few lines of the song...

Rick kneels on home plate in full catcher's gear, takes my left hand and slides a ring on my ring finger. He searches my eyes with his mask up on the top of his head while he holds my left hand in both of his, "Please make me happy and be my wife, Sherry Seno. I promise to do everything in my power to keep you beyond happy for the rest of our lives. I will always love you."

I stand on the field with a microphone in my right hand, in shock. I can't move. It feels like hours pass, though it's only a few seconds. I don't know what the ring looks like, it doesn't matter. I love him and I want to be with him and I never want to hurt him and I've wanted to be Sherry Seno for longer than I should admit. "Yes! Please!" I have tears in my eyes.

Rick squeezes my hand and stands up, squeezing me, and kissing the daylights out of me right there in front of everybody.

EPILOGUE

I didn't realize how badly I wanted it. This man keeps making my dreams come true. My fantasy world, only better than I ever imagined, and real. How did I end up being what makes my fantasy baseball boyfriend happy in real life? This can't be happening. I must be dreaming again. Somebody pinch me or wake me up. No. Don't wake me up. I like this dream.

Text from Sam - Did I just see what I think I saw?

Text from Sam - Was that you at home plate with my brother kneeling in front of you and then kissing you?

Text from Sam - I swear that looked like a proposal.

Text from Sam - It looked like a yes.

Text from Sam - Why aren't you replying to me?

Text from Sam - I need to see the ring.

Text from Sam - Answer me already!

Text to Sam - Why are you texting me in my dream?

Text to Sam - What game are you watching?

Text from Sam - I'm watching the Seals game, just like always. The team my brother is the catcher for and you were on the field and I swear he proposed. Take a picture of your left hand and send it to me now!

Text from Sam - FYI you're not dreaming!

I look at my left hand, take a picture and send it to Sam. If this is a dream it doesn't hurt anything. Then I really look at my left hand, the ring looks like a queen's crown with a diamond solitaire at the center, surrounded by numerous smaller diamonds decorating the crown all the way around my finger. I'm his queen.

I'm not sure what to do. Is this reality? No way. We've been together less than six months and I'd never move that quickly, besides he's a professional baseball player. There's no way I fit in that equation! Fuck! It's what I want. Brain repeats—You want this. Heart celebrates—We love him! Everything Rick does is because he knows it will make me happy.

I totally miss the bottom of the eighth and the top of the ninth, realizing the game is over when the announcer says the Seals won and congrats to the Senos!

Text from Sam - You did say yes! OMG, you're going to be my sister! I can't wait!

I look up and Rick's standing at the net in front of me. I move to meet him there as fast as I can. He reaches for my hands at the net. I gaze at him, "Is this real or am I dreaming?"

"I hope it's real, because you're my dream come true. I love you, Mrs. Seno." He says happier than I've ever seen him. I'm warm all over and I don't know what to do with myself. "I'll be at the car as quick as I can." He takes off for the clubhouse.

Rick steps into the garage with his huge grin and beelines for me. He kisses me senseless. "Let's go home, my queen," as I slide over to be next to him for the drive home.

DIAMONDS IN PARADISE

AN ALL ABOUT THE DIAMOND ROMANCE #3

My baseball fantasy came true.

For the next two weeks, I get to have him all to myself in my favorite place.

I love Hawaii. The North Shore has always felt like home.

Relaxed Rick with a tropical tan. Shaggy and unshaven. Days without putting a shirt on. His strong chest and abs exposed.

But, when our vacation turns into more, it's life changing.

I want to give him everything. All he wants is me.

Diamonds in Paradise (a novella), is available for pre-order now.

MUFFIN MAN

A STANDALONE NOVELLA

Robbi

"Everybody out!" The manager yells, running through the salon as we all ignore her. She's not the owner. Problem is the owner is out of town and she's in charge. She stops and at the top of her lungs, "Evacuate now! It's going to explode!"

The salon freezes instantly, the calm before the storm. There's a sudden frenzy of women gathering their necessities, and their clients as they run outside hysterically. I casually get up out of the salon chair and walk out with Deanna, my stylist, close behind me, and avoid the trampling stampede of frantic, high-pitched women.

We all gather outside for the details, but the manager is still in there! She comes running out with the massage therapists and their clients wrapped in robes. It triggers me to survey the scene for what stages of beautification we're all in. I mean, we all go to the salon for different things. Personally, it's how I stay blonde and that's not changing any time soon because I can prove blondes have more fun. The stylists are brushing out their hair, fixing their make-up, taking off aprons. I overhear what's happening and empathize for some of the poor women in the middle of getting services, when it hits me—I'm one of them.

The building had started to make a banging noise. The manager, Shawna, had taken it upon herself to find the problem. She was left in charge after all and the ship was not going to sink under her direction. This isn't some basic barbershop, this is Michelle's Salon and Shawna would not be responsible for damage to the custom European style decor Michelle has taken years to refine. It was the water heater. The water heater was making the loud noise, like it had air in the line or was trying to pass bad Chinese food. It was also emitting gas fumes and sparked every time there was a bang. The bangs were getting more frequent.

Which brings us to the bunch of women now standing outside in the shade of the building's front awning. It's almost lunchtime and the parking lot of the strip mall is starting to fill up with patrons to the food establishments, eyes peering at the motley crowd of women in smocks milling around helplessly. Shawna's on the phone with 911 trying to get, yes, you guessed it, the fire department.

911: What's your emergency?
Shawna: There's going to be a fire
911: Is there a fire now?
Shawna: No, not yet.
911: Sorry, we can't help you yet
click

At least, that's how I imagine it from the story Shawna told. There were others calling, it would be fine. Help would show up. Hopefully. Deanna, the only person I will let near my hair, is getting fidgety and twirling her soft brunette curls between her fingers. "I'm sure they'll be here quick. We still have ten minutes before we have to wash the bleach out of your hair. Everything will be fine." For those of you who are not salon savvy, leaving chemicals on your hair too long isn't good. Hair will break off, fall out, burn. I've seen it smoke. All kinds of horrible things, and I take pride in my long platinum blonde hair. So, let me translate what Deanna said: Ten minutes until utter disaster. Others have half a haircut, shampoo or conditioner in their hair, extensions partially tied in. The people who were getting massages are relaxed, even if their clothes are inside the building and they're outside wearing only a robe.

Everyone that could primp, had primped for the firemen to show up. It's a lineup and I can imagine the firemen walking the line, *"I'll take this one, and this one. You don't mind sharing, right?" The senior firefighter steps up and says, "Sorry, I get first choice. Seniority gets perks. I'll be taking this one from you."* Anyway, you get the idea. It's a beauty pageant and then there's me with a plastic bag on my head and a lady with foils sticking up off her head like she could receive radio transmission.

The sound of sirens fill the air as the long red ladder truck pulls into the parking lot, stopping in front of the salon. The important thing here is the possible fire, but I appreciate firemen as much as the next girl, maybe more. Definitely more. I love a hot guy, even on days like today when I only get to drool from a distance because I look like a bag lady compared to the stylists. The first guy is a bit older with short salt and pepper hair. He's fit and fills his navy blue uniform nicely. The second guy is shorter, still at least 5'9" and wearing one of those bulky yellow jackets with reflectors. His face is adorable, but the jacket hides every-thing else—not a hint of a single ab or muscular arm. The third reminds me of Goldilocks, he's just right. Thick, dirty blonde hair and the mustache to match. His navy blue uniform pants are topped with his station T-shirt which stretches across his chest and shoulders, yet loose where it's tucked into his Dickies. I'm busy imagining the things I could do to him. Naked. With my tongue. Deanna stomps her boots and drags me into the dog groomer next door.

"Firemen? Hot firemen?" I whined questioningly, not wanting to give up my view.

PLAYLIST

"Thinking Out Loud" by Ed Sheeran
"Come Home" by OneRepublic
"Never Tear Us Apart" by INXS
"All Right Now" by Free
"Yesterday" by The Beatles
"Oh, Sherrie" by Steve Perry
"Sherry" by Frankie Valli & the 4 Seasons
"Take Me Out to the Ball Game" Jack Norworth & Albert Von Tilzer
"We Belong" by Pat Benatar
"Love is a Battlefield" by Pat Benatar
"Million Reasons" by Lady Gaga
"Voices Carry" by Til Tuesday
"Never" by Heart
"We Got the Beat" by The Go-Go's
"One Way or Another" by Blondie
"Lola" by The Kinks
"Won't Stop" by OneRepublic
"Seek and Destroy" by Metallica

"Caught Up in You" by .38 Special
"The Stroke" by Billy Squier
"Fell in Love With a Girl" by The White Stripes
"Blow Me Away" by Breaking Benjamin
"Perfect" by Rick Springfield
"Feels Like the First Time" by Foreigner
"Kashmir" by Led Zeppelin
"Let's Hurt Tonight" by OneRepublic
"Shape of You" by Ed Sheeran
"If I Lose Myself" by OneRepublic
"Shadows of the Night" by Pat Benatar
"Ex's and Oh's" by Elle King
"The Warrior" by Pat Benatar
"Love Runs Out" by OneRepublic
"Victorious" by Wolfmother
"Carry Me Away" by Rick Springfield

ABOUT THE AUTHOR

Naomi Springthorp is an emerging author. King of Diamonds is An All About the Diamond Romance, the second book in what she hopes is a long series of baseball romance. She's also writing other contemporary romance novels and novellas featuring firemen, Las Vegas, and more.

Naomi is a born and raised Southern California girl. She lives with her husband and her feline fur babies. She believes that life has a soundtrack and half of the year should be spent cheering for her favorite baseball team.

Join her newsletter at www.naomispringthorp.com/sign-up

f facebook.com/naomithewriter

🐦 twitter.com/naomithewriter

📷 instagram.com/naomispringthorp

a amazon.com/author/naomispringthorp

g goodreads.com/naomithewriter

👻 snapchat.com/add/naomithewriter

ALSO BY NAOMI SPRINGTHORP

All About the Diamond Romances

The Sweet Spot

King of Diamonds

Diamonds in Paradise (a novella)

Also coming soon...

Betting on Love

Just a California Girl

Jacks!

Other novellas and standalone novels

Muffin Man (a novella)

Confessions of an Online Junkie

Finally in Focus (a novella)

Made in the USA
San Bernardino, CA
14 January 2019